CAT LADY

DAWN O'PORTER lives in Los Angeles with her husband Chris, her two boys Art and Valentine, and cats Myrtle and Boo. Dawn is the bestselling author of *The Cows* and the Richard and Judy Book Club pick *So Lucky*, and her non-fiction title *Life in Pieces* was also a *Sunday Times* bestseller.

Dawn started out in TV production but quickly landed in front of the camera, making numerous documentaries that included immersive investigations of Polygamy, Size Zero, Childbirth, Free Love, Breast Cancer and the movie *Dirty Dancing*. Dawn's journalism has appeared in multiple publications and she was the monthly columnist for *Glamour* magazine. She is now a full-time writer of eight books, Co-Founder and Director of Choose Love Inc., designs dresses for Joanie Clothing, LOVES Instagram, and has a large following on her Patreon blog.

www.patreon.com/Dawnoporter
@hotpatooties
/DawnOPorter

CAT LADY

Limited signed edition

CAT
LADY

DAWN
O'PORTER

HarperCollins*Publishers*

HarperCollins*Publishers* Ltd
1 London Bridge Street,
London SE1 9GF

www.harpercollins.co.uk

HarperCollins*Publishers*
1st Floor, Watermarque Building, Ringsend Road
Dublin 4, Ireland

First published by HarperCollins*Publishers* 2022
1

A catalogue record for this book is available from the British Library

ISBN: 978-0-00-838539-2 (HB)
ISBN: 978-0-00-838540-8 (TPB)

This novel is entirely a work of fiction.
The names, characters and incidents portrayed in it are
the work of the author's imagination. Any resemblance to
actual persons, living or dead, events or localities is
entirely coincidental.

Typeset in Berling LT Std by
Palimpsest Book Production Ltd, Falkirk, Stirlingshire

Printed and Bound in the UK using 100% Renewable Electricity
at CPI Group (UK) Ltd

Dedicated to Sniff, Nin, Tiku, Minu, Acre, Fluke, Twiglet, Suska, Lilu, Potato, Myrtle, Boo and all the pets I have yet to meet who will no doubt add as much joy to my life as you all did. Your lives were short but perfect, a lesson to us all on how to live for nothing but pure love.

(Honorary mentions to Daisy the tortoise and all the geese, ducks and family and friends' cats and dogs who I have borrowed over the years. Especially Waffle, Caroline's cat, who saved me from all the mice. Legend.)

No such thing as just a pet.

[Everyone is playing a part]

Contents

Part One

Mother

For my eighth birthday my mother made me a cake. She was frail at that point, very thin. But it meant a lot to her to bake the cake. I was allowed three of my friends to come for a party. My sister, Liz, was there too. The party involved a small paddling pool in the garden and a sprinkler that we could run through. It was fun, I remember laughing that day because it was unusual to laugh that much in our house. My dad sat on a deckchair on the patio reading a newspaper. Every so often he'd bark something along the lines of 'Quieten down,' or 'Quit that screeching.' I pretended I couldn't hear him and carried on playing with my friends and sister in the water. Such fun to be had in the simplest of things.

Mum came outside holding the cake. She wasn't a very good baker, but – even at that young age – I recognised that she'd put that aside and done her best to make my party special.

Because she was my mum – and that's what mums do.

Her purple dress was so pretty, I remember feeling special because she had dressed up for me despite how ill I knew she was. She started singing 'Happy Birthday' and walked towards me with the cake. My friends and I gathered round; they sang too. My father stayed on his chair.

After I had blown out my candles, my mother cut the cake

up. When she handed me a slice on a plate, I didn't keep it for myself. Instead, I took it over to my father and gave it to him. I wanted him to look at me and say something kind. I wanted him to wish me a Happy Birthday and to tell my mother that her cake was delicious. I was trembling as I handed it to him. So much so that I tipped the plate and the cake fell, getting frosting all over his grey cardigan. He stood up and I knew my birthday was over.

'Look what you did, you idiot,' he yelled.

'Oh come on, David. It's her birthday,' my mother begged. But nothing could get in the way of his rage. He tore off his precious cardigan and threw it on the floor. He stormed out of the garden and my mum had to call my friends' mums to come and pick them up.

But that isn't the important bit that I remember.

It's me and Mum and Liz all sitting round eating birthday cake when everyone had gone, our faces smeared with chocolate, our fingers covered in frosting. And Mum cheering as she relit the candles so I could blow them out again and make a birthday wish: that it could just be the three of us, forever.

1

I arrive at the Methodist Church on the high street bang on 7 p.m. I'm not sure why I came or what I intend to say.

There are five of us in the room, all sitting in a circle: a group leader, one man and three women other than myself. The man is very tall and thin with a bald head and is covered in tattoos. He doesn't look like the sort of person who would come to a group like this, I wonder if he came to the wrong session and instead meant to attend the Anger Management Group. He has a tattoo of a snake going around his neck, it's quite hard to look at him without frowning. Luckily, I've had quite a lot of Botox in my forehead so get away with it. One of the women looks like a character from a children's book. Far too caricatured to be real. She's pale, she looks old, but more like she is in costume, dressed up as an old lady. Exhaustion may have aged her more than the years themselves, like the very act of being awake is the greatest achievement of her day. She is wearing a lot of clothes – a hat, a scarf – although it's quite hard to make out the individual items because they're all a similar shade of earthy green. She wears trousers with thick long socks pulled over the top and shoes that look like slippers. On top there are numerous lengths and fabrics. A jumper, a cardigan, a shirt. It's not cold outside, but I imagine this is what she wears every single day. She sits with her hands clasped on her thighs. On the rare occasion she looks up, her big brown, doe-like eyes try to grab some sunlight from under the heavy resistance of her eyelids. Someone else sits inside of her, I wonder if she even knows it.

The other person is a black lady in a pink dress. She is eating biscuits from a packet and occasionally wipes tears from her cheeks. She seems very much in her own world, and the reverse of the lady in green. Her happiness is all on the outside. You'd walk past her in the street and think she was jolly because of her bright clothes and effort in her appearance. But watery eyes and comfort eating tell a different story. By virtue of just being in this room, I am sure her happiness is a façade, or else why would she have come?

There is also a younger woman who I estimate is in her early thirties. I'd guess of Indian descent, she is very pretty and dressed in fashionable clothes, her hair is perfectly preened and her make-up is flawless in that dedicated

'Instagram tutorial' kind of way. Surely someone like her has a social media following they can pour their feelings into? Or a group of millennial friends who have been raised to talk about their emotions? But I mustn't judge, that is the entire point of this group. Or at least, that is what the flyer said.

The group leader, a small, white woman in her fifties with a pretty blue skirt and a cute, cropped sweater, takes her seat and begins the session. 'OK, if everyone is settled . . . My name is Tiana, I'm your group facilitator. You're here because you have lost someone very special to you. Losing pets can be a truly devastating experience and everything you are feeling is normal and valid. We love our furry friends like family. When we lose them, our hearts break just as they would if we lost a human. I'm here to help you navigate your grief. This is a safe space to express yourself, there is no judgement and we are all here to support you. You don't need to deny your anger, guilt or pain when you're in this room.'

The black lady is nodding in agreement, relentless tears falling from her eyes while the rest of her denies them. I get the impression this is not her first time. The lady in all the green clothes stares intensely at the floor, as if too afraid to move in case her sadness attacks her. The man is vibrating, which I'd guess is what happens when he tries to sit still. The young woman pretends to turn her phone off so she can send a text. I've seen that move before from the staff at work.

'I recognise most of you, but why don't we all go around

and say who we are here to remember. Shall we start with you, Ada?'

Ada must be the lady in the pink dress. She quickly finishes chewing her biscuit – Crawford Custard Creams – swallows and begins. She isn't in a rush.

'I'm Ada, this is my third time coming here. My kitty, Mrs Jones, died a month ago. In my arms, I thank God for that. My husband left five years ago, my son still lives with me but he needs to go out on his own now. He lacks a lot of confidence, ya know?'

Tattoo man nods.

'Is he feeling low about Mrs Jones?' Tiana asks.

Ada wipes away tears with the entire palm of her hand. 'Yes, not that he admits it. He says I should just get another cat, but I can't do that yet. He thinks I'm crazy being this upset about it but it's how I feel.'

'This is a problem we see all too often in the world of pet grief. Others think that animals can just be replaced, and they don't understand that isn't the case for many people. Have you told him he's not to say that?'

'Yes, I have. And then he tells me to stop moping around the place. I think he thinks I am sadder about the cat than I was when his daddy moved out and . . .'

There is a pregnant pause as we all wait for the next part of the sentence.

'I am.'

Wow, that is quite the admission and Tiana doesn't even flinch, this really is a space where you can say anything.

Well, almost anything, I don't plan to speak. On the flyer it said you don't have to if you don't want to.

'Animals give us a very special kind of love,' Tiana says. 'A loyalty that knows no bounds. They don't argue with us or make us feel bad about ourselves. They don't . . .'

'Snore, drink, never use a toilet brush!' Ada butts in.

'Yes, they mostly spend their lives doing whatever it is they can to make us happy. And so it isn't unusual to miss that more than you miss complicated relationships.'

'Complicated all right. For him, anyway, managing all those women,' Ada says, eating another biscuit.

Tiana turns towards the man with the snake tattoo. 'Greg, how are you this week?'

'Shit.'

'Can you elaborate on that?'

'Can't get over it. Can't move on.' Greg starts to cry. 'He wasn't just a snake.'

I do an involuntary cough. It was just so unexpected, but I guess a pet is a pet. It's not like I've got a picture of my cat Pigeon tattooed on my neck. He obviously really loved that snake.

'It sounds like the two of you had a very special bond.'

Good for Tiana, unshakable on all levels.

'I'm a very stressed person,' Greg says. Which isn't a surprise. His image looks like one giant reaction to stress. 'I'm allergic to all animals with fur. I got a mouse once, even that set me off. But animals help me, ya know? They calm me down. Something about that other heart-beat being around meant I weren't on my own. Girls don't want me. Who wants to take this back to their mother?'

I look around and no one is shaking their head in disagreement.

'I know snakes aren't known for being affectionate or nothing, but he used to get excited when I went up to him. And when I got him out, he'd slither over my shoulders and it just felt good. To have something that wanted to be with me. Who else would want to be with this pile of shit?'

He seems so self-aware. Embarrassed to be here, embarrassed to be crying. Embarrassed to feel this way about a snake.

'I don't want to be like this. Someone who only has a snake, but it's who I am. I don't take well to humans, and they don't take well to me.'

'Well, you're here, with us. And we all understand. Don't we?' Tiana says, turning to the group. People give varying levels of support. Just a nod from the lady in the green, an enthusiastic 'Absolutely' from Ada. I give my best smile. The young woman just stares at him, studying his tattoos, I presume.

'Love is love,' Ada says, finishing another biscuit then handing just the one to Greg. He takes it and eats it all in one go but looks like he regrets it and spends a very long time masticating until he is able to swallow.

'My son is gay,' Ada continues. 'His dad didn't like it but I don't care who he loves, I just want him to find someone who's good to him.'

'I ain't gay,' Greg says, defensively.

'Oh no, I wasn't saying you were. But you loved that snake, didn't you. Love is love. That's all I'm saying.'

'I wasn't doing anything weird with my snake,' Greg says, not getting Ada's point at all.

Tiana moves on, which we all agree is the right move. 'OK, Martha, how are you today?' She is talking to the lady in all of the green clothes. She takes a long time to answer, which is quite awkward for us all. Just the sound of Ada's crunching to pass the time. 'How long has it been now?' Tiana pushes.

Martha lifts her chin up as if it's on a piece of string and being controlled by someone else.

'Six months. I still put her food down every morning. It's gone rotten by the evening, so I throw it away, but I still do it, every day.'

It would not be appropriate of me to mention what a terrible waste that is, I'm sure she must be aware. Her head flops back down, as if even the person holding the string is now exhausted.

'I put a pillow on top of me when I go to bed because she used to sleep on me and now, without her weight, I can't sleep,' Martha says, looking at the floor to avoid eye contact.

We all wait to see if she has anything else to say, but her energy suggests she's done. It's a mix of despondency and shyness, maybe. This clearly isn't her first time here, but she's not ready to share much.

Tiana steps in to make a professional transition. 'So much of what we miss are the habits that we formed. Those creature comforts that we maybe took for granted are the hardest things to lose.' She turns to the young lady with the nice clothes. 'And you are?'

'Nicole.'

'And who are you remembering today?'

'Umm, my mum's dog. He died and now I don't want to go home because it won't be the same. His name was Rover.'

'Oh, well I'm sorry to hear that. I can appreciate that is hard. To know that your family home won't be quite the same.'

Nicole nods. 'We got Rover when I was a teenager. I'm sort of dreading going to visit, I just can't imagine my mum's house without him.'

She seems sweet enough. I'm surprised she's here, but grief is grief. And how funny to hear of a dog called Rover. Such a cliché, but also, so few of them around.

'Is there a particular reason you came today?'

'Maybe to get some tips on how to talk to my mum about it. She's really upset. I mean, I am too. Really, really upset, but my mum, you know, she's inconsolable.'

'Well, it's very kind of you to want to gather the right words to help your mother. I'm sure this group will be very helpful for that. And hello, we got to you in the end,' Tiana says, looking at me. 'And you are?'

'I'm Mia. Mia, my name is Mia, and I am forty-five.' I blush when I realise there was no need to tell anyone my age.

'And who are you remembering today?'

A hundred things I could say rush through my head. My eyes well up, as if they know I need help to pull this off. I wasn't sure what would happen today, or how many people would be here. I thought maybe I could disappear into a larger group and not have to say anything at all. I once went to an AA meeting where there were around a hundred people sitting on chairs looking at a stage. I hoped for that. I suppose pet grief support is a lot more niche than alcoholism. I am silent a while, and no one seems to mind.

'Take all the time you need,' Tiana says.

I take some long, slow breaths. Do I lie? Do I tell the truth? I don't want anyone to think I'm strange. The silence and stillness of the room seems to be activating Greg. His breathing becomes heavier and the energy coming out of him feels explosive. And then he erupts.

'He wasn't just a snake!' he shouts, standing up, picking up his chair and throwing it at a wall.

'No one said he was just a snake, Greg. Please pick up your chair and sit down,' Tiana says, calmly.

'I might as well kill myself. What's the point in anything?'

'Don't say that. Don't talk like that,' Ada says, putting her biscuits in her bag, possibly to protect them.

But he is having a full-scale episode. Everyone stands up and he throws all our chairs against the wall. Nicole runs out of the room. Martha also slopes out in her baggy green clothes. Ada talks calmly to him, unafraid and with so much love. Tiana repeats, 'Shhhh, shhhh.' I just watch. It's a display of the rawest emotion, I am not threatened, and I am not scared. Greg's heart is broken, this is just a reaction to that. He doesn't mean us any harm. And I am not here to judge. How could I be? My cat isn't even dead.

2

It's very rude, I think, to bring food to a dinner party. It's polite, of course, to send a message earlier in the day asking if there is anything you can bring. But having received the 'No, just yourself' response, to then go out and buy a ginormous and extremely indulgent pudding and show up with it is just vulgar. I don't know why I am surprised that my husband's ex-wife Belinda has done just that. It's exactly the kind of thing she would do.

I left work early today to prepare the food for tonight. We're hosting a dinner party with people who don't particularly care for me, but with whom I continue to make a great deal of effort because it makes my husband happy. I am perfectly aware that they long for my husband and his ex to still be married, and for me to silently exit out the cat flap, but nonetheless I do what I can in the hope they might change their minds. It's not unusual for me to be the odd one out, but I think I have become quite good at finding a way to fit in. Tonight, this comes in the form of me cooking. Guests must always appreciate the cook.

The most time-consuming part of the food was the vegan sticky toffee pudding. I worked exceptionally hard on it so no one will complain about it being vegan, as I will be the only plant eater at the table. I couldn't be happier with the result. Not only does it look fantastic, but it tastes incredible. Therefore, when Belinda turns up with a pavlova so enormous and non-vegan that putting another dessert on the table alongside it would be utterly pointless, I feel extremely triggered. Belinda knows her pavlova will overshadow whatever I have made. It's so typical of her that I'm mostly annoyed at myself for not predicting it.

'How lovely,' I say, taking it from her. 'You really shouldn't have.'

'Oh, it's nothing, I just thought I'd make sure there was something for the dirty animal-eating heathens at the table too,' she says with a cackle, passing a bottle of wine to my husband. 'Is Oliver in bed?'

'Yes, but still awake. He's waiting for his goodnight kiss,' Tristan tells her. She heads up the stairs to her son's bedroom. The bedroom that used to be hers before she cheated on Tristan and moved out in pursuit of something more exciting.

'You look nice,' Tristan says loyally, coming into the kitchen and opening Belinda's wine despite me having a perfectly nice bottle already on the go. 'Very smart.'

I'm wearing a black blouse and black trousers. It's not very adventurous but Tristan seems to like that. I think he associates smart dressing with being smart, and who doesn't want people to think their partner has brains?

'I was worried I'd get food on myself so thought black was probably best. Nothing worse than a hostess covered in beef juice.'

'You're cooking beef?'

'Yes, steak, why?'

'It's just that . . . well, that seems ambitious. Steak for six people, when you don't even eat meat. How will you know when it's cooked?'

'I'll just wait for it to stop mooing?'

He laughs reluctantly. He's always quite enjoyed my sense of humour, possibly because Belinda doesn't really have one. 'Well, if you pull it off, I'll be very impressed. What will you have?'

'The same as you but with tofu instead of steak.'

'Tofu? Rather you than me. Aren't I lucky that my plant-eating wife cooks me steak?' He kisses me on the cheek and asks if there is anything he can do to help. Knowing that he is incapable in the kitchen, I give him a more practical task.

'Yes please, take these through,' I say, handing him a plate of bread rolls.

'Yes chef!' he says, eating one on the way. Something I find quite irritating as I'd arranged them into the perfect peak. I say nothing and unwrap the steak. I read that it's a good idea to beat the meat with a hammer, so I do that.

And despite being faced with the raw flesh of an undeserving animal, I find it quite therapeutic.

Tristan likes to keep in touch with his old friends, and so I am giving tonight everything I've got to do him proud. There are two couples plus Belinda, me and Tristan. The other two are Matthew and Alice and Dorian and Mark. Matthew and Tristan went to school together, and Dorian and Belinda used to work together. They were all quite a tight group, pre me. Matthew, a large, sweaty pig of a man, announces on arrival: 'Out of all of the divorces yours has been the easiest. We never had to choose between you because you're always together.' After which Alice leans into me and says, 'You're very good, you know. I'm not sure I could have the ex over all the time.' To which I say, 'We all do what we need to do for Oliver.' To which she says, 'Well, it's very admirable.' To which Belinda says, 'Oliver needs his mumma. He's a real mumma's boy.' To which I head back into the kitchen to scream into a bowl of mashed potato.

Mark starts sneezing almost as soon as he walks through the door. 'Have you still got that cat?' he asks, blowing his large nose into a cotton handkerchief, which is something I thought men stopped doing a hundred years ago because of how disgusting it is.

'Yes, she has,' says Belinda, coming back down the stairs. 'The everlasting cat.'

'Pigeon, she's sixteen,' I say, as she miraculously appears. Alice kneels down to her. 'Ahhh hello.' But Pigeon doesn't like strangers so rubs against my legs instead.

'She's not very friendly,' Belinda says.

'She's a real mumma's girl. Would you like a Claritin, Mark? It might help with the sniffles?' I ask.

'No, it won't work. Nothing does. I'll just have to cope with it,' he says.

I grimace and bite my tongue.

'Maybe you could put her in another room for the night?' Mark suggests. I want to remind him of the time we were at his house and his son hid a handful of cold ratatouille in another guest's handbag. Should we have put him in another room for the night too?

'Yes, eating around animals. Icky,' Dorian says, looking for any excuse to speak badly of food.

'She won't bother us,' I say with a polite smile, 'no need to lock her away. Shall we eat?'

I make melon and Parma ham to start, leaving off the ham for me. Belinda has drunk almost an entire bottle of wine to herself and keeps standing up to salsa dance, which is quite embarrassing. Matthew is sweating so much that it's coming through his blazer. He doesn't seem bothered by it, which baffles me beyond comprehension.

'So, have you always been vegan?' Matthew asks, with a thread of ham hanging from his mouth. He doesn't consider how many times I have been asked that question by almost every non-vegan I have ever met.

'For about twenty years, it's a lot easier than it used to be.'

'She eats a lot of vegetables,' Belinda says, as if announcing groundbreaking information.

'Oh dear, pffffft,' adds Matthew, making a series of horrible fart noises. One of which I think comes out of his actual bottom.

'I can assure you that your farts are worse than mine,' I say, which makes Tristan laugh. I love it when he laughs at the things I say.

'And why are you vegan?' asks Dorian, who is extremely thin and pulling the white fat off her ham with her knife and fork.

'It's a personal preference. I don't judge anyone else, I just started to find the notion of eating animals unpleasant. I did some research into it and didn't like what I found so stopped eating meat then progressed to all animal products. It's really no big deal.'

'I wonder if sometimes people use things like veganism to hide eating disorders,' Dorian says, with a very small piece of melon in her mouth. 'It's an excuse not to eat.' She nods knowingly. Mark sneezes then rolls his eyes.

'I eat, Dorian. I eat a lot. I just don't eat animals,' I say, calmly.

'I second that. She eats like a horse. Quite literally, sometimes. Lots of carrots and apples,' Tristan says, knowing I find it tiresome the way meat eaters like to challenge me.

'I suppose you think we're all disgusting,' Matthew says with his mouth full. I notice he's eaten all of the ham and a couple of bread rolls but no melon. I wouldn't be surprised if he had a heart attack right here and now.

'Of course not. Each to their own. How do you all like your steak cooked?' I ask, getting up without waiting for an answer because I wouldn't know the difference anyway. I hurry into the kitchen for a moment's reprieve.

'What's that?' Tristan asks, joining me in the room as I am crushing a pill in a pestle and mortar.

'It's a Claritin, I'm going to put it on Mark's steak. His mucus is making me feel unwell.'

I start to sprinkle the powder onto the meat.

'You can't drug him,' he laughs.

'It's antihistamine, not Rohypnol.'

'He said he didn't want one.'

'I know that, but he's suffering on purpose and it's tiresome.'

'You're a terrible person,' he says, the look in his eye suggesting my terrible side thrills him.

'Is that why you married me?'

He puts his arms around me and kisses my neck. I stop sprinkling so my husband can enjoy me.

When the steaks are on the table, Dorian comes back from a long trip to the bathroom looking disgusted. 'Ohh, well that wasn't very nice.'

Are we supposed to know what she's talking about? 'Did you vomit?' I ask her, finding it interesting she's being so open about bulimia.

'No, the kitty litter in there. Horrid place for it.'

'In the bathroom?' I ask, surprised.

'Yes, not very pleasant for us humans is it, to have to pee alongside that.'

'The cat has to go somewhere,' Tristan says, knowing how defensive I can become about Pigeon. He's sticking up for me, but he's also hoping I don't get upset and make a scene.

'Where do you think I should put it, Dorian, out of interest? Rather than in the toilet. The room with one purpose?' I say, as Tristan rubs my leg furiously as if I am a cat and it will distract me and calm me down. He doesn't need to worry, I know better than to cause arguments. I return to smiling and nodding and just being polite because it's easier.

'Outside!' she exclaims, like she's some undiscovered genius and this is her moment to shine.

'She is an indoor cat, so that wouldn't work,' I say. 'Do start.'

'She doesn't go outside?' pipes up Alice. 'Oh, that poor thing.'

My hand tightens around my knife. This is a very sensitive subject for me. I often feel immense guilt about not letting Pigeon out, but the alternative is opening her up to a life of constant danger and risk. Keeping her in was a decision I made when she was a kitten and I have stood by it ever since.

'Yes, doors and windows closed at all times in case the damn thing escapes,' Belinda says, as if she's finally been allowed to let it out. 'The place could do with a good airing, with all those smelly candles you burn in there.' By 'there' she means my bedroom. By 'smelly' she means my favourite scents, which are leather, musk and tobacco. I turn my head slowly to Alice who has more to say on the matter. I am determined to hold my smile until they're done.

'A cat should be able to live. Run around outside, be free. It doesn't feel right to keep them locked up inside.'

'Hear, hear,' says Belinda, just agreeing with anyone who says something horrible about me or Pigeon.

'I'm not sure why you'd have one in the first place. I don't see the appeal at all. You can't trust them,' Dorian says, hiding some potato under her steak, no concept of how rude and insulting what she just said is.

People who hate cats are like atheists, they cannot get through a conversation without telling you their views. There is such a righteousness that comes with it. You tell someone you have a cat, and they tell you, to your face, that they hate the thing that you love. There are so few instances in life where this is acceptable. But cat haters can't wait to unleash their claws. They like to make you sound strange for loving an animal they don't understand. They tell you cats are not loyal. They shake their heads while you explain the loyalty you have experienced from your own. The madder they can make you look, the more satisfaction they seem to gain. People who don't like cats are scared of them because they don't know how to touch them, and therefore they question themselves and their abilities to feel safe. Or they are dead on the inside. It's one or the other.

'You could put it in your room for the night?' Belinda suggests confidently.

'You want me to put the litter tray in my bedroom?' I reply loudly, my smile still stretching across my face.

'Just an idea,' Belinda replies. Her smile so fake she looks like she got attacked with fixing spray and can't move her face.

'For a group who don't like cats it seems to be all you can talk about,' Tristan says, wanting this to be over. He knows how much I love Pigeon, and how the suggestion to lock her away would upset me. 'How is the steak?' he asks his friends.

'It's quite tough,' answers Mark, chewing and blowing his nose all at the same time. I just need him to get half of that Claritin inside him, that should stop him snotting everywhere.

'I think it's wonderful,' adds Dorian, delighted she can spend the entire evening chewing one lump of beef before downing her knife and fork and claiming to be full. Matthew cuts his in two, stabs his fork into one half and takes a big, animal bite. For the next five or so minutes the room is largely quiet as people chew with varying levels of difficulty.

I finish my meal long before anyone else. I go into the kitchen and get the pavlova but don't bother taking it out of the box. As I walk back into the dining room, I drop the whole thing on the floor. Cream, meringue and berries splatter at my feet. As it falls, I wonder to myself how much of an accident it actually was.

'MY PAVLOVA!' Belinda screeches. Our rug being the least of her concerns.

'Are you OK, Mia? What happened?' says Tristan, rushing

into the kitchen to get a towel. I appear to be glued to the spot. The rest of the guests stare at the mess, wondering what on earth to say next. But there is no need for someone to fill the silence because Pigeon takes care of that. She strolls into the dining room and starts to make the most hideous hacking noise. Before I have the chance to realise what's going on, she heaves up a huge pile of vomit onto another corner of the rug.

'Oh fuck!' barks Mark.

'I think I might be sick,' says Dorian, rushing back to the bathroom.

'Shall we go and sit in the garden?' Belinda suggests, as Tristan gets down on his knees and starts to scrape large lumps of thick cream back into the bowl. He's useless at cleaning and is making it worse. I seem to have frozen in position. Pigeon is now sitting triumphantly on the dining table licking her paws. It's almost like she planned it.

3

'I planned for sex tonight,' I say to my husband a few days later after a TV dinner of pasta and pesto for me, the addition of chicken for him.

'How kind of you to schedule me in,' Tristan says, teasingly. I know he finds it annoying that I schedule our love-making, but I think it's a very useful tool to ensure we do it. Life is exhausting, if a plan isn't made then one of us will fall asleep in front of the TV and any chance of fornication is dashed. So I plan it, and like everything else on my 'TO DO' list, I make sure I get it done.

'Would you rather we didn't?' I reply, coyly. 'I'll use my finger.'

He turns off the TV and finishes the glass of wine on the coffee table. 'You know how much I like that.' He grins, getting up and going to his room.

I walk behind him, Pigeon following me. I pick her up then put her down on the other side of the door. 'Won't be long,' I whisper to her, as I shut it. Tristan starts undressing and lies down on the bed.

There are a few rules to be observed when having sex with my husband.

1) It must happen in his room because he thinks mine smells of cat.
2) Pigeon must not be in the room.
3) I must lie with him until he falls asleep.
4) I must orgasm or he will get upset. This means the length of our sessions varies considerably, depending on my mood.

Tristan and I met eight years ago at a charity event where he talked about his recent divorce all night. We left the party together and, following a series of strange and quite un-flirtatious conversations about his ex, Belinda, I somehow ended up in his bed. The sex was interesting and felt like something I might not get elsewhere. A good mix of intrigue and intimacy. He'd guide me with instructions that began with, 'And now you're going to . . .' Or 'What I'd like next is . . .' I liked that. When someone tells you what they want in bed it's much easier to believe that you satisfy them. In return I got everything I needed. He is the kind of man who likes to perform well. We keep some lubrication in his bedside drawer that I have to replace quite often, presumably because he masturbates a lot. He's never once turned down sex, I'm certain he'd want a lot more of it if I was willing.

'Please get me hard,' he says as he lies on the bed. I appreciate the use of the word 'please', so I do as he asks by using my hand.

'Get yourself ready,' he tells me, becoming very excited. He watches me as I apply some lube. I don't worry too much about trying to look sexy as I do it. I think the act of applying lube is suggestive enough, without some big performance. I put some on my hand too, which I continue to rub his penis with. He tells me to stop because it's too much, and so I sit on his face for a while instead. This is where I orgasm. It never fails. It feels good to still be doing things like sitting on my lover's face well into my forties. I think the pride of it is a big instigator of the orgasm. I feel like a rockstar when I'm up there.

When I've stopped shaking, I wiggle down so my vagina can find his penis. It slides in beautifully, and I move slowly up and down. He likes me to go on top so he can look at my breasts. He pulls my uncomfortable lacy bra down so he can see my nipples. One of the perks of never having had children is that I still have quite buoyant breasts.

'Great tits,' he says breathily as I move up and down on top of him. 'Fuck me hard.'

He's not the kind of man who talks like that any time other than when he's having sex. But men like to think they're porn stars when they're in the moment. I bounce a little quicker.

'Touch yourself,' he tells me. Which I do, entirely for his titillation.

'Grab my balls,' he says, as he ramps up. I use the other hand and somehow manage to stay upright.

'Put your tit in my mouth,' is his final command. For which I release both of my hands for fear of falling flat on his face. As he ejaculates, he opens his mouth releasing my breast. His head presses back into his pillow, his mouth wide as he gasps for breath. I remain on top of him until I'm sure he's done, then roll onto my side and rest my head on his shoulder. I run my fingers through his chest hair. He stops my hand with his and we lie still while he stares at the ceiling.

'Will you stay?' he asks, turning away from me to sleep on his side.

'I might.'

I stroke his back until he falls asleep. It doesn't take long. I think about how it would be nice to fall asleep against his body. To wake up and feel his warm hands stroking me as my eyes open. We haven't shared a bedroom properly for nearly four years, an undoubtable bone of contention in our marriage. Maybe I'll treat him to it tonight. But then Pigeon starts clawing at the door and reminds me why we split rooms in the first place.

Sneaking out of Tristan's room comes with many challenges. If he wakes up, I stay. If I manage to get out, I'm clear to head to my own room for the night. He's a light sleeper. I need to tread carefully.

Pigeon stretches an entire leg under the door and is waving

28

it back and forth like a window washer. I've never put it to the test, but I imagine she'd do this all night if I decided to stay. Poor thing. It must be hard to have only one person on the entire planet from whom you get affection. I take that responsibility very seriously.

I slide one leg out from under the duvet and reach my foot down to the floor. The rest of my body follows like I'm one of those inflatable tube men they have outside businesses to attract attention. When both feet are on the ground, I spring up again and tippy-toe to the door. The hall light is on, and the door opens in a way that will aim blinding light right at Tristan's sleeping face. I need to block as much of it as I can with my body. I open it ever so slightly and shove my foot out to hold Pigeon back. A little more so I can squeeze out. But it was too much. Pigeon shoots past me and runs straight under the bed. I reach into the hall and turn the light off before dropping to all fours.

'Pssssss ppssssss.' I do it as quietly as I can. Rather than come to me Pigeon begins to purr exceptionally loudly. Tristan's digital alarm clock is giving off just enough light that I can see her grinding herself against the legs of his bed. I chuckle to myself. Just moments ago, I was doing a similar move against my husband. Maybe she saw me through the crack under the door and thinks that's what we do in this room. She's so rarely been allowed to come in. He thinks sleeping with animals is unhygienic.

'Pigeon, come on,' I whisper. But the sound of my voice seems to send her totally beside herself and she flops down. Rolling from side to side.

Tristan moves. I hold my breath. He rolls over and faces the other way, his breathing deep. It's OK.

'Pigeon, please, come,' I say, a little louder and a little more desperately. I scratch my fingers on the carpet and she finally comes running. I pick her up, step backwards into the hall and gently close the door. Success. I performed my wifely duty and made a stunning escape to solitude. The perfect night.

'You almost ruined that,' I tell her, kissing her head. 'Much more of that and you'll be sleeping alone.'

In the bathroom I put Pigeon down and pee so I don't get a UTI. I've learned that mistake many times. I wonder if men would roll over and fall asleep so quickly after sex if they were also threatened with pissing needles as a punishment for their pleasure? Women have so much detail to consider when trying to keep life simple.

I wipe myself between the legs with a flannel and smell my husband's sperm before I rinse it and hang it over the side of the bath. I enjoy intimacy, I just have my own versions of it.

My bedroom is a room that only myself, Pigeon and our cleaner enter. It used to be Tristan's office, so is a little boring in tone. But I intend to decorate at some point. I sleep naked in brushed cotton sheets (Tristan likes crisp cotton, which I have never understood) and no matter what joy I have experienced during the day, getting into my bed is always the best part of it. The pressure is off. No more pleasing to do for anyone but me. I can finally be myself.

Pigeon's fur against my naked body sets my endorphins

off. I always masturbate after sex. In the past I lay next to Tristan as he slept and quietly brought myself to another climax. These days I get to do it alone. A reminder to myself that I can be borrowed, but I cannot be owned. I fall asleep shortly after.

4

I am woken the next morning by the loud vibrating of my phone. I have five texts from my sister, Liz:

1. *Why didn't you pick up yesterday? I wanted to go for a walk or something?*
2. *I know you don't think we should mark the day but I do, she always loved a party. Should we have a belated party?*
3. *I'm too tired for a party. Lunch though? Or a walk? Did I already say that?*
4. *Sorry baby's been up since 4. Kids spilled the breakfast they made on the bed so had to change all the sheets. Maybe we should just talk?*
5. *Hope these texts didn't wake you. You won't reply anyway, I know you*

I decide to surprise her with a response:

Can't sorry, big day at work. I'll have cake for lunch. Happy belated Mother's Day x

I kiss Pigeon on her soft head and get out of bed. It's 6.45 a.m., five minutes before my alarm usually goes off on a weekday. I don't normally get to the office until 9 a.m. but I wake up early enough that I am ready to work when I get there. Nothing irritates me more than staff turning up and spending the first fifteen minutes of their workday making coffee and breakfast. Why not get up earlier and have it at home? So, to set a good example, I don't drink or eat a thing until at least 11 a.m. in the office. That means, for the few hours I have at home in the morning, I drink lots of coffee and eat a substantial meal. If I leave the house unprepared for my day, it won't go well. And when days don't go well, everything suffers.

I put on my dressing gown but let the cord trail behind me so Pigeon can chase it. I go out of my way to make her life as exciting as I can. It's the least I can do. In the kitchen I put the kettle on and empty the dishwasher while it boils. I do this as quietly and gently as I can so as not to wake anyone. These precious moments in the morning, before the others wake up, are often the best moments of my day. From the dishwasher I take Pigeon's favourite bowl. I know it's her favourite because, when I give it to her, she licks it entirely clean, but with any other bowl there is always food left, as if she can't stand to look at it any longer, and just has to walk away. One of the things I love most about cats is the way they rely on routine. If you do something at a certain time for just three days, that's it. The cat is locked in and you'll have a hard time changing things up. This suits me perfectly. I long for routine.

While she eats, I make my breakfast. Brown bread in the toaster. While it's in, I make my coffee. An inch of oat milk on top of a heaped teaspoon of instant coffee. I stir that around until it's dissolved as much as it's willing in cold milk, and then I pour hot water on top of that. For my toast I measure a level tablespoon of sugar-free peanut butter and slice half a banana, laying the pieces symmetrically on top of the peanut butter. I sit at the kitchen island to consume this extremely well-balanced and highly nutritious breakfast while Pigeon sits on the stool next to me and watches my every move.

'You said you'd sleep in my bed,' Tristan says, entering the kitchen. I pull open my dressing gown so my naked body can distract him from a conversation I need at least two coffees to have.

'Pigeon was pawing to get in.'

'You could spend one night away from that cat,' he mutters to himself as he re-boils the kettle and loads a huge scoop of ground coffee into a French press.

'She'd claw at the door and keep us awake.'

'I like waking up with my wife.'

I get off my stool and walk over to him. I turn his face so he's looking at me.

'Do you know how many times the average couple in their forties has sex? Once every two weeks. Do you know how many times we have sex?'

'No.'

'Twice a week. Unless one of us is unwell. Every week, twice. Where we sleep doesn't matter.'

He puts both hands onto the edge of the sink. He is wearing striped pyjamas like he's in a 1950s sitcom. I imagine him in a sleep hat, it would suit him. 'My needs aren't just sexual, Mia. If you gave me a hint of the affection you give to that cat . . .'

'Pigeon.'

'Pigeon. I am forced to say Pigeon a hundred times a day. I want a wife, not a lover.'

'A lover? Me? What lover makes sure there is always food in your fridge, does your admin, folds your clothes, pairs up your socks, teaches your child how to read and somehow tolerates your intolerable ex-wife. Come on now.'

'I like to cuddle in the mornings, you know that.'

'And so do I. But we have separate rooms because you won't let Pigeon sleep in a bed with you and if she can't get to me she howls outside the room and keeps us all awake. Allow her in, and I'll sleep with you, it's not complicated.'

That isn't true, I love having my own room and would be devastated to give it up.

'I'm still upset about the time she licked my balls.'

How am I supposed to not laugh at that?

'Some men would pay good money for that. Go back to bed, I'll bring you coffee.'

'I can't, I have to shower. I have an early meeting.'

Tristan is a property surveyor and often has to leave early for site visits.

'Will you have to wear a hard hat?' I ask, flirting. 'You look so sexy in a hard hat.'

'Yes. I'll have to wear a hard hat,' he says, enjoying that I find him sexy.

'OK, well you get dressed. I'll leave your coffee on the kitchen counter in a takeaway cup.'

'Thank you.'

'You're welcome. I love you.'

As soon as he's gone, Pigeon jumps up onto the kitchen counter and we finally get on with our morning. I lean down to her so she can rub her face on mine. I love the way she taps her mouth onto my lips then slides her soft cheek across mine. We do it over and over, her purrs becoming louder, my eyes crossing a little. Our routine is seamless. Tap, slide, tap, slide. Her softness still amazes me. It also makes me proud. I've kept her in such perfect health for all these years, she is gorgeous. My girl. My very important girl.

'Can I have some breakfast, Mia?'

I am startled back to the real world by the sound of a tired nine-year-old boy. Even though Oliver spent most of Mother's Day with Belinda, he still insisted on coming over in the evening like he does every Sunday – something which I'm trying not to feel too smug about. I tie up my dressing gown. Pigeon jumps onto the floor and rubs against my ankles instead. Her support knows no bounds.

'Of course, did you sleep OK?' I ask, but Oliver doesn't answer. He helps himself to a bowl without shutting the cupboard. He pours Cheerios into it until they spill over the side. He finishes the milk. Leaves the fridge door open.

'I washed your sports kit. It's folded up on the chair in your room,' I say, reaffirming my position in his life because it's hard to define what it actually is.

'I know,' he mumbles. 'Thanks.'

'Any lunchbox requests?' I ask. His little face lights up.

'Marmite and peanut butter,' he replies as he sloshes milk onto the floor. 'Oops,' he says, with a face that signals, 'Do I have to clean that up?'

'You go get ready,' I tell him. 'I'll sort that out.'

He smiles and walks back to his room, more careful not to spill his bowl now. When he disappears up the stairs, Pigeon immediately runs to clear up the milk. Where would I be without her. Alone, with all these men.

I get to preparing Oliver's lunch, a morning ritual in which I take enormous pride. I listen to Radio 4 while doing it. First, I cut the sandwiches into circles and make faces on them with pieces of dried fruit. I cut grapes in half and put them on sticks with chunks of cheddar. I cut holes into slices of cucumber and fill them with cherry tomatoes, and finally I hide a piece of chocolate underneath a lettuce leaf. I always do that; hide a treat. He always finds them as they're always gone when he returns the lunchbox. I like to imagine the moment he realises he's been tricked again. A little smile spreading across his face, which he maybe tries to hide from his friends. A little reminder that I love him very much, because telling him so seems to make him uncomfortable.

The doorbell goes but before I have the chance to get the door, it's been opened, walked through and shut. Belinda is heading towards me, and even though she is in our home far too often, her presence first thing in the morning feels particularly invasive.

'Gosh cat food, why does it smell so awful?' she blurts, coming into the kitchen.

'Belinda, you're here,' is all I can manage.

'Of course I'm here. I want to walk my child to school.'

It's an extremely strange dynamic between the three of us, and none of it is my choosing. Or Tristan's, from what I gather. They both have fifty-fifty custody of Oliver, but since Belinda lost her job as an executive (for having sex with another married executive in the stationery cupboard) she has struggled to find another that satisfies her need to feel powerful. Therefore, she spends at least thirty per cent of Tristan's fifty per cent here with us, relentlessly stating that it's what is best for Oliver.

'The cat food just smells like fish really, so you could say the same about human food,' I say with a strained smile.

'Did you sleep OK? You look tired?'

Belinda enjoys putting me down, but she has a very specific way of doing it. This is shot number one.

'Very well, thanks,' I reply. She tries harder.

'So who does your Botox at the moment?'

I've never told her I get Botox, so this in itself is a dig.

'I found a guy in Clerkenwell who I really like. He's sparing, which is good.'

'Mmmm, sounds like a cheapskate. You should go to my

guy, Dr Stilwell, on Harley Street. He's the best. He'll sort you out, honestly. I wouldn't go to anyone else.'

'I like my guy. Not fancy, just really good at what he does and I'm happy there, but thanks.'

'No seriously, Stilwell teaches people like your guy how to do it. Why go to a pupil when you can go to the master? I'll email you his details. Tell him I sent you, I'll get twenty per cent off. Not that I need it.'

I nod. She does this about almost everything. From where I buy my fruit to the candles I like to burn. I am determined not to be the wicked stepmother in this family, so I grin and bear it the best I can.

'Oh look at that,' she says, noticing the contents of Oliver's lunchbox. 'What a silly amount of effort.'

'I don't think so. Just a bit of fun.'

'I make him big sandwiches, he's a growing boy. I cut large slices off a bloomer and load them up with all sorts of fillings. What's in those little things?'

'Peanut butter and Marmite, his favourite,' I say, not rising to it.

'Oh God, Marmite. You might as well eat the cat food if you're going to eat that. I hate it.'

'I know. Which is why on the mornings I make his lunches, he gets it.'

She turns on her heel.

'Oliver darling, come down, Mummy's here,' she calls up the stairs. He obediently obliges, coming down with his near-empty bowl of cereal.

'Oh dear, breakfast in your room? Do you not want to sit here with Aunty Mia? What's the matter?'

'Nothing,' he says. 'Mia lets me have breakfast in my room on school days.'

Belinda looks very disappointed that he didn't express hate for me.

'Yes, the view is fun from up there. He likes to sit at his desk and look out the window, don't you? I don't see anything wrong with that,' I say.

'OK,' Belinda continues, desperate to find something to make herself feel superior. 'I saw your lunchbox. Will those little sandwiches be enough?'

'I never finish the ones you make.'

This is excruciating.

'OK, well if you'll excuse me I have to get ready for work,' I say, walking towards my room.

'Mia, do you want to see the card that Oliver gave me for Mother's Day?' Belinda calls. 'It's so sweet, you have to see it.'

Did she actually bring the card all the way here from home? She wants me to see this because it is one giant symbol of the role she plays in Oliver's life, and the role that I do not, according to gift cards. Last year, he made her the most enormous card and, of course, I got nothing because I am the stepmother. It's something I have learned not to be sad about; Mother's Day is already loaded enough. If there was such a thing as a 'Stepmother's Day' I'm sure Oliver would make me something lovely.

Belinda pulls the card out of her bag. '"I love my mummy.

Love Oliver",' she enunciates loudly. 'I love it. And I love you too, give me another hug, Oliver.'

But Oliver doesn't hug her. Which no doubt sends a chill down her spine. Instead, he goes back to his bag and pulls out another piece of paper. 'I forgot to give you this yesterday, but I also drew this. It's our family.' He holds up a card. It's both fascinating and flattering. The picture is of three grown-up stick figures, one child and one cat.

'Bless him,' Belinda says. 'He's never really progressed with drawings. There is little artistry in his bloodline.'

I ignore her. It's the first time he has drawn a picture that includes me. And furthermore he has included Pigeon, which warms my heart right up. But the most stunning detail of all, and the one that is causing my heart to swell, is the only colour detail on these human figures: my hair. A fiery red mop upon my little pin head. I wear my hair up and orderly almost all of the time. The fact he chose to depict me in this way feels intimate. Much more so than it would if he had presented me in my other guise; the career woman I am by day. This is how he thinks of me. Relaxed and at home in the morning, making him his favourite sandwiches with my hair all messy.

'It's wonderful, Oliver. So lovely. I'm going to put it on the fridge.'

I walk past a quivering Belinda, take a cat magnet that Oliver once got me for my birthday, and attach the picture. 'There, who knew this was what our kitchen was missing.'

Oliver looks very happy with himself. More so with the picture than the card. I've had enough of the mum battle now and really need to get ready for work.

'Have a lovely walk to school. Bye, Belinda.'

'Say goodbye to Aunty Mia,' Belinda says. Not seeing me roll my eyes as I disappear into my room. She has referred to me as 'Aunty Mia' since the very first day we met. She buckles at the term 'stepmother' and sees my position in Oliver's life as an extreme threat. It's a shame and unnecessary as I'm not trying to move in on her role as his mother at all. Belinda is an incredibly insecure woman and it must be exhausting to be her. I do my best to communicate with her as little as I can, knowing that one wrong move could activate her unstable mental state.

Unfortunately for her, the man she left Tristan for couldn't muster the same confidence to leave his wife. The realisation that she had blown up her own family, lost her job and was then rejected by the person she did it for triggered a spate of extremely unhealthy behaviour. All of which resulted in her lover coming to our door to tell Tristan he would be getting a restraining order if she didn't leave him and his family alone. Tristan was so embarrassed by the arrival of his rival that he could hardly speak. I suspect he had imagined himself exercising some extreme machismo should he ever come face to face with him, but in fact it went quite the opposite way. I really felt for him. He was very nice to the man, who spoke to Tristan like he was Belinda's father. Tristan, feeling sympathy for Oliver mostly, told him that he would talk to her. I hid in the kitchen with Pigeon and pretended not to be home.

When Tristan came back in, his face white from the shock of it, I led him to the window seat where he laid his head in my lap and cried. He's a very sensitive man, who really cannot function without a wife. He had a very overbearing mother who did absolutely everything for him. Since she died, he's tried to find the same thing from his female partners. He needs to be adored and looked after, he's very basic really. What you learn from your mother can set the tone of your entire life. I hope my influence on Oliver means he will turn out all right.

When all three of them have finally left the house, I go into the bathroom and turn on the shower. I leave the door open so Pigeon can come in and out, an indulgence I enjoy very much when everyone else is out. I don't know why she has such an obsession with running water but every morning when I turn it on, she gets inside the shower and hovers gingerly at the edge while she drinks from the basin. Luckily for her, our hot water takes a while to come. I always know when the temperature is just right for me because she leaps out like she's being attacked and jumps straight into the bath to lick herself all over.

While I wash, she sits on the sink to watch me. I always give her a good show and wipe a heart-shaped patch of steam on the glass door so she can see me clearly. She tilts her head from side to side as I spread soapy bubbles all over myself. She claims a certain ownership of my body and obviously questions what on earth I'm doing. I sometimes lick my arm to show her I'm washing. She seems to appreciate that.

My shower routine has been the same for many years. Firstly I shampoo my hair twice, rinsing it to the point of squeaking before I apply conditioner to my hair, legs and underarms. With a razor I quickly shave my body and then I rinse off the conditioner from my hair, stopping just before it's all gone. It seems easier to style with a little of the residue to help it hold. I use a scrub on my face twice a week and a long scrubbing brush for my back. A luxury so heavenly that if I wasn't so conscious of the environment and the need to save water, I'd stand under the shower and do it for hours. But as it stands, I allow myself thirty seconds of this simple pleasure and count quietly in my head to make sure I don't go over.

When I get out, Pigeon licks drops of water from my feet as I clean my teeth. I love her rough tongue and the way it scratches. I've often thought how wonderful it would feel if she was to lick my whole back when I lie in bed. I'd let her do it for hours. I once heard a story about a woman who spread Marmite on her vagina and had her dog lick it off. It came to me through a friend who claims to know the man who walked in on her, so quite a reliable source. I don't dream of anything that perverted but I did consider blobs of cream cheese on my back to encourage her. She loves cream cheese. It would be that or tuna, but I think being covered in tuna would feel revolting and take away from the pleasure of the licking. Also, too much cream cheese makes her sick so, in reality, I should just commit this whole thing to fantasy and get a back scratcher instead.

Tristan never recovered from the time she snuck up behind him and licked his balls as we lay post-coitally on his bed. I'm sure it gave him a terrible fright but, if he dared to be honest about it, I'm sure it actually felt quite nice. Society has taught us such control, I bet in the old days they were all covered in tuna having their animals lick them God knows where. I admire the lady with the Marmite, you can hardly force a dog to do something it doesn't want to do so it surely isn't abusive. It's not like she was doing it to the dog.

I put on some smart black trousers and a blue shirt that I tuck in. Both Stella McCartney. No one needs to know I found them in TK Maxx. I tie my wayward red hair up neatly and adorn myself in Isabella May jewellery because it's important to show off the brand at all times. I put on heavy foundation with brown eyeshadow, mascara, pink cream blusher and lipstick to match. I wear pointy ankle boots and a belt with a big buckle. I dress as I think the MD of a business should. Smart, serious and together. It's a part I have become very good at playing. A much safer version of me than the woman who thinks about her cat licking her all over her body.

There is a reason I have built routine and organisation into my life. Without it I have the kind of mind that could get me into a lot of trouble.

5

As usual, I am at my desk just before 9 a.m. Our office is a sixteen-hundred-square-foot unit in a large warehouse in north-west London. I run a tight ship and like to monitor everyone's arrival times. When the staff come in punctually it reaffirms my employing choices and makes me feel like I am doing a good job. I take my role as MD at Isabella May Jewellery very seriously. I see Fliss is already here. She is one of two designers working out of this workshop, she is never late and her work is impeccable. She beavers away all day with her AirPods in, listening to podcasts that sometimes make her laugh out loud, but she never seems distracted. I smile as I come in, she smiles back. I appreciate the lack of pleasantries and the acknowledgement that we are here to do our jobs and don't need to waste precious minutes catching up on details of each other's lives that we don't really care about, just to be polite.

Isabella May is a small brand, but we have come a long way. Very little of that success is down to Isabella May herself. Other than begging her famous friends to occasionally wear our stuff, her actual role in the business is yet to be discovered. She's always late. Which, I suppose, is one of the many pisses you can take when your name is above the door. I credit myself for our success and the National Jewellery Award for 'Team of the Year, 2019' that sits on a shelf behind me is down to who I employed and the way I run the workshop. Isabella might be the face of this company, but I am its backbone. That isn't to say the past year hasn't been hard for us. Sales are down as more and more brands seem to appear every day and competition gets increasingly fierce. We need something that pushes us to the next level, and our current mission to get stocked in Selfridges is critical to our growth.

Next to arrive after me is Ajay, our 'digital manager'. He created the website, runs all of our social media and pretends to care about jewellery for an uncompetitive salary, while on the side he works on his own empire. He is very open about his development of a 'weed chocolate' that will be good to go as soon as the government decriminalise it and he is allowed to market his winning formula – according to him, anyway.

If only everyone in this office could be as simple as Ajay. When there is only one male in a group of four women, it really highlights what a dramatic experience being female is.

Isabella is determined to employ mostly women because she thinks it makes her look good. The term 'women-run' comes up a lot in the numerous panels she hosts as she touts herself as an executive with a conscience. I don't dispute this, the women we employ are brilliant and work very hard, but a few years ago I downsized the office dramatically. We now outsource Marketing, Customer Care, Fulfillment and have another workshop just outside of London to keep costs down. This took a lot of women out of our office. I know it's hugely anti-feminist to say, but life got a little easier after that. We still only have women doing the jobs, but they don't come here so I don't have to hear about every sleepless night, menstrual cramp and gluten intolerance they experience. Saying that, Isabella makes up for all of them being gone. She is one constant menstrual cramp. She has been handed life on a silver platter and I have very little sympathy for her inability to get through a day without suffering some kind of personal crisis. I keep myself to myself at work. This is not somewhere I come to grab attention for anything other than being good at my job.

'Good morning, Ajay,' I call from my desk.

'Morning babe,' he replies. Something I've planned to put an end to in our next appraisal, but think maybe it needs more of an immediate response. I do have sympathy for the fact that as the only man, there is little Ajay can say or do that doesn't come across as suggestive, flirtatious, patronising or sexual. He's in a very difficult position. But calling me 'babe'? That needs to stop.

'Ajay,' I say, approaching him at his desk as he takes off

his coat, releasing a violent wave of aftershave into the room.

'Whatsupp babes?' he says, totally unaware that his choice of words is the problem. He hangs his coat on the back of his chair, revealing a t-shirt that reads, 'Don't Panic, I'm Stoned'. Ajay's trainers always look new and his hair never seems longer or shorter, always falling just above his ears, with a very nineties centre parting, possibly worn ironically along with the rest of his 'hip-hop' clothing. He is wearing a lot of jewellery, none of which is Isabella May but that's understandable, we don't design for men, despite me suggesting numerous times that we should. Women like to buy jewellery, but it doesn't always have to be for them. If you were to ask me, I'd say that Isabella doesn't like men, which is just bizarre considering her dad has given her everything she's ever wanted.

'Would you mind not calling me "babe", it doesn't feel very appropriate,' I say nicely but with authority.

'Oh, yeah OK. Sorry. I don't even think about it. I even call my mum babe, and the dog.'

'You call your mum babe?'

'Yeah, she doesn't care.'

'Are you sure she doesn't care?'

'Nar, she doesn't care. If someone doesn't care about something then it doesn't matter, does it?'

That is an annoyingly good argument that I have no comeback for.

'OK, well I do mind being called "babe" by staff members. I'd like us to establish stronger boundaries than that. So, if you could just call me Mia instead that would be great?'

'Or boss?'

'OK, if you feel that using my name is hard for you and that a nickname is entirely necessary, then I suppose I can cope with "boss".'

'You got it, boss,' he says. 'Coffee?'

'No thank you, I had one at home. Didn't you?'

'Nar ba . . . I mean, boss. My mum doesn't drink coffee so only buys that instant shit, I like the stuff we've got here.'

'You could buy your own?' I suggest, to the back of his head.

He saunters off to the kitchenette, leaving his computer turned on ready to work, but with no human to operate it. I head back to my desk and watch him through the glass as he takes his time to prepare himself the perfect cup. Fliss has a takeaway cup on her desk that she picked up on the way in. That's why she is my favourite.

I have always found it interesting how vocal the staff are about what kind of coffee machine we have in the kitchenette. Like it is a right of theirs to demand state-of-the-art tech to make a cup of something they should have already had at home. Some of them hate the perfectly silent French press, saying it's laborious and slow. The filter coffee machine seems to make whoever gets the dregs of the jug quite cross. At one point we rented one of the barista machines but got rid of it after a week because the performance of the whole thing nearly drove me to murder. The *bang bang* on the side of the bin to get the used grounds out. The deafeningly loud grinding of the beans, which seemed to always happen as soon as I'd start an important call. In the end, we settled on a large Nespresso pod machine. I hate it. I hate the waste it creates and how many pods we have to order. No one puts them in the special bin to be recycled. I think the cuteness of it makes people drink more coffee than they need. By 4 p.m. everyone is yawning. Coffee really is a symbol of selfishness. I hate everything it represents. I do, however, very much enjoy a cup of Nescafé Gold Blend so feel a distant camaraderie with Ajay's mother. The snobbery around instant coffee baffles me. It's a drink that has fuelled wars. Do you really think soldiers in World War II woke up and dicked about with grinding beans before they set off to defend their country? No. They boiled the water, put a teaspoon of perfectly blended granules into a cup, splashed in some UHT and got the hell on with the job. If Ajay was a soldier, we'd all be dead by lunchtime.

Next to arrive, at 9.06 a.m., is Audrey. Audrey is extremely temperamental and emotional.

'Sorry, sorry, sorry. Nightmare on the Tube,' she says, which may or may not be true.

'It happens,' I say, while giving her a strong look. She looks upset, which isn't unusual. As an employer she makes me nervous; a meltdown always feels imminent. Where other people come to work and present their best selves, she doesn't see the need. A part of me is slightly in awe of someone's refusal to conform to behaviour that other people expect of us. The other part of me is her boss and finds it very annoying.

I sometimes catch her talking to Fliss about the man she is seeing. By all accounts he is a lot older than her and married. Audrey's very pretty and in her mid-twenties, and why she sticks with him I have no idea, he doesn't seem very committed to their affair. I heard her tell Fliss that she sometimes doesn't see him for weeks. You can always tell when they've spent a night together because she comes in skipping and chirping like a bird. On those days she does a reasonable job of making jewellery but mostly her output is mediocre. Isabella refuses to get rid of her though. I think it's because Audrey is the only member of staff she employed without consulting me – keeping her on is more of an act of pride than anything else.

'Does anyone else feel really depressed at the moment?' Audrey asks the room, with no desire for an answer.

'I swear man, weed. When the government greenlights it people are gonna be like, "Fuck, I feel so good,"' Ajay says.

'I can't do weed, it makes me eat too much.'

This makes me laugh. She snacks all day, then lets dirty plates pile up on her desk that stay there for days until the cleaner comes. Another awful habit of Audrey's is that she constantly drops the pillow she insists she needs for her back on the floor. People step over it all day and no one ever seems to see the need to pick it up. Almost every day, at least twice, I storm out of my office, pick the pillow up, hand it to her and say, 'Did you realise this was on the floor?' To which she always just says, 'Oh, thanks.' Older men don't like that, they are too long in the tooth to deal with a young girlfriend's mess. She needs to work on that if she expects to keep him interested.

And finally, at 9.33 a.m., in walks Isabella herself. As always she looks very good. Knee-high boots over skinny jeans. A cropped jacket and dripping with her own gold chains and hoops. Her brown hair is shiny and highlighted to perfection. Her face beautifully made-up, but heavy with the usual frown.

'Urgh,' is the first thing she says, referring to whatever hardship she is revelling in this morning.

'Urgh,' I reply, because she is late.

'Fucking Cressida,' she says, slamming her bag down on her desk. 'She never does anything I ask.'

Ah yes, Cressida, the nanny who can't take it any more. A professional caregiver with years of experience, and a mother herself, who is belittled and bossed around by a clueless ball of anxiety who is jealous that her child loves her nanny more than she loves her.

'What did she not do?' I ask, reluctantly.

'Fucking *anything*. Poppy was awake by the time she arrived this morning. She's supposed to arrive at 6.30 and she came at 6.45. It's not good enough. Poppy was screaming.'

The irony of what she is saying about lateness is totally lost on her.

'So you had to do fifteen minutes on your own?'

She shoots me a 'don't you dare' look. 'I'm a single mother Mia, I need help. I'm not denying that. There is no shame in childcare when you are a single mother and run a business, OK?'

53

'I know, I know.'

'You wouldn't understand.'

'Why is that?'

'Because you're not a mother. And you have a husband. You have no idea how hard it is for someone like me.'

I've had to learn to bite my tongue. She's right, I have no idea what it's like to have a father who acts like a personal bank so I can do whatever I want with my life and throw money at all my problems. It must be awful.

'Happy Mother's Day for yesterday,' I say, to lighten the mood.

'Yeah, like my three-year-old gives a fuck.'

There are multiple versions of Isabella that run alongside each other. One is a jittery ex-coke addict who the press refers to as 'best friend to the stars'. She has been on the cusp of celebrity her whole life, friends with whoever's hot in the room. A party girl, an IT girl. She's the daughter of a wealthy businessman who gave her financial support rather than emotional. To be fair to her she made a good decision at age thirty when she realised she would always be an appendage to her famous friends rather than the famous one herself. She started making jewellery and putting the diamonds around their necks, asking them to mention them in interviews and using her connections to have her designs accompany the dresses at events like the BAFTAs and The Pride of Britain Awards. This is all brilliant exposure, she's always in the party pages named as 'Isabella May, Jewellery Designer', but it doesn't translate into sustainable sales. We need some wholesale to keep us afloat. Getting into Selfridges is what will give us longevity.

Isabella is also relentlessly trying to place herself as a trailblazer. Always on a panel somewhere discussing something useless like, 'Can I get Botox and still be a feminist?' She believes yes, judging by her forehead. That isn't a criticism, I haven't been able to frown for five years, I just don't get the point of standing on a stage discussing whether I let women down by having a tiny injection to smooth out the signs of ageing. This part of her is determined to be a hero. It is woke, feisty and liberal. It is a façade. A pretence. A performance. She is liberal because it's good for business, not because it's what she believes. That's what I think, anyway.

'We have a team meeting at ten, if you're up to it?' I say, never knowing which way she will go.

'Of course I'm up to it, Mia. I just need to make breakfast first.'

Out of the corner of my eye I see Audrey's pillow fall to the floor. Maybe Isabella will trip over it on her way to make the breakfast she should have had at home. I'd say that will teach her, but it probably won't.

The meeting starts late because Isabella is in the kitchenette manoeuvring level teaspoons of flaxseed, then hemp seed, then chia seeds into a bowl of oats and oat milk that she heated up three times before it was perfect. The rest of us sit patiently waiting for her, listening to the repeating BEEP BEEP BEEP of the microwave, wondering when she will declare it the required temperature. Eventually she comes in, a tea towel protecting her hands from the hot bowl. She blows on her food as she walks, and finally sits the fuck down so we can get on with it.

'OK, what's on the agenda?' she asks.

'I want to run over everything we are taking to the Selfridges pitch and make sure it's all up to where it should be,' I say, getting stuck in. 'Also, Ajay, can we discuss the digital pack you're putting together?'

'Yeah don't worry about that, Ajay and I have sorted it,' Isabella says, blowing through the billowing steam rising from the bowl.

'Sure have, babes,' Ajay says, making me buckle.

'Oh, you have?' I say, surprised. It's very unusual for things to happen without me having to push a hundred times. 'I'll tick that off the list then. Can't wait to see it. And now what about the pieces we are taking in, how are they looking, Fliss?'

'Great, really good.'

'Excellent, just what I wanted to hear.'

Fliss is the only member of staff who elevates the business without needing constant affirmation and motivation. Sassy, confident and well adjusted, she is so talented at her job. I'm desperate to promote her to head of design but Isabella thinks that will make people think she doesn't design any more. Which she doesn't. Fliss has taken this brand from boring sentimental necklaces that boring sentimental boyfriends get their boring sentimental girlfriends for Valentine's Day, to being a highly revered fashion jewellery brand that celebrities choose and magazines want to write about. Isabella swoops in to take the credit but it's Fliss who has made this brand what it is. I'm so proud of employing her, she was a real find. A graduate of Saint Martins College of Art, she went on to be a buyer for Net-a-Porter, but she wasn't happy there, she wanted to create. That's when I found her and asked her to help me turn our brand around. She couldn't have delivered on that better. Isabella obviously resents her enormously and goes so far as to make a tutting sound as she speaks, which she tries to pretend is because of her hot food. But Fliss seems unbothered. She is one of those balletic women who carries herself with the kind of grace you're either born with or not. She politely ignores her boss's rudeness and holds up a necklace that I immediately realise is beautiful.

'I wanted to add this to the pitch. I just finished it.' It's a long gold necklace with a large hollow disc-shaped pendant. It's perfectly distressed with a beautiful engraving of a bird on it. It's stunning.

'Sure, it looks great, we can add it,' I say, getting up to have a closer look. I think I hear Isabella growl.

'I made it from Fairtrade metal. I think we could do an entire collection this way. There is such a move towards sustainability and ethical trading. I read an interview with one of the head buyers at Selfridges, it's what they're looking for, so it might be good to have something in the pitch that shows we are heading in that direction too.'

'But we're not,' Isabella snaps. 'I realise you want to save the world, but sustainability is expensive. I employ mostly women; we can't be everything to everyone.'

'We'd make in sales what we'd spend on materials. It's what people want.'

Fliss has clearly done her research. I've been trying to talk to Isabella about this for a long time. It's like trying to sell a hairbrush to Boris Johnson.

'Brands that have stories seem to be doing really well. I thought you could build a story around the people that you employ,' Fliss says, trying as hard as she can to make Isabella see sense.

'The brand has a story. My story.'

Isabella will never see sense. Her father taught her not to bother.

'I see what Fliss is saying,' I venture, realising Fliss needs back-up. And because I'm not sure 'rich white girl gets lots of money from rich dad and gets all her famous friends to wear her stuff' is the kind of story that people are looking for. 'The worry is people might see you as quite privileged and not get behind the brand, I suppose.'

'Well you could say that about loads of people, what about Stella McCartney?' Isabella says, fighting her corner.

'She's so much more than just her dad's daughter,' Audrey says, abruptly.

'Excuse me, so am I!' Isabella snaps back. 'I don't think of my story being about me and my bloody dad. I think of it as being me and the connections I have made, and my position in the fashion and media world. How I have built this brand from scratch.'

'Yeah, with about four million of your dad's cash,' says Audrey, digging even more. Her confidence when answering back to Isabella is astounding. But she's achieved what she wanted, Isabella is now silenced.

'Look,' Fliss continues, 'Stella created an entirely vegan brand. That's the story really, not her dad. I think we can do something like that here. Around sustainability and the people you employ.'

'Well, I love it,' I say, for a big bolt of positivity.

'I like it too,' adds Ajay, 'I think a collection inspired by my mum would be well nice.' Isabella rolls her eyes.

'I was also thinking maybe I could come to the pitch, seeing as so many of the designs are mine?' Fliss says, standing firm. This is like a masterclass in how to get what you want, it's just such a shame for Fliss that she is speaking to a brick wall. 'I could talk through the design ideas and tell them my inspirations. This one is based on something my grandmother had. My grandad had it made for her when they got married in Trinidad and it's so stunning. The original had a hummingbird engraved on it too, there have been eighteen species of them spotted on the island. My grandad used to call Gran his hummingbird and they were married for sixty-four years. I've always had a thing about them because of that.'

'Maybe you could bring the original to show them that too?' I say, encouragingly.

'Oh wow, yes I'll ask my grandmother, I'm sure she'd love that. I also thought we could discuss the idea of collections based on all of our favourite animals. For many of us it will take us back to our childhoods and our different cultures. I thought it would be a really lovely way to introduce all of us to our customers. We won Team of the Year, but no one really knows who we are. We could show them?'

'I'm so into that,' Audrey says. 'I could do cats.'

I nearly choke. 'Actually,' I say, in a polite voice, 'I'd be doing cats. I have a cat. Do you even have a cat?'

Pigeon's existence is probably the only part of my personal life that I ever share in the office, so Audrey saying that makes me feel quite invisible.

'No, but that doesn't mean I don't like them.'

'Yes, well I have one so I guess that means I get cats,' I say, like a child. Everyone is looking at me strangely. I ignore them by pretending to write something down.

'Er, OK, I'll do sloths then,' Audrey huffs. 'I haven't got one of those either, do you?'

'Sloths?' Isabella says, hating this entire conversation. 'Who wants a sloth hanging around their neck?'

'I do,' Audrey says, and they stare at each other for longer than is comfortable.

'I'd be up for dogs. Dog ID tags for guys. That would be cool,' says Ajay.

'It's a no from me,' Isabella snaps, as if the sound of our voices has become intolerable. 'Sloths, cats, dogs, birds, who cares what animals the staff like? You can't be in the pitch, Fliss, it's too many people in the room. And you know I support black stories and black women being elevated because I have done multiple panels about it, but this isn't relevant to the brand,' she says, sounding like a moron. 'And are there even hummingbirds in the UK? I think you'll find that's a no.'

'Not relevant to the brand? It's relevant to me and I am a part of this brand,' says Fliss, sticking up for herself. 'And I know there aren't any here, that's the point. My story takes us back to my grandparents in Trinidad. I would like to design a collection using the bird as a symbol of them. That is a story. My story!'

'Well one day you might have your own business and you can talk about birds and go to all the meetings that you want, but right here, right now, you are employed to design and that's all I need you to do.' Isabella looks at Fliss briefly but can't hold the stare, she knows what she is saying is terrible.

'Will you at least mention the necklace to them? Show it to them?' Fliss asks, her shoulders square, her back straight. Holding herself. I'm so impressed. When I was her age, I had no such decorum. I'd have overturned a desk by now or thrown a coffee in the air. She's handling Isabella perfectly. I stay quiet and let her take up all the space that she needs.

'I just don't get why we are suddenly connecting ourselves to Trinidad. It's a bit random, don't you think?'

'It's not random if your Trinidadian member of staff designed it,' Fliss says, looking at me for back-up. I can't think of what to say. I'm trying to come up with the words to support Fliss, to put Isabella in her place without making her more defensive and ultimately making this worse. My pause goes on for too long. I fail Fliss in this moment, and I know it.

'I am not from Trinidad though, am I? And the company is called Isabella May, not Fliss . . . Fliss . . .' Isabella can't remember her surname. This is shameful. 'You are not the face of this company, I am, and I would like the product to represent me, not you. OK?'

'Fine,' Fliss says, standing up. 'Would you mind if I go? If I'm not coming to the pitch I don't really need to be here, do I? I'll just get back to finishing my pieces.'

'Yes, go,' Isabella says.

'Can I go too?' asks Audrey, who has been on her phone for the last few minutes. 'I need to call my boyfriend back real quick.'

'Get out!' Isabella snaps, making me jump. She really shouldn't talk to the staff like that. So then it's just Isabella, myself and Ajay in the meeting.

'Anything else I can do for you ladies?'

'You can go too Ajay, thank you,' I say, and sit calmly and quietly until he is out of earshot.

'Are you looking for a racial discrimination case to be filed against us?' I say, after shutting the glass door and trying to keep my face neutral.

'She's fine. We pay her well.'

'I can assure you she is not fine. Her idea was really good. Different staff members doing collections inspired by their favourite animal? It's cute and original. You should think about it.'

Isabella ignores me and pretends to do something official on her computer. 'I might add my original collection of birthstone rings to the pitch.'

'I think that's a bad idea, we've come a long way since then.'

'They are part of my origin story. I thought that's what you all wanted . . . story!' she says, as if that was a winning line. 'We don't have a bottomless pit of money, Mia, I want to get the current collection off the ground, then see where we are at. No big changes for a while, OK?'

'You realise how important this is, don't you?'

'Yes, Mia, it's my business. I *am* Isabella May, remember?'

Why isn't she getting it? By behaving like this, she's denying Fliss her right to bring her cultural heritage into her work. We're interrupted by my phone ringing. It's Tristan. I don't answer it because his calls are always trivial, and I want to dig deeper with Isabella and explain to her the damage she is doing. We stare at each other until it rings out. He rings again, which is unusual, so I wonder if it is serious.

'Aren't you going to answer that?' she presses. 'It might be your cat.'

I answer the call.

'Hi, you OK?' I ask, concerned. I head over to the kitchenette for a little privacy and put the kettle on. 'What's the matter?' He must be somewhere busy, I can hear a lot of noise. 'Tristan, are you OK?'

'I don't know what meal deal to get,' he says eventually. 'There are so many choices.'

I shouldn't have answered my phone.

'Where are you?' I ask.

'M&S. I can get a sandwich, drink and crisps or a bar thing for £4.99. It's a good deal but I can't choose. I wanted soup but the soup place is shut because they had a power cut and couldn't get the soup made in time.'

'It's very early for lunch, you could go back to work and decide later?' I say, wondering if maybe the gift of time will enable him to make up his own mind.

'No, I want it now as I have a call at 12.30. I wanted tuna but they only have tuna and sweetcorn, and I don't like sweetcorn. What else do I like?'

Christ.

'What about prawn mayo?'

'I think maybe I should avoid fish. It doesn't feel right so soon after watching *Seaspiracy*.'

I won't argue with that. I've been a vegan for twenty years, even before it was easy or fashionable. It's a great way to avoid chaos. Less options, less chaos. Also, I find meat revolting and have occasionally vomited after watching him consume dead animals.

'You had a steak a few nights ago,' I remind him.

'Yes, but I haven't watched *Cowspiracy* so don't feel so bad about that.'

'OK, well get the ploughman's with salt and vinegar crisps. You've always liked it. Brown bread if you can. And a kombucha instead of pop and, rather than the bar for dessert, grab a banana and then we can have something nice after dinner tonight. OK?'

'OK, thank you.' He doesn't hang up while he gathers his items.

'I think I'll get the cheese and onion crisps.'

'Whatever you fancy. I better go love, busy day.'

'What's your favourite flavour, I can't remember?'

Make it stop.

'Plain ole ready salted, but you already know that.'

'I just like the sound of your voice. You sound sexy on the . . . FUCK!'

'Tristan, what? What happened?'

'I dropped my kombucha. It rolled under a display unit. Yes, yes it's mine. Thanks, yeah, I'll get another one.'

Someone has obviously picked up his drink and now I am listening to them discuss it while making a cup of tea that I don't want.

'Tristan, I better get back to work. I have to take Pigeon to the vet this afternoon so have a lot to do before that.'

He doesn't hear me due to the kerfuffle he has caused.

'I better go Mia, sorry!'

He hangs up as Isabella storms past me. 'Let's sort the pitch out on Zoom. I have to go, Cressida called. Poppy just threw up and won't settle.'

'Oh dear, I hope she's OK. Let's Zoom this afternoon, I have a vet's appointment at lunchtime.'

'During work hours?' she says under her breath.

'The perils of motherhood!' I say, with a what-are-you-gonna-do smile.

Isabella is gone.

'Fliss, give me the necklace,' I say, striding over to her workbench. 'I'll take it to the Selfridges pitch and do my absolute best for you.'

'Thanks boss.'

I pick up Audrey's stray cushion from the floor and throw it at her on the way back to my desk.

6

I get a cupcake on my way to the vet's and sit eating it as I wait for Pigeon's appointment. I know this would make Liz happy, so I take a rare selfie and send it to her.

For mum x

She texts back with a smiley face and a love heart.

I've always liked taking Pigeon to the vet. She's generally very well behaved and in perfect health, and it makes me very proud. I also like to be around people who love animals, and it's never more apparent than in a vet's waiting room. I particularly like ours. The walls are covered in happiness-inducing posters of humans cuddling their pets. There's even one picture of a man aged around fifty cuddling a tortoise. There's another poster showing '100 Breeds of Dogs' and another showing '100 Breeds of Cats'. I could look at the cat one for hours. Pigeon is a mix of a few breeds. I found her on the street when she was very little so will never know exactly, but she has the blueish grey coat of a Russian Blue and a brilliant stripy tail like a tabby cat. Her nature fits the description of both. Calm, affectionate, loyal. Really, I don't know what more you could want from a cat.

I do worry I'll never be able to feel this way again. Of course, I am not blind to the fact that my beloved girl is sixteen and that any time we have from now is a bonus, but the inevitable isn't something I can avoid. I am fond of all cats, but I do see Pigeon as exceptional. I fear another cat would just be disappointing. I do try not to think about it, but it's there in my mind somewhere. A fear I try to swallow back down when it tries to get the better of me. I simply don't know how my life would continue without her.

You get all sorts in a vet's waiting room. There is a real tough-looking guy, probably around thirty. He's wearing a singlet and has tattoos up his arms. His head is shaved, and he has multiple piercings. You'd expect him to have a huge status dog, but actually he is sitting cuddling a very sweet Jack Russell. This man, with so much to prove with his image, has nothing to prove with his dog. He strokes it and holds it tight. The dog looks up at him lovingly, making squeaking noises if his owner stops scratching him, even for a second. The man laughs, a sweet smile for someone so angry-looking. He kisses his dog on the head, clearly adoring him with all his heart.

There's an old man with a cat in a basket on the seat next to him. The cat looks older than the man. The man seems very sad, but occasionally sticks his finger through the bars of the carrier and says, 'It's OK, I'm here.' The cat meows and sniffs his finger. His daddy, the person who has kept him alive all these years. I glance down to Pigeon, she's sitting happily in her carrier. No sounds, no panic. She can see I'm here and that is enough for her.

There is a woman, likely in her forties, also with a cat. She is tapping away on her phone, busy busy. Like me, she is dressed in smart clothes and has probably stepped out of the office to take care of her baby. She looks irritated by whatever is happening inside her phone, but every now and then a white paw comes jutting out through the wire grid and she stops tapping, her nose scrunches up as she smiles and taps the paw with her finger. The paw tightens around it; a little thing they must do. It makes her smile even more. 'Good girl,' she says. 'Won't be long.'

And then there is another man. A businessman, in a suit. He sits patiently with his hands clasped next to a cage with a little yellow bird inside. Every now and then the bird makes a sound, and the man laughs. When the bird makes the sound twice in a row, his laugh turns into a guffaw that he tries to hide from the rest of us. He finds his bird absolutely hilarious. Is he also like that at home? Just walking around in hysterics every time the bird makes a noise? How charming. He thinks his bird is the best bird in the world, and the dear little thing just loves to make his daddy happy.

I love being around pet lovers. People brave enough to lower their walls and admit that the joy they get from their furry friends is sometimes far more plentiful than what they receive from humans. I realise I feel very at home here, with people like me.

'Pigeon,' says the vet, coming out to get us. I just love how he uses her name instead of mine. I stand up, pick up the carrier and follow him into the little room with the metal table. I let Pigeon out and she sits calmly, waiting for whatever will come.

'Such a good girl,' says the vet.

'She really is.' This must be how mothers feel when their children get straight As.

'So, it's just shots today, is she doing all right other than that?' He picks her up and puts her on the scales, she doesn't make a fuss.

'Yup, just shots. She's been great, no change.'

'That's lovely to hear. Her weight is perfect, her coat looks lovely and healthy.'

'I give her steamed fish twice a week.'

'Lucky girl.' He has a little silver tray behind him with two syringes. He starts to unwrap one. 'I had a cat in this morning who's twenty-one. She's great, no signs of illness. She still eats well, she's a little blind and needs more grooming but, other than that, perfect. It's so good to see.'

'Well I can only hope she'll make it to that age, that would be wonderful.'

Suddenly I hear a kerfuffle in reception. The vet is about to inject Pigeon but is obviously concerned.

'I better just make sure . . .' he says as he goes to leave. But then the door bursts open. The receptionist looks stressed.

'Ben, we've got an emergency and you're the only vet here, can you?'

'Absolutely. Sorry, Pigeon, back with you soon.' He asks me to put her back in her carrier but she jumps down and hides under the table. I'm forced into the corner of the room when the receptionist comes back in with a man and a cat. The man looks so upset. I can't leave because they are blocking the door and Pigeon is still under the table that they are surrounding. The vet looks very concerned about the emergency cat, so I just step back and try to go unnoticed. Pigeon is being very still. So am I.

The man is crying, he's struggling to catch a breath. The nurse rushes out, shutting the door behind her.

'What's your name, pal?' asks the vet.

'It's Lee.'

'OK Lee, can you tell me what happened?'

'I found him under the sofa. He'd been missing for a few hours, I couldn't see him anywhere, then I saw his tail poking out. He wouldn't come when I called him, my mum was screaming for help.'

'It's OK, he's here now,' says the vet, calmly. He is pressing the cat, stroking it. The cat isn't moving.

'Is he all right?'

'Would you like me to perform CPR?' the vet asks, creating an air of terror in the room.

'Yes, it's my mum's cat. Do whatever it takes.'

As if the nurse knew this would happen, she comes in with tubes and forms and hands one to the man. 'We will need your permission here,' she says to him. He wipes his eyes and signs his name. He's crying so much, he didn't even read what it said. The vet is getting ready to do something. The man starts stroking his cat. The vet asks him to take his hands away for a second. He holds his hand to the cat's chest.

'What? What's happening?' the man weeps. The pace of the room has slowed right down, the vet has lost his sense of urgency. He takes his hand away from the cat.

'I'm so sorry, it's too late.'

Oh God no, this is awful. The poor man, his poor mum. The poor cat. I shouldn't be in this small room at this extremely intimate moment.

'No, this can't be happening. Oh no, Plimsoll. No.' The man is sobbing into his cat.

The vet puts his hand on the man's shoulder and the nurse puts her arm around him.

'We're so sorry,' they both say. 'He was clearly very loved.'

Pigeon moves towards me so I pick her up and put her in her carrier. I manage to slip out and wait in the waiting room to be called in again. About ten minutes later, the man comes out carrying his cat in his arms.

'Are you sure you don't want to leave him here, Lee?' the nurse asks, sweetly.

'No, my mother will want to say goodbye. She always said she wanted to bury him in the garden when it happened. How long do I have before he starts to . . .'

'About twenty-four hours, please don't push it longer than that. We offer a full service for ashes. We're here if you need us.'

The man breaks down again. Standing in the reception area with all of these strangers watching him. I wonder if he feels safe in here, in a roomful of people who all understand. A safe space. Everyone is looking at him sympathetically. There is a chorus of 'So sorry', 'God bless' and 'Oh dear, poor kitty.' Even the man with the bird stops laughing.

The nurse opens the door for Lee, and he walks out, his dead cat hanging on his forearms. It's the sorriest, saddest sight.

'All the best to your mother,' the nurse calls after him.

He stands outside as if he's been frozen. Holding the cat, looking at it, just the running of his tears proving he's alive. And then he starts to walk away. A slow walk, the kind of purposeless walk you do when you don't want to arrive anywhere. Everyone in the waiting room is feeling the moment. Fingers are poking through cages, dogs are on laps. All of us knowing that one day, that will be us, just so grateful that our day is not today. I look out of the window again, he's almost around the corner. I feel an uncontrollable urge to run after him.

'I'll be right back,' I say to the nurse, making her aware I am leaving Pigeon for a moment. She says it's OK, I know Pigeon will be safe. I run down the street after the man. When I reach him the weight of his sadness hits me like a wall of thick smoke.

'Excuse me,' I say. 'Hello?'

He stops walking and turns around slowly. I first notice the cat. Eyes open, draped, dead. I move my eyes up to the man's face. His eyes just open, his shoulders slumped, lifeless other than the essential acts of breathing and standing.

'It's Lee, isn't it? I am so sorry about your cat.'

I can see he wants to say thank you but can't manage it.

'There is a support group. We're meeting tonight. It's every Tuesday at seven p.m. at the Methodist Church on the high street. A pet bereavement group. I know it sounds silly but it's real grief and there are people who understand. It might be useful for your mum, or you. I just wanted to tell you that.'

He manages a nod.

'I'm Mia, by the way. Mee-ah.' I don't know why I spelled that out.

'It sounds like "meow".'

'I've never thought of that, but I suppose it does.'

We stand opposite each other looking at the cat. If I didn't need to get back to Pigeon, we might have stood like that for hours.

'I'll be thinking of you and your mum,' I say, turning around and walking away.

'Did your cat die?' he calls after me, taking me by surprise. I turn back to him, I don't know what to say. I don't want to lie to him. That wouldn't feel right.

And so I say the first thing that comes into my head. 'All cats die, right?'

'Right.'

Kicking myself I head back to the waiting room. *All cats die.* What a stupid thing to have said.

'Pigeon,' the vet says, calling me back. 'Sorry about that, do you want to come back in?'

'Yes. Yes, absolutely,' I say, following him again. The room feeling much less calm this time. Plimsoll's little soul clinging to the walls.

7

That evening I'm back at the Methodist Church. I told Tristan I was working late to prepare for the Selfridges pitch. I walk in and sit down. The leader, Tiana, is already here, making a cup of instant coffee on a trestle table in the corner where there is a kettle, a box of Tetley, a pot of Gold Blend and a saucer full of little plastic pots of UHT milk. That really is all a kitchenette needs. I mean, I wouldn't grumble about the addition of a vegan milk option, but really, that is absolutely it.

'Welcome back, Mia,' she says, remembering my name, putting me at ease.

'Thank you.'

The chairs are already arranged in a circle. There are eight of them. I wonder if the group changes from week to week. Will Greg return, or will the shame of his outburst keep him away? I wonder if Lee will come. It felt good to pass on the knowledge of a group like this. But I probably scared him off with my doom and gloom 'all cats die' nonsense.

'Help yourself to tea and coffee,' Tiana says, not asking how I am or inviting anything that might kick off the session before the correct time. Still four minutes to go. I respect the timekeeping on her part, very professional.

I've been to a few different kinds of groups over the years. AA wasn't for me, neither was anger management – largely considering I am not an alcoholic nor unable to control my anger. Control is what my existence is based on. It's something I have endless amounts of. You have to, when you come from the kind of background that I do. I've attended a few eating disorder groups but felt far too guilty being there among so many young women, and a surprising number of men, who were actively in such distress. I'm hardly the world's most authentic person but lying about an eating disorder felt like a betrayal to the brave people seeking help. My cat might be alive and well, but my fear of Pigeon dying is profound enough for me to justify my place in this group.

'So, how did you end up doing this? It's quite a niche form of therapy, isn't it?' I ask Tiana as she sits down.

'It is. I used to run a group for people who were experiencing loneliness and over time realised that pets dying seemed to be the cause of loneliness for so many people. But there was a shame that came with it. Or if not shame then just a feeling that their grief wasn't worthy of the attention it needed. So, I created this group. I have left a few flyers around but mostly it's a word-of-mouth situation. I've never had less than four people attend.'

'I told someone about it today. A man at the vet, I watched his cat die and I told him about the group.'

'Oh that's very sad, I hope he comes.'

'Me too. It was his mum's cat, he seemed very upset for her and . . .'

'You know, Mia. In case he comes why don't we let him share his story himself.'

'Oh, yes. Of course,' I say, embarrassed by my gossiping. 'Are you an animal lover yourself?'

'Let's hold tight. It's 6.58 p.m. and the session will start soon.'

'Right. Absolutely.' Again, I'm struck by the sense of order that Tiana exudes. It has a calming effect on me.

First in is Martha, who I'm surprised to see is wearing different clothes. Baggy trousers with a loose-fitting sweater. Her clothes look very comfortable, but they don't look cheap. She sits down on a chair, seemingly unaware of her surroundings. Still looking at the floor. It's been months since she lost her cat, should she be over it by now? It doesn't seem like she wants to be and yet every week she comes here, to a place where people understand her, maybe with some hope of moving on. I wonder who she is when she isn't in this room. Is this Martha when she is in or out of her shell?

Next in is Ada. This week in a very nice red dress that nips in at her waist then sprawls and flares out over her hips. She has a red fabric tote bag over her shoulder, and when she sits down she pulls out two packets of biscuits. She keeps one packet and passes the other one to me.

'I brought some for all of you today. Sharing is caring,' she laughs to herself. 'Gotta find joy where you can. Haven't you?'

'That's very kind,' I say, taking them. I won't have one myself as the cream filling isn't vegan but I open the packet and offer one to Martha. She takes a biscuit but holds it in her hands rather than eat it.

Nicole walks in looking like she's come straight from work. I admire her for being here. It's not a cool place to be, but she comes because she is going through something that maybe her friends don't understand. It feels good to be in a group that makes you feel better.

At 7.02 Tiana begins. 'Hello again everyone, no new faces today which is nice for us all as we can get right back to where we were.' She doesn't mention Greg, or that he isn't here. His empty chair feels ominous and sad. I wonder if he killed himself, like he said he might. Maybe we will never know.

'Mia, seeing as we didn't get to you last week, would you like to begin?' she asks.

Of course she was going to start with me, that's the polite thing to do. Imaginary animals run through my mind. I could say my dog died, a hamster. I could say Pigeon had died but I can't think about that. Suddenly the door bursts open, offering me a few more minutes to think. It's Greg. He strides towards the circle and stands behind the chair that we all left for him. Exactly where he sat last time.

'I want to say I'm sorry . . . for how I ended things in the last session.' His lip wobbles. He's trying to be brave. 'That wasn't cool. I'm sorry.'

'Thank you Greg, why don't you sit down and we'll get started,' Tiana says.

He slaps his hand to his face and wipes his cheeks, sniffs and sits. He's nodding, as if to say well done to himself. It's clear that took a lot of courage. Ada edges her chair closer to his and puts her hand on his back. 'I'm glad you're here. I was worried about you,' she says, kindly.

Greg thanks her with a nod, as if words would make him cry. Ada leaves her chair where it is. 'I don't really wanna talk, OK?' he says to Tiana, who seems untroubled by the thought of someone sitting here silently, which bodes well for me.

'My son can be a bit that way,' Ada says, her hand still resting on Greg. 'He gets very upset. His dad let us down, it made him think he wasn't good enough, I think. I'm always telling him he's a good person. He can do whatever he wants, but he thinks no one will love him like I do. I think that's why he won't move out. Mopes around. Doesn't lift a finger and blames it on his mind.'

'I 'ave to wash up cos I don't live with anyone,' Greg says. To which Ada nods emphatically as if he just told her he was training for a marathon.

'That's good. You've got some motivation then. Don't knock yourself down, that's good, that really is. Some days my son doesn't even get out of bed.' She turns to us all. 'It's why I needed Mrs Jones, she made my house feel less sad. Without her around I sort of just wallow with him.'

'Animals bring joy. Dogs, cats, snakes, hamsters, it doesn't matter. That's what pets are all about,' Tiana says. 'I once had someone come to this group for six weeks, do you know why?'

There is a quiet chorus of 'Why?'s.

'Because his fish died.'

Everyone chuckles, even Martha. Nicole laughs properly, I join her. Greg says, 'I thought a snake was stupid' with a smile that changes his entire face. And Ada laughs so loudly that none of us know where to look. Something tells me she was just waiting for an excuse to laugh like that. It's quite the show.

'Oooo, I'm sorry,' she says, opening her eyes and realising everyone is looking at her. 'Any excuse to laugh these days.' She eats another biscuit to force her mouth into another position.

'No grief is stupid, OK?' Tiana says, using our reactions to make a point. 'Nothing that any of you are feeling right now is unusual, stupid or unjustified. When a pet dies, no matter what the pet was, how long you had it or what happened, grief is the response and no one should tell you it isn't real.'

'I walked out on my job yesterday,' Greg says, everything from his mind, heart and body opening up. Tiana looks to me as if to say she's sorry, and it will be my turn soon. I shrug my shoulders, the more time Greg takes up the better for me. 'One of the lads noticed I'd been cryin' and took the piss and I got so mad. I wasn't gonna say nothin' but I yelled, "My snake died," and they laughed their 'eads off. So I did what I always fuckin' do and threw shit. I quit before they sacked me. Now I'm unemployed as well. I'm a fucking joke.'

'My son is unemployed and he's not a joke,' says Ada, like this conversation plays on a loop in her own life. 'You're more than your job. You're more than your anger. You're more than that snake, no matter how much you loved him.'

'What was your job?' asks Nicole, speaking for the first time today.

'I'm a carpenter,' Greg says. 'Only thing I'm good at. Fucked that up as well though, didn't I?'

'Sometimes a pet symbolises a person and that's what makes it so hard when they pass,' Martha says, raising her head to the highest it's ever been in here. 'Bessie was not "just a cat" as so many people say. My husband and I got her together. We never had children. It wasn't a choice we were able to make, but getting a cat was. Can't imagine a parent loving a child more.'

Tiana seems energised by Martha opening up but looks at me. 'Mia, I was going to come to you but . . .'

'No, it's OK,' I say, suggesting she must follow up with Martha. I don't want to be in the spotlight, yet the more this group lay their hearts on the line, the more of a fraud I feel.

'Go on, Martha,' Tiana prompts.

'I've had two great men in my life.' She unclasps her hands and sits up straighter. 'My husband and my father, who was a vet. A lovely man. Back then having your dad as the local vet meant our house was a drop-in centre for all local pets. We had a giant turtle living in our bathtub for a few days. Birds in the wardrobe, snakes in the basement, all sorts.' Greg even cracks a smile for that, he sits a little taller.

'But we had our own pets too. A few cats, a budgie and a dog called Wally. Wally was the love of my life when I was a kid, I played with him for hours after school. He used to run off, probably looking for rabbits or squirrels or something. One day he didn't come back, I was so upset. Weeks went by. I'd sit at the end of the drive and wait but nothing. Dad drove around at night, Mum left food out. After a few weeks a woman called. She said she might have our dog. My dad and I got in the car and went to the address but when she answered the door she was sobbing. She said the dog had been with her for weeks, that she'd wanted to call but couldn't bring herself to. I was cross, I remember wanting to shout, "Give me my dog," but my dad was good with people too, he knew something wasn't right, or that she wasn't bad or whatever. She asked us to come in. She said her husband was very ill, he'd been so down and nothing cheered him up – not until Wally turned up. She opened a door to a room where a man was sitting on a chair and Wally was lying across him. Wally didn't even look up at me. The man looked heartbroken as he said, "Is this your dog?" And do you know what my dad said?'

'I hope he knocked him out for nicking your dog,' Greg blurts, spitting testosterone all over us all.

'No. He said, "That isn't our dog. I hope you feel better soon." And he took me by the hand and we left.'

'He gave up your dog?' Nicole asks, with a faint look of disgust on her face.

'No,' Martha says. 'He gave him to someone who needed him more, there is a difference.'

'That was incredibly kind,' I say to Martha. 'Your father sounds like a really nice man.'

A memory rises up from my childhood – my own father going ballistic and shouting at Liz and me when we asked if we could get a puppy. I swallow the memory back down.

'He was. I've never forgotten it because I saw how powerful a relationship with a pet can be. That man had hope, because of Wally.'

'And what about you?' Tiana asks. 'You must have missed him terribly.'

'I did. But I also had three cats, two birds, a hamster, a goat, another dog and a donkey called Plonk. And I had my dad. I was happy to know Wally was so loved.' Martha's body slumps again. 'If it's OK, that's enough for today.'

'Of course,' Tiana says, clearly knowing not to push. 'Well done, Martha. It was really good to hear you speak so freely.' The whole group nod in agreement as Tiana turns to me.

'Mia, what would you like to share today?'

I look at the door, feeling sad and frustrated that Lee hasn't come through it. I wanted to see him again. I wonder if he is home right now with his dead cat. I wonder how his mother took the news. If they are both OK. I don't know why I care about a stranger, but I do. I watched someone experience the thing I fear the most. I think about it a lot.

'Mia,' Tiana pushes. 'Would you like to share anything with us?'

They all look at me expectantly. My mouth is suddenly so dry I can hardly move it. 'I feel quite nervous,' I say.

'That's how I get,' Greg says, supportively.

'It's hard to know where to start,' I say, meaning it. Where does my story even begin? 'I come from disorder.' That feels like a good start. 'That maybe means I have a disorder, I'm not sure. But I come from chaos. Chaos that I created and chaos that was pushed upon me by my dad.'

A crushing comparison overwhelms me again. I try to imagine my dad exhibiting the sort of kindness Martha's had and it's so impossible to imagine that I give myself a headache trying. I start to cry hard, messy tears.

'Sharing is very hard for me,' I say, looking up at Tiana. 'But I will try, it's why I'm here.' I take a deep breath. Maybe I can tell just a piece of my story, and that will be enough. 'My cat, Pigeon, well, she saved me from the chaos. My husband tolerated her,' I shudder as I speak about Pigeon in past tense, 'but I suspect he didn't really like her very much. He's a good man, Tristan, but I'm not sure he gets *all* of me, that he understands the things that have made me who I really am.'

Everyone is looking at me intently. It feels unfamiliar to be the focus of people's attention in this way. By the looks on their faces, they seem to want to hear what I have to say. I continue.

84

'Before we met, I was never in hot pursuit of a boyfriend. I had more lovers than relationships and I enjoyed the ones I had. I could have coasted along like that until my libido had had enough.' That makes Ada laugh again, but much more controlled this time. 'But people didn't like it. The closer I got to forty, the more comments I would receive. "Are you married?" "No." "Engaged?" "No." "In a relationship at all?" "No." "Well do you want to be a mother?" "I don't know." My answers would often be followed by sympathy or questions as to why Mr Right was yet to appear. They wouldn't believe me when I told them I was OK alone.'

Tiana nods, encouraging me to continue.

'When people learned I had my cat, Pigeon, I became subject to the "cat lady" label. Something that is bashed around quite casually, but it's extremely insulting because no one means it as a compliment. People are not commenting on the love you feel for your furry friend, they are insinuating that you are lonely and isolated. Possibly even unlovable. There came a point where it felt easier to slide into what society deemed was normal for me to do. My sister Liz was married, any friends I had were coupling up, settling down. So I opened my mind to the idea of marriage, and then I found Tristan. We do love each other, I'm a good wife, he's a fine husband, I think I'm a good stepmum . . . But I don't feel very . . . me. I don't know if the life I am living is the right one. In many ways, maybe "cat lady" suited me better.'

'People need each other, it's why we're all here. But that doesn't mean it's easy,' Tiana says. 'Would you like to go on, Mia?'

'No, thank you. That feels like enough for today.' I know I'll need to talk about Pigeon at some point, and I don't want to ruin this yet.

As Tiana moves the group on, I take them all in. How is it that in this roomful of strangers, I feel more myself than anywhere else?

When the group is finished, I see Nicole standing on the street outside, texting furiously. When she sees me approaching, she puts her phone away.

'Are you OK?' I ask her.

'Yeah, fine, why? You?'

'I'm OK, I suppose. How are you finding the group?'

'Good, yeah, nice. You?'

'Yeah, same.'

We stand awkwardly. Any camaraderie we felt inside the church not happening out here on the street. I wonder if that's just how it is. The group really is a safe space. Vulnerability in the real world is dangerous.

'Maybe I'll see you next week,' I say, walking away.

'Mia, wait,' Nicole says, calling after me. I turn back to her. A connection. I like the feeling. 'I'm single, and all my friends have boyfriends. What you were describing in there, about feeling a bit left out, that resonated with me. Do you regret getting married?' she asks.

'No, I don't regret it as such. My marriage brought a lot of nice things into my life, but sometimes I do feel I have to be someone else to keep it going. It's not necessarily a bad thing, I think maybe it's even quite normal. But it nags at me.'

'So if you could go back, would you have stayed single?'

'I don't know. And it doesn't matter because this is the life I am living. So even when I feel like it isn't really me, I remember it's a choice I made. And maybe a small feeling of displacement is even healthy.'

'Do you regret not having kids of your own?'

She asks a lot of questions. But I suppose if you're at a crossroads in life, that's what you do. And it's flattering that she thinks I might have all the answers.

'No. Between my stepson and my cat my maternal instinct is adequately satisfied. Some women don't need to be mothers, but it doesn't mean they can't love. See you next week?'

'Yes, I think so.'

I start to walk away, then quickly turn back. 'Oh, how's your mum doing?' I ask her.

'Fine, why?'

'Rover, her dog?'

'Oh, yeah, sorry. She's doing well, thanks for asking. And you? Are you missing your cat?'

'Absolutely,' I say, confidently. 'Very, very much.'

Part Two

Career Woman

I'll always remember the night with Mum sitting at the dining table making something out of a huge pile of pink fabric. She had a needle in between her teeth and was humming to herself. She'd have been smiling, if it wasn't for the needle. Liz and I were sitting on the floor watching Sesame Street.

Mum loved to make our clothes. She'd probably have run her own fashion label, if it wasn't for our dad.

'OK girls, nearly ready,' she said, threading the needle and hand-stitching. Her eyesight had got worse lately, she never used to wear glasses, but she had thick ones now. They sat so close to the end of her nose I wondered if they would slide off.

'OK, TV off please.'

We did exactly as she said and rushed to the table. She had laid out three pink dresses. One for her, one for me, one for Liz. 'We'll be like the Pink Ladies,' she said, looking so happy with herself. 'Who wants to try theirs on?'

We all immediately stripped down. It had been a while since I'd seen her body. She was wearing a camisole but her chest was now completely flat. She knew I was looking but didn't engage. 'Come on, Mia. Put it on.'

The outfits were cute, a different style for each of us. She'd made Liz's – who was more of a tomboy – into culottes. Mine

*was a pretty sundress with straps that I could tie myself, and
Mum's was loose-fitting and long.*

*'We look like a band,' she said, laughing. 'What shall we
call ourselves?'*

'The Raspberries,' Liz shouted, making us all laugh.

'Strawberry Surprise,' I said.

'The Pink Apples,' Liz said. 'Or Heart Stoppers.'

*'You're so good at this,' Mum said to Liz. 'But I feel like it's
not quite there, what about . . .'*

*And then, as if all tuned into the very same frequency, the
three of us shouted, 'The Love Hearts!' making us laugh so
much we all landed in a heap on the sofa.*

*'Quick,' Mum said, getting up. 'Dad won't be home for
another hour. Go and get your favourite cassette and let's make
up a dance routine before he gets back.'*

*We laughed and danced for precisely fifty-eight minutes to
the sound of Billy Joel's 'Uptown Girl'.*

*When Dad arrived home, Mum slid back into her role of
obedient wife.*

8

It's not very often that I get to go to large fancy events for work. Usually, it's just Isabella who gets invited and that's OK with me. For the most part, 'industry' nights are pretty horrendous. Lots of people pretending to be interested in each other, constant selfies for Instagram and everyone getting so hammered it's a miracle they turn up to work again with the shame they must carry. But tonight is different as it's a huge fundraiser sponsored by Isabella's dad's private bank. And as I am managing director of his daughter's business, I'll feel quite important. It's a power trip I'm happy to ride, and it's also for a good cause so well worth the effort.

I have one dress that suits the occasion perfectly. 'No Pigeon, off that,' I say, picking her up and putting her on the floor. I don't know what it is about me laying a clean dress on the bed, but she immediately thinks she has to sit on it. The dress is a knee-length, black pencil shape with three-quarter sleeves and excellent shoulders. It's much more sexy than anything I would wear to work, but still has enough structure to it that I look like the boss I am. I wear it with four-inch black heels and put my hair up into a neat bun. I apply quite a lot of make-up with strong blusher and a red lip. I squeeze some face powder, a lipstick, my phone, some business cards and a house key into a small clutch bag and then I'm ready.

'Whit-woo!' Tristan hoots, as I walk confidently into the kitchen. 'You look incredible.'

'Why thank you,' I say, taking the glass of wine from his hand and having a gulp.

'How about I book somewhere for dinner next week? You wear that so I can show you off?'

'That sounds lovely. I better go, can't be late. We're all meeting outside the venue so we can walk in together.'

'Have fun. Don't talk to any men,' he calls after me.

'I only have eyes for you,' I shout, shutting the front door behind me. Ending one scene and entering another. My character adjusting accordingly.

Theo May is one of the most notorious finance people in London, always making it into the Forbes 100. He has the kind of money where homes are like fully staffed hotels and commercial flying is a concept he doesn't need to bother himself with unless he is considering buying the airline. He's been married to Isabella's mum, Alice, for forty years. She doesn't come to events like this and stays mostly at home. I've always respected that: why should she pretend to be comfortable in his world when she is happier behind the scenes? They're a young family, Isabella herself is only thirty-six. She is an only child and, from what I gather, has lived like a princess her whole life. Theo is magnetic. I wonder if every piece of money in the room is dragged towards his chest when he takes his clothes off.

When I arrive at the venue, five minutes early, I notice Ajay is already there and talking to someone just inside the door. When the conversation is over, he heads out. He's wearing his usual baggy ensemble with an oversized black jacket, as if that suddenly makes it a suit.

'Woah boss, look at you. Fuck yeah, you can be seriously hot when you want to be.'

'OK Ajay, thank you. Didn't we talk about boundaries?'

'Yeah we did, but that was at work, right? This isn't work, this is a party. That guy just took two of my weed chocolates off me. This crowd is gonna be lit.'

'Ajay, you can't sell drugs here. It might not be the office but this is a work night and we are representing the brand.'

'Chill, bab . . . boss. I didn't sell anything. I'm giving these away for reviews. It's market research, always working boss, don't worry about me.' I give up.

Next to arrive is Fliss, shortly followed by Isabella. We all wait another seventeen minutes for Audrey. Mostly in silence as we're all so annoyed. When she eventually walks slowly up the steps towards us, Isabella rolls her eyes and storms inside. Ajay and Fliss follow her.

'Audrey, you're so late,' I hiss, feeling I have to say something as this really is very unfair on everyone else. 'You didn't even text to say why, we could have gone in.'

'I'm sorry. Mia, can we talk about something before it starts?' She looks upset, but that isn't unusual. I do feel bad for her boyfriend troubles, but lateness really is my pet peeve.

'No, Audrey. Not now.'

'OK, but I really need to . . .'

'Come see me in my office first thing. We'll talk then. Come on, if we miss Theo's opening speech that will be so rude. Take a deep breath and put your big girl pants on, OK?'

'But . . .'

I make my way up the steps and she follows me inside.

'There they are, my favourite jewellery branding team of all time,' Theo says as we all walk through a grand atrium and approach our table. It's one of fifty in the room, each costing £35k. He gave us one for free, of course.

As is always the case with events that encourage punctuality nothing has started and most people are standing near the bar. I edge away from Audrey though, I don't want to get sucked into her drama tonight, I want to have a good time. She looks really upset. It's hard to know how much attention to give people like that. Are you feeding their drama, or alleviating it when you express concern? I choose to put it on a diet until tomorrow.

'Hello Theo,' I say, kissing him on each cheek. 'It's good to see you.' I tingle a little. He is very handsome.

'You too, Mia. Has my little girl been behaving herself?'

Isabella rudely shrugs him off when he hugs her and goes to talk to two very tall, thin model-like women who are undoubtedly very famous even though I've never seen them before in my life.

'All is well,' I tell him.

I like Theo, there have been a few occasions where I've had to call him directly and ask for money to bail us out because, for some reason, Isabella has refused to ask him herself. He's always agreed. He once said to me, 'There is business, and then there is Isabella May. Call it more of an investment in a peaceful life for me.' I don't think he cares if we make money or not, which is terrible for business but excellent for my job security.

'Do you remember the team?' I say, waving towards Fliss, Audrey and Ajay who are all standing next to me.

'Of course,' he says as he shakes Ajay's hand and then takes Fliss' before kissing her on the cheek. It's impossible to ignore the way he looks her up and down adoringly, but I suppose it's easy to do that. She looks incredible tonight in a very short dress with rainbow sequins and huge batwings. She's got her hair out and is wearing almost every piece of jewellery from the new collection, which would look messy on most people but on her looks like the epitome of style.

'And hello,' he says, taking Audrey's hand and kissing her on the cheek too. She is dressed in a jade suit with patent pumps. It's a chic look that she carries off well. Her teary eyes start to twinkle.

'Hi Theo,' she says, 'you're looking well.' She gazes at him for so long it makes me uncomfortable. But at least the look of misery disappears from her face. Whatever secret power he has just injected her with is a much more appropriate energy for a party.

'Thanks for the table, so generous. Wonderful cause,' I say, breaking Audrey's lingering stare. I am hoping he stays around so I can absorb his charm a little more. But, of course, there's a roomful of people waiting to be made to feel special.

'Have fun,' he says, as he disappears into the crowd. Audrey melting in a puddle of sexual arousal.

'What?' she says, realising I am giving her daggers. 'He's got that gorgeous old man thing.'

'He's got an old man thing,' Fliss says, as grossed out as I am.

'Fuck me, there's a Fitbit in here,' Ajay says, tearing into the goody bag on his chair. 'My mum is gonna flip. She tries to count her steps in her head. And a . . . wait . . . what's this?' He starts running a jade roller over the tablecloth. 'What's it supposed to do, iron shit?'

'No Ajay,' Isabella says, snatching it off him and rolling it on her cheeks. 'It's for your face, see?' She hands it back to him and he repeats the motion.

'What's the point in that? You women are batshit with all you do to yourselves. I don't even use soap.'

We all wish we hadn't heard that.

'Ooooh, what else have we got?' Fliss says, sitting down and opening her own goody bag. 'Perfume, lip balm, oh wow, a voucher for Harvey Nicks, this is awesome.'

I take in the scenery from our table which has 'ISABELLA MAY JEWELLERY' emblazoned on a gold plaque sticking out of a giant flower arrangement – which alone must have cost a few hundred pounds. There's free-flowing champagne and wine, little plates of food constantly appearing and luxurious gift bags on every seat. It's hard not to feel ridiculous at an event that aims to raise money for charity while costing hundreds of thousands to put on. But, according to Isabella, some of London's biggest players are here. For them, these flowers would go in their downstairs loo.

'When you create an atmosphere that makes rich people feel special, their money just pours out of them,' she told me as we waited for Audrey. 'They raise four times what the event costs in the silent auction.'

'Is that how you get so much money out of your dad?' I say, jokingly. 'New Celine handbag one week, crystal-embossed nappies for your baby the next.' I give her a friendly nudge.

'That isn't funny Mia.'

'Sorry, I was only messing around.'

'No, I mean it. That really wasn't fucking funny, OK?'

'OK, OK, I said I'm sorry.'

God, she's so touchy about it. If I had a dad who gave me all that money, I'd at least admit to how brilliant it was. She's never once said how lucky she is.

Aside from the five of us, Isabella has invited another three people to make up our table of eight – they're all either models or of Instagram fame.

'Hi, I'm Mia,' I say to one of them, who is so tall and thin I wonder if she'll grab onto my hand for support when I hold it out. She shakes it like she's a germophobe, it's almost offensive.

'Those shoulders!' she says, referring to my dress. She then sits down, not bothering to tell me her name – no doubt presuming I already know it.

'And you are?' I press, both my hands out, palms up.

'I'm Britney Spears,' she tells me, turning away to talk to an equally lofty Barbie doll who I don't waste my time being insulted by.

Isabella rushes to my ear. 'She's Jemima Plat, Mia,' she whispers. 'Jesus, the supermodel? Do you live in a barn?'

'You only know if you know. And I didn't know. She's quite rude.'

'She's not rude, she's just famous,' Isabella says, defensively. 'And if she wears the Isabella May necklace I just dropped into her goody bag and posts it to her twenty-five million followers, it would be huge for us. So please, if you don't know someone's name here tonight, just nod.'

Modern fame is so ugly. It used to be that special people made it to the top, but the Internet means literally anyone can gather a crowd. In one way I think it's better. Why should only a select few experience the joy of recognition? In another way I think it has made too many unworthy people very rich and recognisable for all of the wrong reasons.

I recently learned there is a young woman who is followed by forty million people and makes millions of pounds for opening boxes of things on TikTok. Surely, I can't be the only one who thinks that's problematic?

I sit down before I get myself into more trouble. 'Who is that?' I ask Fliss, referring to the other woman who Jemima is probably bitching about me to.

'Hattie Garfield. An influencer,' Fliss says, knowing the information but gloriously unbothered about being in her presence.

'And what does she influence?'

'Make-up stuff, mostly. The occasional dance routine. She's got to a point where she can do anything, really. Make-up, unboxing, playing with her cat. She makes so much money.'

'Maybe I could make loads of money playing with my cat on Instagram?' I say.

'Go for it. I'm not really on there any more. I got into an argument with a Trump supporter in Arizona who said the LGTBQ+ community was polluting the water and decided to save my soul after that.'

She's got so much self-control. It's highly admirable. Even I dabble with the funny cat accounts on Instagram.

Ajay seems delighted to be sitting next to the third young woman who has joined us for the night. She's in a shiny green dress and resembles Kim Kardashian. Her breasts could double as a plate. Her nails can't be less than two inches long.

'And this one?' I ask Fliss, nodding in her direction.

'Never heard of her. Probably a model or something.'

I wonder how upsetting that would be to hear for the girl we're referring to. To be described so vaguely.

'Fuckin' hell she's well fit,' Ajay says, leaning into me. I pretend not to hear him. I may have to resign myself to the fact that a professional relationship with Ajay may never exist.

'She's a bad bitch as well. CEO of Click Nails.'

'WHAT?' I ask, genuinely agog. '*She* is a CEO?'

'Yup, and look at that rack.'

I go back to ignoring him. It's less stressful.

Theo then gets up on stage and the room goes silent. 'I'm not going to take up much of your time, as the important part of tonight is about what you give, not what I say. But as you know, tonight's funds will be going to an organisation very close to my heart: the Theo May Foundation. Over the past ten years we have raised fifty million pounds that has gone directly to supporting women and girls around the world. What you might not know is that I have personally matched that amount and so the total donated is actually a hundred million.' He pauses for applause. 'And seeing as it's been a good year, I have decided that tonight I will not only double, but triple whatever we raise in this room. So, I ask you to give what you can, and seeing as I know what most of you earn, I'll know whether you did or not!'

The audience are laughing so much. If anyone else was saying this they'd be throwing tomatoes. He really is the kind of man who can get away with anything. It's a good job he's nice.

'So, if you don't want me calling you at midnight asking

for your credit card details, DIG DEEP,' he says with a flourish before leaving the stage.

Almost immediately a plate of smoked trout is placed in front of me. I do my best to pick around it.

'Wow, this is such an amazing cause,' says Britney Spears, or whatever her name is, as she pretends to eat. 'It just makes me think about me and how my life could have been. Don't you think? When you hear stories of women who are told they can't be what they want to be and you just realise how hard we've worked?'

She raises her glass of champagne and clinks it with Isabella's. 'To women,' she says.

'To women,' they say in chorus.

I feel very proud of Ajay, Fliss and Audrey because we all just look at them like they're mad. But Ajay is almost immediately enraptured once more by Miss CEO's boobs.

Over the course of dinner Audrey can't have drunk less than two bottles of white wine. Her head is beginning to flop.

'Audrey,' I say, assertively. 'Maybe drink some water?'

'Fuck water,' she slurs. Isabella shoots her a very disapproving look.

'Come on now, just a sip,' I push. 'It will make you feel better.'

'I don't need to feel better,' she splurts, standing up and wobbling all over the place. 'I have an announcement to make.'

It's clear she is unstoppable, so we all resign ourselves to listening to whatever this announcement will be. I'm guessing she has finally dumped her boyfriend and wants a slap on the back for being so brave.

'I'm pregnant,' she says, finishing off her glass of wine. Causing me to drop my head into my hands.

The influencer, the model and the Kim Kardashian look-alike don't seem fazed by Audrey's alcohol consumption and all immediately shower her with lots of high-pitched 'Congratulations!' Fliss and I look at each other with terror in our eyes. Isabella stands up and rests her fists on the table.

'You're fucking what?' she says, making all of our eyes pop open.

'Pregnant. It's when a man puts his penis into a girl's vagina and they make a baby,' Audrey says, like a child.

Isabella looks livid. To be fair to her this is very unprofessional, but we need to handle it with a little more care.

'Audrey, you've had quite a lot to drink,' I say, concerned.

'Oh, don't worry, I'm not keeping it. I'm booked in for Friday to get this little sucker sucked out.' She makes a terrible sucking noise, then a pop.

'I'm sorry, did we discuss you having a day off?' Isabella asks, angrily.

'Is it a problem?' Audrey says, as if about to start a fight.

'Well, she can't keep it now, it will have two heads,' Fliss says, taking the bottle that Audrey is trying to pour out of her hand.

'Crack whores have babies,' says the woman in the green dress, making Ajay nod along.

'It's true, my aunty was a crack whore and I've got three

cousins. One of them even has a job,' says the influencer, proudly.

'Can we stop using the term "crack whore", it is highly derogatory,' I say, wishing the two of them would shut up.

'"Abortion Audrey", that's what you can call me. Abo Aud. Audrey, the Abortion Queen. This is my third.' She holds her glass high in the air. 'All hail the Queen of Abortions. Cheers!'

None of us are quite sure what to say.

'Can someone get her the fuck home?' Isabella snaps.

'I will,' says Fliss. The most responsible one, other than me, but I really don't want much more to do with Audrey, Queen of Abortions, she's far too wasted.

'I think that's a very good idea,' I say, wondering if I can make a break for freedom myself. 'Do you need any help?'

'No, we'll be fine. I'm used to doing this, if my girlfriend drinks white wine when she's got her period she wants to fight everyone. If I can get her to leave a party, I can do anything.'

She puts an arm around Audrey and leads her out of the room. Eventually the sound of Audrey singing 'I'm Abortion Girl' to the tune of 'I'm a Barbie Girl' fades out.

'Right, well I'm going for a dance,' says the model, grooving off. Hattie the Influencer follows her.

'I'm going for a smoke,' Isabella says. 'That was bullshit.'

'I thought you quit?' I ask, knowing that another huge box of Nicorette gum has just arrived at the office.

'Stop judging me, Mia!' She storms off. And then it's just

me, Ajay and the CEO at the table. She's managed to eat a whole meal with absolutely none of her lip gloss coming off.

'I need to pee,' she announces, unnecessarily. And when she gets up and walks away, Ajay follows like a dog on its way to the park. I suddenly find myself alone.

I sit for a minute, wondering what I should do. I could go into the big room with the dancefloor and do what I do brilliantly – playing the part, networking, spreading the good word about Isabella May. But I'm feeling flustered with all this rising havoc around me, I don't have the energy to be impressive. My warm bed and my cat seem far more inviting right now.

I make for the exit and head to the toilet, spotting Ajay at the end of the corridor. He is facing a wall, one hand pressed into it holding his body back, so he doesn't crush the woman in front of him. It's the CEO in the green shiny dress from our table. I hardly heard them say a word to each other, and now they are here, like this? She's whispering things to him that are making him smile. Her waist is tiny, her hips enormous. She wiggles them like she is being controlled by a console. Then, without any acknowledgement of who might be looking, she grabs him between the legs. He leans forward and they start kissing. I don't want to see this. I hurry into the toilet before he spies me. What must it be like to be a girl like that? Living life with the aim of being as fuckable as possible at all times? It looks absolutely exhausting, and so uncomfortable too.

As I am waiting for my Uber I notice Isabella smoking a cigarette under a tree. Theo is with her, they look like they're arguing. As I get into the car, I see him head back inside, leaving his daughter alone and upset. It strikes me that even in a family where they seem to have everything, fathers and daughters can still be complicated. I find that quite comforting.

9

Despite the late night I am in the office the next morning by 8.54 a.m., having consumed both coffee and toast. I am surprised to see that Ajay is already here.

'Good morning,' I say, seeing him in a very different light after last night's escapades.

'Morning boss,' he says. He has changed his clothes, at least, which is a good sign that he went home. He has a mug of coffee in front of him and two empty mugs on his desk which tells me he needs a lot of caffeine today. 'Mad night,' he says.

'Mad? Why mad?' I ask, hoping he doesn't tell me too much, but also wanting to know what happened after I saw him in the corridor with Fake Kim.

'You know, all that money in one room, and the chicks were sick!'

'Sick?'

'Yeah, sick!'

I presume he means attractive. 'Oh, meet anyone nice?' I don't know why I am asking these things. I don't even want to know.

'All right, boss. Boundaries, remember?'

'Oh, yes, absolutely,' I say, shuffling back to my desk, embarrassed by myself. 'Get on with work then,' I add, trying to reinstate my authority.

'Hey, want to see something sooo funny?' he asks, ignoring me and settling himself next to me.

I already know it won't make me laugh. 'Sure,' I say, to be polite. I sit at my desk and wait for whatever it is to not blow me away. He presses a few things then comes behind me, leans down and shows me his phone. I am overwhelmed by the smell of alcohol on his breath. A musty smell from his body that is both gross and familiar. My sensory memory takes me right back to my twenties, walking back to my flat smelling of sex. It always used to amaze me how repulsive a lover can smell the next morning after their pheromones had driven me to sexual euphoria the night before. And that is exactly what Ajay smells like: yesterday's sex. And of course I now know he doesn't even use soap.

A video plays showing Audrey just behind him at last night's event. Something strange is happening with her lips. Music starts and he begins to mime along to 'Bongo La, Bongo Cha Cha Cha'. His lips are also imposed on Audrey's lips so, even though she isn't singing, it looks like she is, but with his lips, not hers. She has no idea.

'That's very funny,' I say, not laughing. He seems to believe me. 'Maybe don't show that to Audrey today. Also, maybe delete it.'

I pick up some pieces of paper hoping that will be enough to discourage more conversation.

'Such a sick filter. I did it on my dog too, look.'

I hold my breath again. He scrolls down and shows me a video of exactly the same thing but, instead of Audrey, it's his dog. I have to admit, that one actually does make me smile. He's very close, I've not been this close to him before.

'I now know never to stand behind you,' I say, getting up because the smell and thought of Fake Kim's juice all over him is making me queasy.

'You dress well, boss,' he says out of nowhere. I look behind me, as if he could be talking to someone else.

'Pardon?'

'You dress well. It's good, yeah? Smart, together. Like you've got nothing to prove with your clothes. Always ironed. Sharp. I don't have an iron. Well, my mum does but she never uses it either. You are the kind of woman who irons your clothes. That's a good sign.'

'A good sign of what?' I ask him.

'That you've got control. I like women who are in control.' He doesn't realise it, but that's the biggest compliment someone could pay a person like me. But really, this chat has gone on long enough.

'Ajay, could you go back to your desk now please?' I say, asserting some of that control.

He does as I ask, laughing at his phone until he sits down.
He puts on some headphones and finally gets on with his
job.

Fliss is now in the workshop. She looks as fresh and put
together as ever.

'You get Audrey home OK?' I ask, heading over.

'Yup, all the way to bed. I bet you a fiver she won't be
in until lunchtime.'

I feel rage but also know that isn't fair. Audrey is going
through something and as her boss I have to offer support.
But I'm going to have to reprimand her in some way, she
can't get away with behaving like that at an industry event,
no matter how pregnant she is.

It seems like everyone, at some point, becomes chaotic.
I certainly come from that place. And the problem with
coming from bedlam is no matter how much you take on
to keep yourself distracted, its persistent little voice will
always be calling you back.

My phone vibrates with a text from Isabella.

I won't be in today. Was networking until 4am. Wrecked.

Sure, networking on coke with Instagram influencers. Nice
one Isabella, that's going to really elevate our business. The
Selfridges pitch is tomorrow, and she should be here so we
can rehearse it, not bunking off work to go to a bouji yoga
class and having 'clean eating' smoothies that cost the same
as my weekly shop. Yet again, I have to be the responsible
one because she knows that whatever happens, Daddy will
have her back. I wouldn't wish my childhood on anyone,
but one good thing that comes out of being raised by a

neglectful father is you work hard to get to a better place. If you're not reaching to get somewhere, what's the point in getting out of bed in the morning? That's Isabella in a nutshell. I do wonder what they were arguing about last night, though. He probably lowered her allowance or something.

I realise I need to find a materials receipt so that I can properly calculate some costs for the pitch. The last I saw it I'd left it on Isabella's desk for approval. Getting Isabella's approval is an entirely pointless process but it's something I still must go through the motions of doing. She doesn't know how to approve an invoice because she has no concept of what is expensive and what is reasonable. She stares at them for as long as she can bear and eventually says, 'Fine,' every single time. Generally, I file paperwork right away, but the invoice I need mustn't have made its way back to me. I text her back.

Where might I find a missing invoice?

I get a message saying she has silenced her notifications. I don't see that I have any other choice but to go looking for it. Stepping behind someone else's desk can feel like walking into their house when they're not home. I never come over here, even though I sit looking at it all day. Seeing the office from a new perspective is quite exciting. I am proud of how tidy my side looks in comparison to Isabella's. I look in the trays on her desk, but it's not there. There is a pile of paper on the cabinet behind the desk, so I check that too. I slowly open a drawer, it's full of make-up and a powerful smell of cosmetics clouds my face. I open the drawer underneath, which is full of every kind of herbal tea on the planet, and finally the bottom drawer, which looks promising and is full of papers and cardboard files.

I find myself looking up to make sure Fliss or Ajay aren't watching me, then I go through the pile. There are quite a few things I've been looking for for a while. Plus numerous returns labels for clothes that I know for a fact she never returned because they are still in boxes next to her desk. I find the invoice I'm looking for, but as I'm about to put the papers back, I notice a letter. It's from a law firm called Partridge's. I've heard of them because Isabella once had to take them on to fight off an ex-boyfriend who tried to claim she'd slapped him on a night out and he wanted £500k in compensation. This letter is dated from last week. At the top in bold, underlined letters it reads:

CASE AGAINST THEO MAY FOR SEXUAL MISCONDUCT CLAIMS

'Oh my God,' I say aloud to myself. 'Fuck.'

I sit down on her chair and just stare at it. So shocked my eyes can't read, they just lock onto those words in big bold letters. I honestly cannot for a second believe what I am seeing.

'Mia, can I have a word?' says a very dishevelled-looking Audrey who is approaching the desk. I quickly put the letter exactly where it was and shut it back away in the drawer. My hands are shaking like I've drunk fifty cups of coffee.

'Yes, absolutely,' I say to Audrey, guiding her away from Isabella's desk and towards my own. 'What is it?'

'I just wanted to say that I am very sorry about last night, I was very unprofessional, and it won't happen again.'

I had planned to be strict but all I can manage is, 'Don't worry about it, we all have nights like that.'

'You've had a night like that? I can't imagine that. You're so strong and together. But I really am sorry, I don't know why I behaved that way.'

'It's fine, let's just move on. I'm sorry about the pregnancy, if it's not what you want. And of course take Friday and any time you need.' I just want her out of here so I can process the words I just read.

'Thanks. I don't know why I did it, I . . .'

'Honestly, it wasn't that bad. Just go to work, all forgotten.'

'No, it was, it was really, really bad. Is Isabella coming in today? Do you think she told her dad what I said?'

'No, and no, honestly it sounds like you have the fear. It happens to us all with a hangover. Have a chamomile tea. You'll be fine. I really need to crack on, OK?'

'All right, will you tell me if she says anything?'

'Absolutely not. Let's just move on.'

'OK. Would you like coffee? I'm going to make one.'

'No thanks, I had one at home. Did you not?'

'No, there wasn't time.'

It's gone 10 a.m., but I'll let this one slide.

Audrey heads back into the workshop. Her performance last night now the least of my worries. Theo is being done for sexual misconduct? I think back to his face against mine

114

last night. A kiss on each cheek. I wanted three. His hands holding my forearms, his charm burning through my dress. Not a single woman in that room didn't feel it. Should I have seen through him? Is his sophistication and gentle touch just an act? The real Theo May is a perverted sex pest? Urgh, how could I get him so wrong? How did he fool us all? And how could Isabella not tell me? She would rather protect her father than be honest about what he's been up to.

Partridge's have a long history of making stories go away, but if this ever gets out, Isabella May could be over. My job is on the line, everything I have worked for could be taken away. The Selfridges pitch must be a success – it's now more important than ever. If they stock our collections, we'd need less money from Theo. And maybe, just maybe, the business could survive.

I can't lose my job, and I'll do whatever it takes for that not to happen.

10

'It's just that she loved a party,' my sister says as we chat on the phone on my way home from work. She's right. Mum did love a party. If she had lived the life she was supposed to live, with a man who allowed her to be herself rather than seeing her happiness as something he needed to destroy, she'd have spent it in bright-coloured kaftans, with a martini in one hand and a microphone in the other. I think about that a lot. How different her short life could have been if she'd been married to the right person. I suppose you could say that about lots of people. But my mother's relationship made her life particularly tragic. At least her death got her out of it.

'The day she was born still exists and I want to celebrate it, that's all,' Liz says, annoyed with me for being evasive about plans for Mum's upcoming birthday.

'I know, and I'm sorry. Things are just really busy at work. Maybe next year, OK? We can go for lunch, somewhere nice.'

'All right,' she says. 'I bet you don't, but OK. How is everything with you?'

'You know, fine. Work is exciting enough, home is . . . it's fine.'

'You said that on your wedding day.'

'Said what?'

'That everything was fine. I remember wishing you'd said it was the best day of your life, but you just said it was fine. I thought, "Right then, fine it is."'

'OK, sorry for my choice of words. How is your stunning, mind-blowing, Hollywood-movie-style romance of a marriage going?'

'OK, no need to be sarcastic,' she says, defensively. 'I just want you to be happy, that's all.'

'I am happy, Liz. Some days I even laugh, imagine that!'

'OK. It makes me happy that you're happy,' she says.

'I know. I'm home now. Chat soon, OK?'

'Promise? I love you.'

'Bye Liz.'

There is nothing I love more than coming home to an empty house. It's so rare. On Thursdays Oliver has football practice after school, and Tristan works then goes to therapy with Belinda. They are still working on their marriage even though it's been over for nearly a decade.

'Piggles,' I call, as I come through the front door. The silent house immediately feeling too quiet. She usually runs to me at the door. 'Pigeon,' I call again. 'Pig Waffle. Piggy Pops. Pigeon Toes . . . ?'

Nothing.

I hang up my bag and take my coat off. 'Pigeon,' I call more gently. 'Where are you?' I look in my room, she isn't there. Very unusual. I look in the kitchen. Her bowl is full, she isn't in there either. I look in the living room, nothing. 'Pigeon,' I call, with a little more urgency. This has never happened. Is she trapped somewhere? I walk up the stairs to Oliver's bedroom. It is supposed to be the master but when we decided on separate rooms Tristan suggested we take the lower bedrooms so we didn't disturb Oliver when we passed from room to room at night. I'm fine with it, but there is something very wrong about a nine-year-old having a huge bedroom with an ensuite and a balcony with park views. I look under the bed, in the bathroom, out on the balcony and in the cupboards. Pigeon is nowhere to be seen.

'Pigeon,' I call again. 'Pigeon, come here.'

I hear the front door burst open and slam shut. Multiple voices fill the house. *Thud thud thud* as more than one child runs up the stairs towards me.

'Why are you here?' Oliver asks, looking confused and flanked by a friend of his who looks at me like I've ruined everything.

'I was just looking for Pigeon,' I say. 'But she's not here. What happened to football practice?'

'Coach is ill. Mum came to pick me up.'

'Is she here?'

'Yes I am, helloooo,' shouts Belinda from halfway up the stairs. I feel immediately annoyed.

'Hello Belinda. I could have picked him up, it's our night,' I say, coming out of Oliver's room and squeezing past her on the stairs.

'You're busy, I know how hard it is. And anyway, Tristan and I have therapy, so I was coming here anyway. Our therapist isn't well so isn't in the office. He's doing sessions on Zoom this week. He can't be that unwell, or at least I hope he isn't. I don't want to talk about the perils of parenting and divorce while he sneezes at us. Did you ever get a therapist in the end?'

Classic Belinda.

'Did I ever say I needed one?'

'Oh, sorry I thought you did. Silly me. Well, if you do, I know a great one.'

'I don't feel like I need a therapist,' I say, to which she rushes into the kitchen after me.

'I don't *need* one, Mia. I have one because talking to men about anything is so damn hard. I need a mediator to get through to Tristan about Oliver. You know how he gets.'

I hate these chats. Where she gets all 'sister wife' with me.

'Pigeon? Come on Pigeon, where are you?' I continue, trying my best to ignore Belinda.

'I can help,' she offers, opening a kitchen cupboard as if the cat will be inside. 'Where shall I look?'

'Honestly, don't worry, I'll find her. She might run away when she hears your voice.'

'No she won't. The other day she came up and sniffed my toe. It felt like progress. Maybe one day we might even be friends.' I don't know why she's being so nice to me, it's making me feel uncomfortable. I brush past her and head down the corridor to Tristan's room, it's the one place I haven't looked.

I open the door and Pigeon runs out immediately. The cleaner must have shut her in there this morning. I am so relieved, I pick her up and let her lick my hands and cheeks.

'Ewww, that's not hygienic. Having her lick your face. Cats lick their bottoms.'

'Lucky them. Thanks for your help,' I say, heading into my room and shutting the door.

'I'm going to set the computer up in Tristan's room,' Belinda shouts. 'Wouldn't want to disturb you.'

An hour later, Tristan comes home. I open my bedroom door to say hello. 'Your ex-wife is waiting for you in your bedroom,' I say, with a cheeky smirk. 'When it's over, stay in there, take off all your clothes and wait for me. I think you'll need it after an hour with her.'

'I better get this over with then, hey,' he says, with a wink.

Tristan knows I'm not jealous of his ongoing marriage to his ex-wife, I see no reason why he would choose her over me. I just find her a pain in the arse and wish she would leave our fifty per cent to us. I often feel more like a lodger in my own home. Who has sex with her landlord and makes exceptionally cute sandwiches.

Tristan shouts hello to Oliver who is being eerily quiet with his friend and goes into his bedroom, shutting the door behind him. Pigeon and I take this opportunity to head to the kitchen together. I love being in the kitchen with Pigeon, she finds me preparing food fascinating. As Belinda is here, I presume they will take Oliver for dinner after therapy. They like to do that. They get the chance to explain to him how fantastically they think they're doing.

Being vegan in a house full of meat eaters isn't so hard, I can easily prepare food that suits us all. But when I don't have to handle dead animals, I enjoy my food much more. Tonight, I am making a quinoa bake. I put the quinoa on, then chop spring onions, cherry tomatoes and green olives. I fry those up and sprinkle with garlic powder. When the quinoa is done I tip that in, mix it up then sprinkle chopped walnuts on the top and a little vegan Parmesan. That goes into a baking dish and I pop it in the oven. Just as I am shutting the oven door, I hear Belinda come screaming out of Tristan's room, the shock of it making me slide my arm against the edge of the hot oven and my skin shrinks and splits immediately.

'FUCK. NO,' I shout. It really hurts. I get it under the cold tap. Belinda is now in the kitchen looking repulsed.

'LOOK at me.'

I don't want to look at her, so I don't.

'Look at me. Your cat pissed on Tristan's bed. I lay on it. I am covered in cat piss. It's the worst smell.'

'Wait, what?'

I wrap a tea towel around my arm and run to Tristan's room. He is standing by his bed. He points at his duvet. I notice that his laptop is closed, and then I notice a huge wet patch in the middle of his bed.

'Oh my God,' I say, genuinely horrified. 'She was trapped in here all day, she must have been desperate.'

'It's very smelly,' he says, trying not to get too mad.

'I know, it's a terrible smell. Irina must have locked her in here this morning. She was stuck, she had to go somewhere.'

'GET IT OUT,' screeches Belinda, coming back into the bedroom.

'She's doing it,' Tristan says, supportively. Even though I know he is fuming. 'Keep calm.'

I wrap the duvet into a ball and get out of his room. I feel disgusting, like I was the one who pissed on the bed. Belinda is now down to her bra and pants in the kitchen. Her dress in a heap on the floor. She is looking at it like it's infested with rattlesnakes. I've never seen her body before. It's a lot nicer than I imagined. I put the whole duvet into the washing machine. It hardly fits, I have to really cram it in.

'I have nothing to wear,' Belinda yelps. Oliver and his friend appear in the kitchen too. Oliver runs off with embarrassment, his friend stays to look at the woman in her underwear.

'GET AWAY,' Belinda screams as if she's being abused. Although it was a bold move in the first place to strip off, I guess that's a sign of how comfortable she is in this house.

'I'll lend you something,' I say, hurrying to my room.

Pigeon is hiding under my bed. She knows exactly what she's done. I am in my wardrobe looking for something to cover up my husband's ex-wife. She is suddenly behind me.

'Nothing that smells,' she says, as if that would be normal for my clothing. 'I don't want to look like some crazy cat lady.'

Those words stick to me. How am I the crazy one because I have a cat? She's the one standing there in her pants screaming.

'What about this?' she says, picking up the dress I wore to the industry event.

'It's not clean, I wore it a few nights ago.'

She smells it. 'Well at least it smells of perfume and not cat piss. I'll take it.'

She steps into my dress. She looks really good in it. Which is annoying.

'Oh, there you go. You look very nice,' Tristan says, as she walks down the hall. 'I didn't realise what a similar shape you both are.'

I don't know what it is about him saying that, but it makes me feel icky. Like he has a type, that I just happen to be.

'I'm going home to shower. I'll smell of piss for days,' Belinda says, storming out of the house. I gather clean linens and get to sorting out Tristan's bed.

'Your real mum is fit,' I hear Oliver's friend say in the kitchen. I kick the door shut.

11

A few days later I'm back at the Methodist Church – and this time I've come determined to share. Martha is lighter this week, brighter, experiencing relief from opening up perhaps. I want that. I want to get things off my chest and out into a room of people because once a secret has been told, it's no longer a secret, it's a story. And everyone has a story.

Martha, Ada and Greg are all here tonight. Tiana too. No Nicole. I feel sad not to see her, I enjoyed the way she asked me questions after the last session. It made me feel wise. I came prepared for more.

When I walked in I had my eyes closed and only opened them when I knew I was through the door. I hoped to see Lee sitting there. I tried to surprise myself with his presence. A small thrill, like when a package arrives that you forgot you'd ordered. I imagined him seeing me and saying, 'I came because of you. It's good to see you again.' But it's not how that story played out.

Tiana comes to me first, indicating that I should speak. I feel Ada's warm hand on my back. Her signature move. Heat radiates from it and I feel her support sweep in waves around my body. But the door creeps open before I have a chance to begin. My heart flutters like I was just asked to dance. It's Lee.

'Hello everyone,' he says nervously. 'Room for one more?'

'Yes, of course,' says Tiana, walking over to him, shaking his hand and guiding him to a seat. 'You're very welcome here, what is your name?'

'Lee. Hi, hi, hello, hi,' he says, looking everyone in the eye as he goes round the group. I am staring at him, amazed.

'Hello again,' he says to me directly. His gentle eyes burning a little hole in my hard shell.

'Hello Lee,' I say, warmly. 'How are you and your mum?'

'Not great, but I'm glad I'm here.'

'Us too,' says Ada. 'We need more men around. Poor Greg stuck with all these chicks.'

I find that funny, so does Martha. Greg blushes, which I think is very sweet. His stupid tattoos hiding his soft side.

As Tiana explains to Lee who she is, what the aim of the group is and what he can hope to achieve, I take him in. A tall, heavy-set man. Short hair, good skin under considerable stubble. I don't recall that being there when we met, so maybe it's a response to his sadness. He has an inexpensive-looking watch on one wrist, a thick copper bracelet on the other suggesting he aches in places. His eyes are brown, his teeth not straight, his lips thin, his smile is kind. His voice sounds gentle and soft. I shouldn't be staring at him the way I am, but I can't stop. I compare a man like him to a man like my father. If Lee was a ball of string, you could grab hold of the end and watch it gently unravel, never letting go. If my dad were a piece of string, you'd fight for the tiniest piece and in the end just give up and kick it away.

'And who are you remembering today?' Tiana asks him.

'My mum's cat, Plimsoll. Well, he was my cat too, I live with my mum. And no, before you think it, that doesn't mean I'm a freaky weirdo.'

The whole group laughs. Greg in particular. 'Freaky weirdo,' he says. 'I like that. Freaky weirdo. That's me, or what people think I am.'

I wonder if Greg regrets the version of himself he has painted on his skin, making it impossible for people to see anything else, the real person beneath.

'Plimsoll died very suddenly a week ago. I took him to the vet thinking he'd be OK and next thing I'm carrying him back through the front door and he's dead.' Lee cries immediately.

Greg puts a tentative hand on Lee's back. 'It's OK, you can say anything here,' he tells Lee. 'I'm here because my snake died and everyone's well nice about it.'

'I love snakes,' Lee says, smiling at Greg. Teardrops showering his top lip and running into his mouth. 'Had one when I was a kid.'

Greg looks so happy that he almost seems proud.

'My mum is not doing well and I'm doing my best to hold it together for her, but I kept thinking of this group and in the end I needed a place to let it out. Online forums just don't feel right.' He breathes out three times in a row, then takes one long breath in. 'I feel like I'm reliving my dad dying. Like ever since he left us, I've held it together for my mum but Plimsoll dying just brought it all back again. Slap in the face. Right back to where I was the night he died, but this time I can't keep it in. I feel so stupid. He was just a cat, I know that, but . . .'

'No such thing as just a cat,' Ada says, defensively. 'When I found out my husband was having it away with other women that cat became everything to me. I swear if my son was brave enough to admit it, he'd agree he's the way he is now because the cat died. She brought joy into a very sad home. There is no "just" about it. She saved me, I swear it.'

'I agree,' Martha says, growing taller by the moment. Those enormous doe eyes like parasols trying to stay open in the wind. 'I've never thought about my dad more. Bessie dying brought it all back. And my husband. I powered through the grief both times, onwards and upwards, life must go on and all that. But when Bessie died, everything collapsed. It was her but it was everything else too. Years of compartmentalising and then the doors opened all at once and all avenues to me were flooded with pain. That's why it's never just a cat. It's a symbol of how hard you are capable of loving. And when they die, it reminds you of everything you ever lost.'

I had unfortunately just taken a sip of water at this emotional point in Martha's speech and it projects straight back out again and lands on my thighs.

'Are you OK?' Lee asks, despite being the one in tears.

'Yes,' I say, enthusiastically, as I wipe the water off my trousers with my hand. 'I'm fine. Sorry. That was just so poetic. Your words, Martha, so beautiful.'

'Thank you. When I'm not here I'm a writer, of sorts.'

'You are? That's so fancy,' says Ada, her hand on her chest. Still agog at the beauty that just flooded our ears. 'It's like a Brontë sister just flew in through the window.'

'I love *Jane Eyre*,' says Greg, causing the room to go dead still from shock. 'What? I got no mates, what am I supposed to do but read?'

Everyone laughs. Greg doesn't know whether he should be offended or not.

'What do you write?' I ask Martha.

'I'm a journalist. Opinion stuff. It's been hard for the last few months. Very little inspiration.'

I can hardly hide my shock. Martha, a high-flying journalist? I thought she was going to say she wrote the odd poem or cosy short story. But it goes to show you never really know someone.

'Maybe you should write about your cat Bessie,' Ada suggests. 'Something you really know about. It could unlock your creativity.'

'I don't think so. I fear the comments underneath would make me regret it.'

'That's terrible,' I say. 'That a writer holds back from

spilling something truly emotional for fear of what people might say.'

'I worry I'd become a bit of a joke if I wrote about my cat six months after she passed. It's a very unique group of people that allows you to be honest about this pain.'

'I'll second that,' Greg says. We all nod and smile sweetly at each other. This strange little team that we all rely on so much.

'I'm very happy to be here,' says Lee. 'You all seem . . . very nice.'

I am amazed by the ease with which he's slotted in and opened up. I think that's a real sign of a strong person, to speak so freely about their feelings and not be afraid. He's the furthest thing from a 'freaky weirdo' I can imagine. It's inspiring. I want to be more like him.

'So Mia,' Tiana says gently. 'Let's circle back to you, is there more you wanted to share today?'

A wave of bravery crashes over me. I do want to share. My cat might not be dead, but I deserve to be in this room. I have a story to tell, and it's about time I did it. I take a deep breath, and begin to speak.

'Sixteen years ago, I jumped off London Bridge in an attempt to end my own life.'

'Oh dear,' Ada gasps, a tear forming in her eye. 'You poor thing.'

Lee can't say anything, he just looks at me with his gentle, caring eyes.

'Sorry, I know this is a lot. Shall I go on?'

'Yes,' nods Tiana. 'It's why we're here.'

'I climbed up onto the side, launched myself forward and plummeted into very cold water. I remember a pigeon was sitting on the edge of the bridge and as I fell it came with me, as if we were playing a game. Almost as soon as my body hit the water it was being dragged out and pulled onto a boat. Like they'd seen me on the bridge or were just waiting for people to fall.

'I remember feeling nothing but rage. How dare they intercept my destiny? The destiny I had tirelessly considered. The only destiny I could imagine for myself. I was so angry. They sat me on a bench and wrapped a towel around me. A pigeon perched on the side of the boat, I was certain it was the same one. The people on the boat didn't say much, just asked a few questions about how I felt. My teeth were chattering, I was either freezing, or livid, I don't remember. Chug chug chug to somewhere and then off the boat. A series of people, a car, police, a cell, where they kept me for the night. They asked me questions about why, but not in a way that made me think they cared. Did I have anyone I could call? A mother? No. A father? No. A partner? No. A friend? No. Eventually they let me go. I remember my clothes being dry, but my shoes were wet. I was heading straight back to the bridge. All they had done was prolong the inevitable.

'I was nearly there when I saw something moving in a bush. A kitten, so small. Maybe two months old. It looked so scared. It was trembling, abandoned, her huge gentle eyes looking at me as if to say, "Please help." I picked her up and rather than walk to the bridge I went home to the house I shared with two other people whose names I kept forgetting. The chaos of my life suddenly began to calm. I called the cat Pigeon. She became my reason to stay alive.'

'Wow. That's a very sad but also beautiful story,' Tiana says, wiping a tear from her eye.

'Thank goodness you found her,' Ada says. 'It sounds to me like that kitten saved your life.'

'She did,' I say. 'She really did.'

'And now you've lost her, of course you must feel such a huge gap in your life. Would you like to tell us what happened to dear Pigeon?' Tiana asks, gently.

I consider lying to them. And then I consider telling them the truth. Both make my presence here inappropriate so, rather than ruin this moment, I decide to do neither.

'I don't need to say much in this group. It's just good to be here, with people who understand. You know?'

'We know,' Tiana says.

'We know,' they all agree.

12

People talk about being vulnerable like it's a good thing. I told a group of strangers my darkest secret last night and, quite honestly, it's left me feeling very shaky this morning. It's unfortunate because today is a big day. The day of the Selfridges pitch. I had really wanted to be at my most brilliant, but a horrible feeling of anxiety is getting in the way of my usual routine. I snoozed well past my 6.50 a.m. alarm. I forgot to make Oliver's breakfast. I put the shower on but forgot to get in it. I went into the bathroom but shut Pigeon out. I've never done that in her life. When I opened it, she was sitting across the hall waiting like I had gone completely mad.

'I'm sorry, Pigeon,' I said, getting on the floor to stroke her. 'Mummy's all over the place today.'

I managed to pull myself together enough to get into

character. Black trousers, a smart pale blue blouse, a black blazer. I didn't seem to be able to get my hair into the usual neat knot, so instead I did a looser ponytail. No matter how many times I stabbed at my left ear I couldn't find the hole for my earring, so I had to abandon that. Everything else came together sufficiently to get me out of the house.

'Wish me luck,' I say to Pigeon as I leave. 'It's a really big day for me.'

When the front door shuts behind me I straighten myself one more time and head off to central London. I have butterflies in my stomach. This must go well. I must not be distracted by my mind trying to pull me back to chaos.

By the time I arrive at Selfridges I feel together and ready. It's thrilling coming to a place like this. It's like fashion's Buckingham Palace. To sell our jewellery in here would be us dealing with royalty.

I meet Isabella and we enter through the visitors' entrance. I'd be lying if I said my heart wasn't thumping. It's exciting to be here. The ultimate retailer. The reception is contemporary and minimal. Slogans on the walls, the woman behind the desk young and chic. I feel like I'm in a movie and have rocked up to the offices of my dream employer. I have no particular interest in jewellery but even I can feel the heat of a place like this. The thrill of it over-rides my self-doubt. I am here to win this pitch, I'll do whatever it takes.

'I feel like I've made it being here,' I say to Isabella, immediately regretting showing any kind of emotion.

'I suppose I'm more comfortable in places like this,'

Isabella says, approaching the reception desk. 'Here to see Rosita,' she says confidently.

'And what company are you from?' the receptionist asks politely, but without looking at Isabella, who takes enormous offence. She expels air from her nostrils and just stands there, tilting her head and opening her eyes wide as if to say, 'It's me!'

The receptionist finally looks up and asks again, 'Your company?'

'Isabella May Jewellery,' I say, unable to take it any more. 'We are here for a pitch.'

'Great.' She tells us to take the lift and wait in the seating area on the next floor. I'm nervous, I can feel my hands trembling. Isabella is nervous too, I can tell, but she would never admit it. In the lift she pretends to read a poster on the wall.

I want to ask her about the accusations against Theo. Is it something that could send us under? I have a right to know before I try to sell us into Selfridges. If the story breaks this weekend, will we look dishonest if we don't mention it?

'That was nice of your dad to give us the table the other night, it must have cost a fortune.'

'He doesn't care. I want to sweep through the accessories hall after this. See if they have the new Balenciaga tote,' she says, shooting a judgemental look at my fabric tote bag that I got for free when I ordered Pigeon's food from a fancy independent cat food company. It's an extra-large size and holds everything I need for the pitch. It's got a cute picture of a cat on it, which I really like.

'I've never seen the point in expensive bags. Too precious to put down anywhere, a big advertisement to thieves that it's full of precious goods,' I say, defending myself. 'These totes are so good. I use them until they fall apart. I have a whole drawerful, it's such a clever idea when brands give free ones away. We could do something like that?'

'The words "free" and "fall apart" are two reasons why we will not be giving away tote bags.'

The lift opens and we take a seat in the waiting area. It's a huge open-plan office. Modern, minimal and chic. There is no clutter. Nothing on the desks. I see lockers and everyone is impeccably dressed. They all look so young and sexy and cool. Isabella takes a copy of today's *Metro* from the coffee table and starts leafing through it. A clear sign she doesn't want to run through the pitch one last time before we go in. She seems to be entranced by whatever article she has stumbled across.

'Did your cat die?' she suddenly blurts, taking my breath away a little.

'Excuse me?'

'Seriously, did your cat die? The woman described in this article could be you, but her cat must have died if she was in some weird . . .' she leans a little closer to the paper '. . . pet bereavement group. What the fuck?'

'Give me that,' I say, reaching for the paper. My heart climbing up my throat and lodging itself at the back of my mouth. The headline immediately jumps out from the page:

DAWN O'PORTER

A BIG BOW-WOW FOR THE
SADDEST PEOPLE IN THE CITY

I recognise the journalist in the picture immediately. It's Nicole, from the bereavement group. Although her name isn't Nicole, it's 'Amy Newton'. I read on.

There is nothing new about the idea of a support group. The likes of AA, NA, Anger Management have been bringing people together for group therapy sessions for decades. But riddle me this, a small group of broken people coming together every Tuesday night to cry together over their dead pets. Has the craze for mental health support gone one step too far?

I took my seat in the circle. The group leader was a nice enough woman. Possibly bumped to the lowest echelon of therapy. You wonder if she moaned and groaned to her superior when she drew the short straw and learned that she would get the pet people, begging for the Angry Men so she could try to fix them.

If the cast of characters were in a novel, the author would have leaned too comfortably on the stereotype. One lady, six months in from losing her cat and still unable to raise her head, spoke in a low and sombre voice about how she still put the cat's food down every day, and slept under a pillow to give the illusion of the cat sleeping on her. It was hard not to suggest the cat wasn't the problem. I wanted to wave Tinder under her nose, there was never a more worthy candidate of a dating app.

136

Next was a woman who mainlined custard creams and admitted to being more upset about her kitty's death than her husband's cheating. She wore vibrant colours that would make you question if her grief was real. More just a place to go to get any kind of attention at all.

There was a man, the embodiment of toxic masculinity, who started throwing chairs around. I know, it was as random and shocking as it sounds. A huge python tattoo wrapped around his neck, representing his beloved snake that died in his arms. That's right, a snake. You couldn't make it up, could you? Some may have seen a heartbroken pet owner needing some friendly support. I saw a violent man let loose in a room of vulnerable people. No control over his emotions, a threat to them all. And yet, we must not question the line between insanity and mental health. When people who are a danger admit to having feelings, do we forgive them for their acts of harm? Not the next week, it would seem. He returned and sat back down, not a stern word offered to him, or security offered to the rest of us. I felt terrified in my seat, like he could attack us all at any moment.

But the person who stuck out to me the most was a woman. Tall, thin, fiery red hair. Dressed in sensible work clothes. A disguise maybe, to shield the cat lady that lay beneath. The death of her pussy was too much to share so instead she used the group as a free therapy session for her many woes. Or maybe she's just a rubbernecker for everyone else's grief. We somehow happened upon each other outside where the confessions kept coming. She married to conform rather than for love. Her stepson and cat are plenty, no need for a child of her own. And maybe the most shocking of all, she thinks the stereotype of a single 'cat lady' is far more suited to her than the role she plays of wife. Well, I'm sure her poor husband wishes her all the best with it!

I want to be sick.

'You've got a doppelganger, Mia,' sniggers Isabella.

'Which one is like me?' I ask her, trying to hide my mortification and struggling to move my tongue around my mouth, which feels like sandpaper.

'Are you kidding me? Red hair, sensible clothes, an under-cover cat lady? You should go to this group, find that woman. You could be friends.'

'Why the hell would I go to a group like that?' I snap back at her.

'God, so touchy.'

I'll see how touchy she is when an article about her sex pest dad comes out. *If* it comes out that is, he has enough money to stop a war.

'Hi, I'm Hannah the assistant buyer,' says a young woman who is dressed in very expensive clothes for someone of her age. 'If you'd like to follow me I'll take you through to meet Rosita.'

I put the newspaper in my tote bag, which Isabella is horrified by, and Hannah raises her eyebrows at. I feel like I just got punched in the gut. Nicole, or Amy, or whatever her name was. Did her mum even have a dog? And I can't help wondering – if Isabella compared me to cat lady in the article, would others recognise me too? I feel the walls I've built around myself all these years start to shake. Deep breaths in, deep breaths out. Focus on work, that's what's always got me through.

I follow Hannah through the office to a meeting room. She says to help ourselves to water. I take some because my mouth is so dry and drink the whole bottle in one go.

'Jesus, chill out will you?' Isabella says between her teeth.

'Would you like tea?' Hannah asks in a way that suggests she'd rather we didn't so we both say no. 'Great, we will be with you shortly.'

I'm still shaking. I feel awful for the other people in the group, I hope they don't see it. Would Martha read the *Metro*? Lee? Greg? Oh God. Greg.

'I've never seen you nervous before,' Isabella says, like it pleases her.

'I'm fine. OK, let's get ready.'

Another deep breath and that's it, I put it to the back of my head. This pitch means more than ever. Work means more than ever. I can feel chaos creeping up on me. Work, focus, success, that is what keeps it at bay. I am determined to win this pitch.

I start laying out some samples on the table and pull out my computer to bring up the presentation that we created. Isabella is carrying the marketing strategy which I haven't seen yet as she was so late to get it over.

'Oh great, can I look?' I say, reaching out for it.

'Yes, it's brilliant,' Isabella says.

I sift through the pages. 'Is this all it is?' I ask, horrified.

'What do you mean, it's incredible.'

'It's all pictures of you with famous people. They're not even wearing our stuff in most of them.'

'Yes, but I am.'

'I know, but . . . Isabella, you knowing famous people isn't enough. This is Selfridges, they want more than this. Why don't you get that?'

'I do get it, Mia. I have achieved a lot, and this shows that.'

She snatches the deck back. I just hope I can get us through this meeting without having to show it to anyone.

The door opens and my heart starts racing. Rosita is a head buyer at Selfridges. She really is top of the game and suddenly I care more about Isabella May Jewellery than I ever realised I could. I want to get this right. I want Selfridges to take us on. Rosita is a stunningly well-dressed and poised black woman who emits restraint and decorum and knowledge. I'm terrified of ways that Isabella will insult her. I make sure I am smiling and that I don't come across as anything but the businesswoman I am. They must not see through my appearance. Not the way Amy Newton did.

'Hello, how are you?' I say, standing up and reaching out a hand for her to shake. Isabella quickly pushes hers out too, Rosita takes that one instead.

'So good to meet you,' Isabella says. 'Finally!'

Rosita and Hannah are pretty unresponsive. They do these meetings all the time, I can tell. This was put in the diary four months ago, it's not easy to get here. I'm sure they only buy a tiny percentage of the products they are pitched. They can't give too much away. Being too nice would be misleading. So they are not very nice at all and do little to calm our nerves.

'OK, shall I get started?' I ask.

Rosita nods and calmly says, 'Please.' Which is very chic and intimidating.

'OK, if you'd like to take a look at the screen, I can talk you through who we are and what we do.'

Rosita and Hannah look aimlessly at the screen as if it wasn't necessary for me to have shown them any of it. When I finish, Rosita just turns from the screen to me with a half-arsed smile as if to say, 'What else?'

'Would you like to hold the samples?' Isabella says, picking up one of the silver pendants and passing it over.

Rosita takes it and looks at it. 'It's pretty,' she says, immediately putting it down. 'We are very keen on story. Without a story, there is no brand. So what is yours?'

'Oh, well, since you asked,' Isabella says, excited to talk about herself. 'Ever since I was a little girl . . .' I shudder at the cliché '. . . I've wanted to make beautiful things. I used to watch my mother get all dressed up with her sparkles and jewels and think to myself, one day, one day I will help

141

women feel as beautiful as my mother looks. And so when I was around twenty-six, I learned how to make things. It started small at first, just pieces for my friends. You know, like Tara Palmer-Tomkinson, Sadie Frost . . . Then when I realised how many celebrities wanted to wear my stuff I realised I was on to something really special. My dad is a huge supporter of women in business so he gave me the money to create my own brand. And here we are today, Isabella May Jewellery. Iconic, really.'

'That's interesting. But I mean "story". Who inspired the brand, why do you make what you do? What do the collections stand for?'

'Well, they stand for me. Pretty, glamorous, unique. Which is how I want all women to feel.'

Hannah picks up a necklace. 'Reminds me of Pandora,' she says quietly to Rosita.

'Do you stock Pandora?' Isabella asks.

'No, it's too mainstream for us,' says Rosita casually. 'We also want to work with brands who see sustainability as part of their plan. How are you working towards being an ethical brand?'

'Oh well that's easy. I openly work with women. I support women, I employ them. I boost them up. We only have one man working for us and he's Asian.'

Hannah is Asian. That doesn't seem to make Isabella feel uncomfortable.

'Your pieces are very pretty, but we really do need a stronger hook from our brands. I think it's very exciting that you've had such big names wear your work, but ethics, sustainability and story are far more important to us than that. We can help build a brand if we have the right material to work with.'

'My brand is already built,' Isabella says, defensively.

Hannah and Rosita start looking at each other as if the meeting is over. Rosita starts to close it up. 'OK, well thanks for coming in. We'll be in touch soon.'

We all know that isn't true. I don't want to leave this room like this. We came here to get our jewellery into Selfridges and that is what I'm going to do. I take Fliss' necklace out of my tote bag and lay it on the table. 'We do also have this.'

Rosita immediately leans in, her eyes widen. 'Oh wow, that really is beautiful.'

Isabella is burning a hole in the side of my head. But I know I'm doing the right thing.

'One of our designers, Fliss . . .'

'She's black,' yelps Isabella like a small dog. It causes everyone to buckle.

'Fliss based this on a piece her grandfather made for her grandmother in Trinidad. She made it from reclaimed metal and found a Fairtrade supplier for the gems. It's all hand-made. She's got ideas for an entire collection inspired by the original necklace.'

Rosita picks it up. 'It's so unique.'

'Fliss is so talented, one of the best we have. I poached her from Net-a-Porter a few years ago, such a find,' I say, determined to win this pitch.

'And would she be willing to promote the range? I'm sure

we could secure some press for her to talk through the origins of the collection. This is exactly the sort of thing we are looking for.'

'Yes,' I say confidently. 'She's not only very smart and talented but also painfully beautiful, I'm sure she'd give fantastic interviews.'

'Great. I'm so glad you showed us this,' Rosita adds; she really does love it, I can tell.

'Well, we just wanted to save the best for last,' Isabella says, kicking me under the table. Letting me know I am in for it when we get out of here.

'OK, well we are very interested. I'd love to meet Fliss. Maybe you could come in again with some more ideas for the collection and we can go from there? I'd love to develop this with her.'

'Great,' I say.

'Fine!' says Isabella.

Rosita picks up a notebook so she doesn't have to shake our hands, says thank you and leaves. Hannah walks us to the lift.

'She never reacts that way,' she says quietly. 'She must really love it. Congrats.'

We get into the lift. Not a word from Isabella. She walks five paces in front of me until we get outside and round the corner. She turns to look at me, hate streaming from every pore.

'What the fuck was that?'

'That was Isabella May getting into Selfridges.'

'No, it wasn't. It was Fliss getting into Selfridges, not

144

me. I told you I didn't want to do that collection; it's got nothing to do with me. But you planned it all along, you and Fliss. You brought the necklace so you could sabotage the meeting. Now I have to spend money creating a collection that has nothing to do with me, that I don't want to make. That changes everything I went to do, why did you do that?'

'Because your brand is in trouble and getting into Selfridges could change that?'

'My *brand* isn't in trouble.'

I realise that by 'brand' she means herself, not her business.

'You employed me to run your business and grow it. That is what I just did.'

'Well, I obviously made a mistake.'

There is a very long and uncomfortable pause as I await more insults.

'You're such an odd woman, Mia,' she says, teeth showing.

'That's not very nice.'

'Well, it's true. You cavort as this businesswoman but you're just like the woman in the article. Aloof, a loner, you never let anyone in. A crazy cat lady in disguise.'

'What even is a crazy cat lady in your eyes?'

'You, but without the husband and the job.'

'Well, I have the husband and the job so I guess I'm just a woman with a cat.'

My phone rings. It's Tristan. It's always trivial. But this time it's like he sensed I need to be rescued. 'I'm going to answer my phone,' I announce unnecessarily to Isabella, who is now ordering an Uber.

'Like I give a fuck,' she snaps.

I turn my back to her and answer the call.

'Hello?'

Oxford Street is loud, I can't really hear anything. I stick a finger over the other ear and scrunch my face up, as if that will help.

'Tristan, hello?' I hear him make a strange sound. 'Tristan, are you OK?' Then I also hear a woman making a strange sound. I stop trying to get his attention and just listen. There is rustling and moaning. A bus pulls up next to me, it's so loud. I find myself covering the receiver on my phone and screaming, 'Shut the fuck up' at it. A number of people, including Isabella, look at me as if I am too much. I go back to the entranceway of Selfridges so I can hear a little better. Tristan obviously didn't mean to call me, but something keeps me listening.

It sounds like he's in the kitchen. Things keep landing on what must be a hard surface. Then I hear Pigeon meow.

'Oh shut that thing up,' says a woman's voice. It's Belinda.

'Ignore it,' says Tristan. 'I've learned to do that.' Then kissing sounds. Rubbing, zips, moaning, groaning. Another meow from my cat. 'Get down, urgh.' And then a thud as my cat hits the floor.

'I don't know why you allow that flea-infested rag to live here.'

'The cat or Mia?' my husband says breathily, finding

146

himself funny. Belinda laughs, it makes me think of Cruella de Vil. A loud, haunting cackle.

'Am I better than her?' she says, when she stops screeching. It's followed by kissing sounds. 'Your crazy cat lady? Can she fuck like me?'

'She's stiff, like a bag of kitchen utensils. Her pussy stinks like a dead cat.'

'And mine?'

'Marshmallow.'

I hold my phone to my ear. My mouth hangs open. I think I am bent right over. I am. I don't have what it takes to correct myself.

Tristan's voice becomes more muffled.

'Then eat it. Eat it all up,' Belinda says.

I hear slurping. Groaning. Moaning. Belinda begins to orgasm. It's frantic and unruly. Tristan sounds like a dog pushing its snout around a pile of rubbish. Belinda orgasms. Long and dramatic groans that verge on wailing. A steady, filmic crescendo. My husband telling her to 'Go there, go there.' Her telling him to 'Eat more, gobble her up.' His sounds make me feel sick. Very sick. And then I am sick. I see it on the floor. Some lumps of it on my phone. I don't move. I am locked in a position just inside the doorway of Selfridges. Sick at my feet. People are coming through the doors and dodging me, dodging the sick. A man's feet appear, he has a bucket and a mop. He starts swirling the mop around in my vomit. I slowly straighten and stumble back out on the street.

Isabella is sitting in a cab looking furious. 'Are you coming or what?' she yells. I see a bus pull into a stop a few feet further down the street. I run as quickly as my jelly legs will take me and jump onto it. I'm still holding my phone so tap it on the reader. I take a seat. I have no idea where this bus is going. I don't even care.

I watch strangers out of the window. People living their lives. Busy busy. I see lovers holding hands and mothers with children. A homeless man with lots of stuff around him but most importantly an empty cup held in both hands and a sign that says, 'Please help me.' People walk past him, catching a glimpse then pretending not to see. It's easier that way. Businesspeople walking from meeting to meeting. Women with shopping bags, some with boyfriends who paid for it all. Independent women with high heels, their own credit cards, bagfuls of swag. Men ogling, the women dismissing. The smell of waffles. So many people. I wonder who out of them is carrying pain, who is doing damage to someone else. Maybe we all are. Maybe an unavoidable part of being human is that we will hurt someone else. We won't love them enough, pay them enough, celebrate them enough. We just won't be enough.

A bag of kitchen utensils.

A woman gets on the bus. She is large, looks younger than she probably is. She sits next to me. The sides of her body pressing into me as she spreads over onto my seat. She doesn't seem bothered by the contact until I rest my head on her shoulder. She gets up quicker than her bones would like, brushes her shoulder as if I've left virus particles on her coat, and moves to another seat. She looks at me as though there will be trouble if I try anything like that again. She doesn't need to worry, I won't. Not with her.

I look back out of the window. Holborn. The business course I did was in Holborn. I was twenty-nine. It took a year. Doing a business course is a generic knee-jerk reaction that a lot of people make to chaos. When in doubt, do a business course. When you weren't blessed with the gift of ambition but need to do something, do a business course. When you have failed at anything you thought you might like to try, study business to make you employable. 'Business' is 'business', it doesn't matter who you work for. Can you crunch numbers, set goals, use words like 'profits', 'assets', 'margins'? Can you manage a team, sound like you know better even if you doubt that you do? If you do those things you can be in business. And then you find yourself with a job. Working for a business you find vacuous and uninspiring. The second in command to the creator who takes your good work and turns it into their own success. I didn't know where that business course would take me. I just came here every day, to Holborn. I sat in a cold room with fifteen other people. Men in cheap suits, women in uncomfortable shoes and tight skirts. Everyone being all serious. Meaning business. I listened to a man a few years older teach me how to do things that didn't interest me but that I happened to be good at. I got the soup and salad deal from a small café on the days that I didn't make my own lunch.

Sometimes I got the Tube twelve stops and ate lunch

along the way, just so I could go home and give Pigeon a quick cuddle before heading all the way back and I was never once late. That was the beginning of my relationship with order. Old habits like lateness or skipping meals became intolerable to me. I was attentive, alert. I learned what I had to do to live a better life. I programmed myself to live differently. I began to collect life goals. A job, then a marriage. I suddenly had value.

I didn't share a room with my husband, is adultery the price I pay for that? Could he tell I loved my cat more than I loved him? Did he know this was a marriage that worked for me because I had to share him? That I never minded because any kind of family was enough to keep me away from chaos? The role of second wife and stepmother was just enough to stop me spiralling back to where I was. Like a drug addict needs a hit, I need focus. When I lose focus, who knows where I could end up.

The driver rings a bell, the sign says, 'Last stop'. I am at Monument, apparently. I have avoided this part of London for a very long time, but here I am. Grounded here by circumstance. Not for the first time, I walk straight down King William Street and on to London Bridge.

Sometimes it's hard to walk straight when walking across a bridge. It's as if the water below is causing it to bounce up and down, twist side to side. I walk slowly, my arm out as if to balance myself. A few metres before the other end, I stand still and face the river. This was my spot. The place I made what I thought was the best decision of my life. The place I jumped.

I stand looking at the water. The bridge is higher than I remember. Maybe because the idea of the fall wasn't so frightening then. How had I been so brave? Could I be that brave again?

My phone rings. It's Tristan. Is he calling to tell me it's over? He can't be calling to have a trivial conversation like usual, that would be pure cruelty after what he's just done. I answer without any feeling in my body.

'Hello Tristan.'

'What time will you be home?' he asks.

'I don't know,' I say, not letting on that I heard him eat his ex-wife's marshmallow cunt in our kitchen just an hour ago. The strange family that I relied on now shattered. The return to chaos consuming me.

'Well should I organise my own dinner or have you planned something?'

'Organise it yourself. Feed Pigeon. A scoop of the biscuits. And fill up her water fountain.'

'Well how long are you going to be?'

I hang up.

13

It took me four hours and thirty-seven minutes to walk from London Bridge to Acton. I didn't rush. I had to take my shoes off and carry them from somewhere just after Hyde Park. My feet went through several stages of pain, ending in numbness. As I walk into the house, I realise I can't feel them at all. Pigeon comes running to me in her usual way. I drop my bag and bend down to stroke her. I sit down on the doormat and let Pigeon lick me. Tristan comes out of the kitchen.

'Where have you been? I kept calling.'

'My phone died.'

With the kind of comedy timing you couldn't make up, my phone alerts me to a text message from within my tote bag. I get it out. A message from Liz: *I have a box of Dad's old clothes. I'll take them to the charity shop unless you want them?*

'Mia, your feet?'

'What about them?' Pigeon is purring very loudly. Poor thing had a terrible day.

'They're covered in blood. Where have you been?'

'Walking.'

'Where from, Scotland?'

I stand up, it's harder than it should be. I walk past my husband and into the kitchen. I slip because my feet are wet with blood. As I fall, I smack my head on the corner of the kitchen island. I hit the floor hard and land on my bottom. It sends a bolt of pain up my back and I have to lie still for a few moments until it passes.

'Jesus, Mia, what's wrong with you?' I put my hand to my head. More blood. 'You could have had your eye out.' Tristan wets a dishcloth and passes it to me, I press it against my head.

'Are you drunk?' he asks me.

'No, but I'd like a drink.'

'I'm not sure that's a good idea. Are you having some sort of episode?'

'Are you?'

'What?'

'Are you having an episode? Or are you just one long bad movie?' That sounded better in my head. My head that really hurts.

'Mia, you're being very strange. Why don't you get up, have a shower and get into bed. You need to sleep off whatever you've taken.'

Tristan starts cleaning awkwardly. He wipes down the

kitchen surface with a damp sponge. I pull myself to standing then sit heavily on one of the stools so I can watch. The sponge is leaving trails of water behind it. Water mixed with Belinda's juice from her big marshmallow vagina. He starts humming to himself, as if there is nothing to see here. But I see it. I see his fear that he's left a clue. That he smells of her.

'How was your day, what did you get up to?' I ask him, all chatty.

'Work. The usual.'

Lies. Or maybe fucking Belinda in the kitchen is usual for him. It's probably been going on for years.

'Why do you keep me?' I ask him.

'Keep you? What do you mean?'

'I mean, what purpose do I serve? You have your son, Belinda, why bother with me?'

'You're my wife.'

'Why?'

'Mia, what's this about?'

I walk up to him. My eyes seductive. I wonder if his beard stinks of her or if he's had time to wash it. Will I taste her if I kiss him? Will she taste of dirty shoes, like I imagine she will? He turns to the sink to wring out the sponge, then throws it towards the plughole and walks off..

I get a fabric tote bag from the cupboard under the sink. He stands back from me and looks out of the kitchen window, pretending to gaze longingly into the garden he takes zero interest in maintaining. He can sense that I am up to something, so starts to whistle an ear-piercing tune to pretend everything is OK.

I open the kitchen utensil drawer and fill the bag. He is

watching me out of the corner of his eye. Too scared to ask me what I am doing. When the bag is full, I start rattling it violently.

'Mia?' he says, nervously. 'What are you doing?'

'I'm just interested to know what a bag of kitchen utensils feels like.'

He looks around him. Like I've planted cameras.

'It's funny, because it doesn't sound like it would make a man wail the way you wail when we have sex.'

'You are drunk, you must be.'

'Look at your phone.'

He slowly reaches to his back pocket as if someone is about to jump out of a kitchen cupboard and tackle him to the ground.

'Go on,' I say. 'Have a little look at the last time you called me.'

He presses some buttons. The blood drains from his face.

'You called me at 3.34 p.m. and the call lasted sixteen minutes. During that time you described me as a bag of kitchen utensils, performed oral sex on your ex-wife and then stood by while she violently pushed my cat to the ground. I heard everything. I was sick on the floor and tried to cuddle a woman on a bus.'

'The cat was walking its dirty feet across the kitchen surface, I have told you repeatedly how that upsets me,' he says, as if that is the most important part of what I just said. He found the only part of it where he could shift the blame away from himself and on to me. Classic man. I pick Pigeon up and put her on the kitchen surface.

'There have been dirtier pussies than her on here today.'

Tristan walks to the other side of the room and stands in the corner, which is very odd. 'What do you want me to do?' he asks. 'You won't sleep in my bed. I can only touch you when you come to me. Otherwise it's hands off, or you recoil like I am revolting to you. I always liked your oddness. You intrigued me. The way you seemed to have your own life, it worked. Didn't it? For both of us. I could still have my family, but I also had you. But you don't seem to ever want me. You give me so little.'

'I made Oliver all of those sandwiches.'

'I'm talking about me, not lunchboxes.'

'I cooked you meat even though it made me sick.'

Tristan huffs as if he's getting nowhere.

'You told Belinda my vagina smells like a dead cat. Does it?'

An eyeroll. 'Of course it doesn't. She needs to hear those things. She's not a secure woman, you know that.'

'What is a secure woman? A woman who is lied to so the truth doesn't destroy her?'

'I suppose a secure woman is someone who doesn't need to be told how good she is compared to other women. I have to do that for Belinda, she needs that.'

'Gosh it must all be so hard for you. Your two wives that you get to fuck. Having to tell us horrible things about each other to make us all happy.'

'We can't go on like this.'

'Oooh, but it's so fun for me.'

I have found a bottle of white wine in the fridge. I drink directly from it.

'You need to be alone, you're happier alone, Mia. You're not the marrying type. You're not a mother.'

'How dare you!' I say, hurt. Wondering if the thick skin I convinced myself I had is in fact transparent. Can he see right through me?

Pigeon rubs against me. Her purrs are so loud, like a rocket preparing for take-off.

'I never sent Oliver to school with odd socks. That's harder than you'd think. I kept all of the single ones and when I found the other I tied them together as a pair. Sometimes it was weeks before I'd find a match. But I never threw one away, and he never once wore odd socks.'

Tristan exhales as if I am just too exhausting.

'I can help you find a place to live.' Tristan's voice is becoming distant to me now. Blah blah blah. Something about me being easier to move than him. LA LA LA. This is Oliver's home, it's a family house. Pigeon's purrs are louder. The rocket is launching. I pick her up and storm to the front door. Sore feet, sore head, but determined. My slippers are in a basket. I slide them on. Relief. I pick up my tote bag. I go to leave but then realise this won't work. I put Pigeon and my tote bag down and open the cupboard under the stairs. I throw things over my shoulder and push things out of the way until I reach it: Pigeon's carrier case. I try to shut the cupboard door but I've made too much mess. Not my problem. I put my cat in her bag, pick up my tote and leave.

* * *

The Tube is busy. I smell, I am carrying a cat. People are trying not to look at me but failing terribly.

One woman is focusing on Pigeon instead of me, she's more comfortable staring at the cat. She is well dressed with a nice handbag. She looks up at me.

'What?' I ask, boldly enough to surprise us both.

'I used to have a cat who looked just like that.'

'Well this isn't it.'

'No, I know that. Mine died. She was fourteen, my heart and soul. How old is yours?'

'Sixteen.'

'Oh, well, my sister's cat lived until it was twenty-two. You never know, really.'

I feel my heart thump. The thought of losing Pigeon isn't something I need on top of the events of the last twenty-four hours.

'You can get pets' ashes now, you know. I have mine next to the bed, I kiss her goodnight every day.'

The train pulls into a station and the woman stands up.

'Here,' she says handing me a ten-pound note. 'For the kitty.'

'What?' I say, taking it despite my confusion.

'And I hope things improve for you soon,' she says, before getting off. I see my reflection in the glass opposite. There is make-up down my face, my hair is a state. I look down at my feet, blood is seeping through the sides of my slippers. I feel like a Tracey Emin installation.

I arrive at my sister's house an hour later, West Ruislip, right at the end of the Central Line. I ring the doorbell, but it doesn't make a sound. Someone has drawn a cock and balls on the front door. It looks like someone else has tried to rub it off. I let myself in and shout, 'Hello?'

The hallway is scattered with shoes of various sizes and Liz's DM boots that she's had so long I can't believe they are still intact. The smell of food, joss sticks and old books fills the air. I step over a pile of Lego, then around a large T-Rex whose batteries are causing it to roar at nothing. The door to the living room is open and the TV is on. A kids' show. No one is in there. Simon, Liz's husband, shouts, 'Hello Mia' from his office off the hallway. The door is shut, he'll be working on the manuscript he's been writing for nearly fifteen years. Giving him constant excuses to step away from family life. Always home, but never present, is how I would describe him.

The sounds of loud lullabies drift from upstairs, which tells me my little niece, Layla, is in bed. My teenage nephew, Tommy, walks toward me holding his nose.

'Hey Aunty Mia,' he says. 'You don't wanna go in there.'

He is referring to the kitchen. He's grimacing but also has a slight smile on his face so I'm not too worried about it.

'How is school?' I ask him.

'Cool yeah, aced my exams,' he says as he disappears up the stairs having maxed out on information sharing with a grown-up for one day. Luckily he didn't look at me long enough to acknowledge the state I'm in.

I ignore his advice and head into the kitchen, a disorganised but homely space with pots and pans hanging off hooks and piles of plates on the side instead of being tucked away in cupboards. Liz painted the cupboard doors a 'fun green' herself, there are plants on every available worktop. A wooden rack hangs above our heads with laundry dangling from it. I couldn't live like this, but Liz loves the madness of it all, making little or no effort to encourage schedules or order. I get a headache just thinking about it. To her this is the epitome of domestic bliss.

Wearing her usual grungy style clothes, as if she walked home from a festival in 1996 and never got changed, Liz sits opposite a little boy who is around Oliver's age. She could be telling him his fortune, but on closer inspection I realise he is in trouble.

'I know you're hurting but we don't do things like that in this house. Do you understand?' my sister says to a boy who ignores her, gets up and runs past me and then heads up the stairs.

Liz sees me and smiles as if all is well and wonderful in her world.

'He's a particularly tricky one,' she says, referring to the boy. 'He won't talk about what happened to him at all. Poor kid.'

My sister, despite having three of her own, fosters children. She is addicted to caring. Our abandonment and co-dependency issues have manifested in very different ways. Where I separate myself and need to be alone, Liz collects people. She and Simon have been together since they were sixteen. She had her first baby at twenty-four, her second at thirty and her third at forty. Over the past fifteen years she has fostered over thirty children. She's been in countless scrapes with them. One left her with a giant scar across her left cheek. Another broke her arm. But nothing stopped her taking more in. She can't have slept more than three hours in one night in eighteen years. She looks after Simon like he is another child. Delivering plates to him throughout the day as he keeps his head down, typing away at the novel that must be a million words long by now. He earns money by copywriting for various companies and Liz marks exam papers for universities. A job she can do from home while the kids watch TV. They also get some money for fostering, but that isn't why they do it. For Liz, this is life at its best. She takes care of people who need her, that really is all she ever wanted. To be needed.

We have little in common other than the long childhood that we shared, where we had to be everything to each other because our mum died of cancer before we were ten and our dad drank himself into a narcissistic stupor until he also eventually died of rot just after I turned twenty-one. Liz and I went our separate ways after that. I went off on a solo rampage around the world. She got married and started making babies to ensure solitude would never haunt her. My sister cannot be alone, I would go as far as to say it is her greatest fear. I was pleased when she married young. It took a lot of pressure off me.

'Mia, look at you. What happened?'

'A lot. Can I stay the night?'

'Yeah, sure. You'll have to take the couch because I've got two right now so no spare beds.'

'I can sleep anywhere. What's that smell?' I ask. Presuming that is why my nephew was holding his nose.

'Poop. Look!' She points at the wall. There are large brown stains all over it. 'He's ten. Dad beat him, mum in rehab. Poor kid.'

'He rubbed shit on your walls?'

'Yeah. Funnily enough it's not the first time one of them has done this. I don't know how they know to do it, like some secret foster kid code. Shit into your hand and rub it on the walls in the kitchen, just so everyone knows you're hurting. Trauma is a very strange thing.'

I feel quite sick.

'Why do you do it, it's so hard for you?' I ask her, bewildered.

'They make me realise I had it easy. Dad wanted nothing to do with us, like he hated us. But at least he left us alone. Some of the kids I've had here had dads who would never leave them alone, and not in a good way. Doing this makes me feel lucky, and whoever thought someone like me would feel lucky?'

There's a banging on the wall.

'WHAT?' she yells.

'TEA,' Simon yells back.

'He's still writing the book then?' I ask, wondering if she is finally tiring of his obsession with it.

'Yup. He says I'll be able to read it soon, can't wait.'

With absolutely no offence taken at all, she gets the kettle on and makes three cups of tea. She won't drink hers. She will be continuously distracted until it's cold and then she'll throw it down the sink.

'Do you need a baking tray and a newspaper again?' she asks me.

'Yes please.'

'Here.' She picks up the baking tray that has cold food on it and goes to tip it into a bin. Just before she does she says, 'Oh, sorry are you hungry? Do you want any of this?'

I'd estimate that it came out of the oven at least an hour ago by looking at it. 'No, but can I have the fish fingers for Pigeon?' I take the tray off her. Put the fish fingers on a dirty plate and tip the chips away. Liz passes me a newspaper, we've done this all before. I shred up the newspaper and put it into the tray, then pull apart the fish fingers, taking the coating off. It creates a small pile of white fish that I top up with some tuna from a cupboard. Liz always has tuna. She eats it straight from the tin.

'Come on Pigeon,' I say, unzipping her carrier. She's very relaxed here, she knows the house well. She sniffs the fish but first goes over to her makeshift litter tray and pees on it. I always feel so proud of her when she does it. So well trained. Then she goes over to the fish and eats it all up. I put some water down, she takes a few sips.

'If only kids were that easy,' Liz says, admiring Pigeon.

Liz is the only person I know who doesn't make me feel gross for having a cat. She used to foster dogs before she fostered children, but the neighbours were always complaining about the barking.

'She's never had to worry from the moment I took her

home,' I say, smiling at my cat. 'And look at her, happy as a clam wherever she goes. Unless it's Tristan's bedroom, she did a massive protest pee on the bed the other day. You can imagine how Belinda reacted to that, she got piss all over her clothes. The atmosphere in the house was awful.'

'Tristan never liked your cat.'

'What? That's not true. It's her, she's too heartless to love an animal.'

'Well, you found yourself a husband with an ex-wife appendage who never liked your cat. Either way, big choice.'

'I suppose I was just amazed that I found myself a husband at all.'

'Talking of protests.' Liz fills a saucepan up with warm soapy water. She takes it to the wall and starts to wash away the brown smears. It's a strange thing about us both, that we dedicated ourselves to the survival of others. I'd do anything to ensure Pigeon's happiness. Liz would take a bullet for any child, hers or not.

'It looks like my marriage is over,' I tell my sister. 'I'm scared of what I will be without it, I know I was never as alone with him as I will be without him.' She's scrubbing as hard as she can, but a few stains will not come off. She huffs, then gets a can of white paint out of a cupboard and just starts painting over it. 'I don't know where to go, or what to do.'

'Well, where is he now?'

'At home. He says I'm easier to move, that he is going to take the house for him and Belinda and Oliver.'

'Belinda? What's that paddlepoop moving into your house for?'

'Paddlepoop?'

'Oh, it's a child-friendly word I found for . . .' she tightens her lips '. . . uptight cunt.'

My sister has child-friendly words for everything. I've seen her drop a boiling hot saucepan on her foot and simply say 'ouchies'.

'He's been cheating on me with her for I don't know how long.'

'What! That horrible . . . turtle brain!'

'Thanks. I'm shocked but also not surprised, which is odd, I suppose.'

'Wait, did you say that Belinda got cat piss on her from lying on Tristan's bed? What was she even doing on there?'

'They were having their usual therapy session in his room. I didn't even question it, it felt too obvious that there could be anything going on. Urgh, I feel like I've got her juice all over me, where else were they doing it without me knowing? I'm such an idiot.'

'Don't blame yourself, Mia.'

'Hard not to really. I'm homeless now. How could I not have known?'

'Look, you paid for half of that house. You maintained it, you kept everything going, you looked after Tristan. It's your house. He cheated, he can get out. You have to fight for it.'

'I don't know if I have any fight in me. I can't be bothered.'

'You can't be bothered to keep your house?'

Pigeon jumps up onto my lap.

'I just go numb. You know?' I stroke Pigeon. 'I could go to a hotel for now. Somewhere easy.'

My sister sits down in front of me. 'Listen to me. You deserve to keep your home. He cheats, he moves. End of story. You need to tell him that, OK?'

'I feel like as long as I have Pigeon, anywhere could be home.'

'We have allowed men to set the tone of our lives for too long. You cannot let Tristan push you out of your home, understand me? He does not get to control your life.'

Another bang on the wall. It makes us laugh.

'Yikes, his tea,' she says, hurrying back to the counter, pouring three cold cups away and starting the whole process again. She delivers his, loyally.

'Doesn't it bother you that he's always in there doing that while you're always in here cooking or cleaning up?'

'There's a lot of love in this house, Mia. That's all I care about. I don't mind what room he sits in or what he's doing as long as he loves us and shows it.' She picks up her brush and starts painting over the shit again.

'Dad really fucked us up, didn't he?' I say.

Another bang on the wall.

'BISCUIT,' Simon yells, with no please or thank you.

'I don't know what you're talking about,' she says, pretending to lick the paintbrush like an ice lolly. 'I'm totally fine.'

14

I wake to the realisation that there is a finger up my nose.

'Layla, no, get off,' I say, waving my hand.

'Play with me,' is all I get in return. She climbs on top of me and grabs a chunk of my hair.

'Not too hard,' I beg, as she yanks it from my head. I release her grip and tickle her on the nose with it instead. She giggles and it's so adorable that I tickle her under her arms too. Her body is convulsing around as I tickle her tummy, her sides, under her neck. Her laughter louder and louder as she forgets herself entirely. It's very cute, until she kicks me so hard in the face I wonder if she's broken my nose.

'Layla, come on love. Let Aunty Mia wake up,' says Liz, coming in and leaving a cup of tea on the coffee table. She scoops her baby up and disappears, shutting the door, giving me a moment to come round.

My back is sore. They've had the same couch for longer than I can remember. It smells, it's sticky and there is more food on it than I've eaten in the last twenty-four hours. I'm wearing one of Simon's t-shirts and a pair of his shorts. Before I went to bed, I had a shower and washed the blood off my feet and the make-up off my face. I rinsed my slippers in the water. The blood didn't come off and they have dried hard.

In the kitchen, Liz is wearing a fleece dressing gown that I got her about fifteen Christmases ago. I got the same one, but I've had four of them since. Simon is still in bed. Layla is making a terrible job of eating scrambled eggs with a spoon. There is a toddler in a highchair that I haven't met yet, and the angry nine-year-old is eating Cheerios and not looking up. Liz looks so tired, but still she doesn't complain. I watch her serve them all with half-open eyes. She receives mostly grunts as thank yous but continues with a weary smile. I wish I could have more of my sister, but she is taken by her need to do for others what no one will do for her.

'I have to go to work,' I say, as I put Pigeon into her carrier.

'OK, well it's been good to see you. I left that box of Dad's things by the door. Finally, after all these years, I could face going through it all. There's a dress of Mum's in there too. Take it.'

'I don't want that stuff.'

'Well then just take it to a charity shop, Mia. Please, save me the job. Oh come on, you didn't help me at all with Dad's place. Can't you at least just take this box?'

I don't want to touch it. And I didn't want to go back to Dad's house when he died. I told her I'd pay someone to go and clean it out, donate anything worth donating, chuck everything else. But Liz is more sentimental than me, she wanted to keep things. I just wanted to forget things.

'Fine, I'll take it. But please stop making me feel bad about not helping, I told you I didn't want to and you made the choice to go alone.'

'Thank you. I still have our dolls' house upstairs, you know. The one Mum got us. It needs a good clean but I'm saving it for Layla.'

A memory of Mum and me bathing all of the dolls then placing them around the little house floods my brain. I used to wish we could drink a magic potion that would shrink us to be tiny enough to live in the little house. So tiny that Dad could never find us.

'They're not expensive, I could just get her a new one,' I say, not really wanting to see the dolls' house for the memories it will bring up.

'But I like that she's got ours. I know there aren't many happy memories, but you have to admit we had fun with that?'

I shrug.

'I better go. Thanks for letting me stay. What do you say, Pigeon?' I hold up the carrier and say 'Thank you' in a cat-like voice. Layla laughs, Liz smiles, the boy rolls his eyes. I'm pretty sure I also hear a fart.

* * *

I'm struggling with Pigeon's carrier, my tote bag and the box of old clothes, so walk to the high street before getting on the Tube. The first thing I see is a charity shop raising money for Age UK. It feels like the right place to leave Dad's old clothes.

The sign says it doesn't open for another hour, but there are a few bags and boxes of things that people have left at the door. Most of them have been rummaged through already. I can't get the thought of my mother's dress out of my head. Will I recognise it? Will it smell of her?

I put Pigeon down and open the box. A familiar smell causes the hairs on my arms to stand up so stiffly they look like they're trying to break free of my body. Smoky and musty, with a hint of crushed-up digestives. The clothes are folded neatly, with more respect than they deserve. I don't want to touch them. I close my eyes and take out a layer of clothing. When I open them again, Mum's purple kaftan is there, folded perfectly. Alongside it my father's grey cardigan. Just the sight of it triggers the most painful of thoughts.

'Are you taking those?' a gruff voice says, pulling me away from my memories. 'Those. Are you taking them?'

It's a homeless man. He's pointing at my dad's trousers on the ground.

'No, not those.' I pass them to him.

He stands about a foot from me and takes off the trousers he is wearing and puts them in a bag. I don't watch, but the smell of stale urine and body odour drowns out the smell of my dad.

'Here, do you need a shirt too?' I say, handing him a white one.

'I don't want that.'

'This? To keep you warm?' I say, handing him Dad's old grey cardigan. Memories of him wearing it burning through my skin. The homeless man takes it, puts it on then shuffles away. An item that was so chilling to me as a child, now a source of warmth to someone else. Is there such a thing as just an item of clothing, when the very fact that they are worn at all makes them such a part of our history? There are a few people milling around now as the high street begins to open. No one seemed fazed by the homeless man changing his clothes so I take off mine – the bland uniform I've worn for years – and put on my mother's dress.

I have no choice but to take Pigeon to work. Isabella will be mad about it, but the staff might quite like it. It doesn't have to be a big deal, I don't have to be embarrassed. I can tell them we are renovating and all the doors will be open all day so it wouldn't be safe for Pigeon to be home. No one will question that. People don't have to know what is really going on. That I've lost my husband and my home and that my sanity is heading in the same direction. How would they know, if I don't tell them?

I have numerous missed calls from Tristan plus multiple messages asking where I am. Saying I can't just leave. Asking when I'll be back to organise my things? Where will I go? All questions I don't have answers for so see no point in answering.

I make a litter tray out of a cardboard box that is sitting

on my desk and fill it with the contents of the shredder and let Pigeon out of her carrier. I got myself coffee and a pastry on the way in, the first thing I've eaten since before the Selfridges pitch. I also acquired some food for Pigeon, which I spoon into a bowl and put on the floor next to my desk. I keep a spare pair of shoes at work because I often walk in and change them when I get here. I'll pop them on in a bit. I feel awful and broken but put on my professional head and am at least pleased I have somewhere to be for the next eight hours. I can distract myself with work like I have for so many years. What happens after this I really have no idea.

Fliss arrives first. I watch her come in. Always impeccable. Pigeon runs into the workshop and straight up to her. 'Oh my goodness, who is this?' she says, kneeling down and stroking her. It's always reassuring when someone you like is into cats.

'Morning Fliss,' I say, coming out of my office.

'Morning, wow, are you OK?' She looks worried.

'Yes, why?'

'Oh, nothing. You just look . . . tired?'

'I am quite tired.'

'Sorry, I didn't mean to be rude. You just always look the same and today . . . God, I'm sorry, I am being so rude. But the dress. It's a new style for you?'

'This was my mother's dress,' I tell her. 'It's from the eighties.'

'Yes. Yes, it is. I mean, I love it. It's just a real departure from what you usually wear, but good for you.'

'Good for me. Thanks. I'm really enjoying wearing it, I feel quite at home in all this fabric.'

'Is this your cat?' She looks confused.

'Yes, why?' I reply. Which is a strange thing to say, considering it was a perfectly valid question.

'Oh, it's just . . . I just read this mad article on the way here and . . . well, I mean, this is your cat so it can't be you who was being described. Anyway, sorry, I'm waffling . . .'

She read it. She knows. Everyone will know. She picks Pigeon up with unusual success.

'She likes you,' I say, surprised. 'You have a cat?'

'I don't, but my gran does. She's pregnant, actually.'

'Your gran is pregnant?'

'No, God, Mia, her cat. My gran is seventy-eight.'

'Of course. How lovely, some kittens.'

'Yes, I can't have one unfortunately. My girlfriend is allergic. I'd have ten cats if it was down to me. Actually, I say "girlfriend", but I should probably say "fiancée". I asked her to marry me last night, and she said yes.'

'Oh my goodness, congratulations. There's champagne in the fridge, why don't you open a bottle. It's not too early is it?'

'It's 9.05 a.m.,' she says.

'Exactly!' I say. 'You know what, I'll get it.'

I head over to the fridge, there are multiple bottles in there. I take one out, no idea if it's expensive or not, I just need some.

'We can save it for lunchtime if you want?' Fliss says, a look of concern on her face that I choose to ignore.

'No, no, we have lots to celebrate.' I pop the cork and pour the liquid into two mugs even though I know there are flutes somewhere.

'So, I probably shouldn't say this without Isabella, but Selfridges loved your necklace, Fliss, and the whole idea for the collection.'

'You pitched it?'

'I said I would, didn't I? It's the best thing we had to show them. You deserve to do well, Fliss. You're very talented.'

'Thanks Mia, that means a lot. My gran isn't well, this will really cheer her up.'

'We'll have a proper talk about it when Isabella is in, but I just wanted to say well done. We really need this and if it happens it will be down to you.'

I finish my mug of champagne and fill it up again.

'Mia,' she says. 'Are you sure you're OK?'

'Yes Fliss, I'm absolutely fine. Thanks for asking.' I brush my hands down my mother's dress to smooth it, I suppose it is quite creased. And then of course there are my slippers. It's a different look for me, I accept that. But truthfully, I don't remember the last time I felt this comfortable in anything.

'Morning,' says Audrey, arriving uncharacteristically close to 9 a.m. Pigeon jumps up onto a desk. 'Woah, whose cat is that?' she asks.

'Mine,' I say.

'Oh, wow. I just read this article where the woman in it was so like you, Mia. I was going to ask if it was you. But her cat is dead, so, I guess it's not you?'

'I don't know what you're talking about,' I say, innocently. 'My cat is alive and well. Sixteen years, as it happens. No dead cats here. And how are you, all OK?' I'm referring to her abortion, as she hasn't been in since and it's been nearly a week.

'Well, I did it. I don't know about "OK".'

'OK, great. Champagne?'

'Pardon?'

'Yes, we're celebrating. Go on Fliss, it's not my news to share.'

Fliss looks awkwardly at Audrey. 'Yeah, I'm getting married, and Mia thought we should have champagne. At 9 a.m.'

'Okaaay,' Audrey says, as I hand her a mugful too. 'Enjoy,' I say, spinning around and heading back to my desk. Pigeon, my cat who's very much alive, follows me loyally. A few minutes later, Ajay comes in and he is very sweaty.

'Sorry I'm late, boss. My bike broke so I had to get the Tube. I never get the Tube, so don't read many papers but someone left this on the seat and check this out. This woman could be you.'

He starts to unfold the newspaper.

'Well, it isn't me, so if you could get on with your work that would be great.'

'No, hang on. Listen to this. *Tall, thin, fiery red hair.*'

'It's not me, Ajay. Please do some work.'

'*Dressed in sensible work clothes . . .*'

'*I SAID IT'S NOT ME, AJAY. PLEASE GO TO YOUR FUCKING DESK AND DO SOME FUCKING WORK.*'

Everyone, including Pigeon, goes still and stares at me. I am trembling, sweat is rolling down my face.

'OK, boss. I just thought it sounded like you. But it's cool, I get it,' Ajay says, heading for his desk as I asked. When he has sat down and turned on his computer, Fliss and Audrey get back to work, I notice they aren't glugging their drinks the same way that I am. I stare at my computer screen. It isn't even on.

By 9.30 a.m. the atmosphere has settled and there is no sign of Isabella. I make a rare visit to the kitchenette to make a cup of coffee, I need extra today.

'Mia,' Ajay says, approaching me. 'I'm really sorry about before, I didn't mean no harm.'

'It's OK Ajay, I'm sorry I shouted. I didn't sleep very well last night.'

'No worries.'

I concentrate on the drink I'm making, because I'd like him to leave me alone now.

'I like what you're wearing. It suits you. What is it?'

'It's a kaftan.'

'Yeah man, I like it. I'm getting a glimpse of the real Mia. It's cool. You're cool. When you're not yelling.'

I watch him walk back to his seat. He puts his headphones on and eats a bowl of cereal, all while still smiling. He's so odd.

At 10.15 Cressida, Isabella's nanny, walks in.

'Can I help you?' I ask.

'I have something for you,' she says, looking me up and down.

'For me?'

This is very unexpected. I have met Cressida once before at a Christmas drinks party Isabella hosted at home. She looked like she was going to have a nervous breakdown because Poppy wouldn't go to sleep. I wait patiently while she rummages around in her bag. She presents me with an envelope.

'Here, from Isabella.'

'Well, where is she?'

'She said I must not say more.'

I take the letter, and Cressida stands and looks at me for far too long to feel comfortable. 'Was there something else?' I ask, politely.

'It's not all her fault,' she says, firmly.

'What's not all whose fault?' I ask, confused.

'Isabella. The way she is. It's not all her fault. I know she is awful, but . . . no, that's all.'

'Is Isabella in trouble?' I ask, worried as to what this letter says.

'No, you are. But it's not all her fault. I just wanted you to understand that. I see more than what you see, but I do get why you argue. OK, I wasn't supposed to say anything.'

'Well I have the letter now, so thank you.'

'She told me I have to stay and watch you open it. So she knows that you've read it. Oh God, is that a cat?' Pigeon has jumped up onto Isabella's desk.

'Yes, it's my cat, Pigeon.'

'I hate cats. They lick their bottoms and have shit on their feet.'

'I can assure you she is perfectly clean. Do you really have to stay here while I open this?'

'Yes.'

I sit at my desk and open the letter.

Mia, I am sorry to say that I cannot keep you on at 'Isabella May'. You have made it increasingly impossible for me to run my business as I wish. You have blindsided me repeatedly with staffing decisions and even at the Selfridges pitch. You obviously planned to reveal the necklace and went ahead despite knowing it was not what I wanted to do.

You have accused me of terrible things in the years that you have worked for me, but it is you who has created a toxic work culture at 'Isabella May'. Your cold and brittle demeanour intimidates the staff and makes you impossible to approach. And then there is the betrayal; taking my business and turning it into something that disconnects me from its core.

As you know, I am a single mother with a high-profile image to protect and a business to run. You have no respect or consideration for the many things I am up against, and I can't be beaten down by you any more.

I'd like you to leave immediately. Take your things. I left a box on your desk for you to use. I will pay you for

six weeks as a courtesy which I have been advised is
extremely generous. In return I expect no fuss from you.
I hope you find peace in whatever you do next.
Isabella.

I just stare at the letter.

'Are you OK?' Cressida asks.

I stand up. I wobble. My head has gone very light. 'Pigeon?' I call, but she's using the litter tray I made her. 'Pigeon, off that.' But it's too late. The smell fills the office.

'Oh no!' Cressida screeches. 'Oh, cat shit is the worst, that's disgusting.'

Pigeon jumps out when she's done. I have so many things in my drawers that I need but I can't pack up now. Is that letter a joke? What the hell is happening?

'Are you going to clear that up?' Cressida asks, reminding me of Isabella and showing me they are more alike than I thought. 'I can't stay in here,' she says, leaving me alone in the office. I want to smash things up – pick up Isabella's computer and throw it at the wall. Empty every single drawer and pull out every piece of jewellery and rip them apart and stamp on them. I want to get a bat and smash the windows, run into the workshop and grab Cressida by the hair. Spinning her round in circles as she screams with pain because she is the closest thing to Isabella that I have.

I put Pigeon back in her carrier. I pick up my tote bag. I walk calmly through the workshop in my mother's purple eighties dress, as if I'm popping out to a meeting.

'So go on then Mia, what's the key to a happy marriage?' Fliss asks, looking so desperately happy that it makes my heart ache.

'What the fuck would I know?' I say, stunning her. I pick up her mug and drink the champagne from it so quickly that I cough violently.

'I'll get you some water,' Fliss says, rushing to the kitchenette. By the time she gets it to me, I have turned what I imagine to be a shade of beetroot and my eyes are pouring with water. I take a sip, but a cough launches the water straight back out of my mouth.

'Is she having a breakdown?' I hear Cressida say.

'No one can be that together all the time, I've been waiting for her to crack,' says Audrey.

Coughing hard and barely able to catch a breath, I stumble out of the office to the lift with Pigeon. When the door opens, three people get out despite it clearly not being their floor.

'Allergic to cats,' I hear one of them mumble.

'TWAT,' I shout, to my own surprise, as the doors close.

I walk a few miles before my slippers become so stretched that they're almost impossible to keep on my feet. I have to slow right down and, instead of steps, do more of a skating move. I have so many things at work, it's amazing what drawers can acquire over the course of many years. I don't know what to do about that. I don't know what to do about anything. I see a park. Parks are good at times like this. When things got tough at home, Liz and I would always go to the park. Sometimes we spent whole days there and Mum would come to find us, until she wasn't strong enough to do that any more. Dad never came to the park, which is why it felt so safe.

I am lost. Nowhere to go. My home, my office, are no longer options for me. In between them is a space I must now wander aimlessly. I can't think straight, what should I do? I'll need to let Pigeon out at some point. I'll need to wash. Where do I do those things now? I had everything so together. I made good decision after good decision, and I ended up here? How can this happen to someone like me, someone who worked so hard for order and routine? Some-one who worked so hard to play the right part.

I walk into the park and look around. A play area to the left, a small rose garden straight ahead, a large grass lawn to the right. I walk over to the play area and watch a mother push her little girl on a swing. She's pushing with one hand, holding her phone with the other. Her child can't see her so she doesn't feel bad about it. She still shouts, 'Weeeeee' and 'Legs forward for up and back for down.' She looks so bored. Living her two lives simultaneously. The role of mother, and the role of whatever it is that she is trying to cling onto through her phone.

There is a nanny in command of two children, one maybe five, one a baby. She sits with the baby, bouncing it, feeding it, making it giggle, giving it love. The older one left to fend for itself. Trying to find fun on some monkey bars that are too high for him. Another mother sits closely next to her child on a bench, they're laughing and eating sandwiches together. I spent so many hours of so many days in playgrounds with Oliver when he was younger. I'd push him on the swing until my arm ached. I must be staring at the mum with the phone because she looks annoyed and turns the other way.

A large dog is suddenly alongside me barking aggressively – it's noticed Pigeon.

'No, go away. GO AWAY,' I shout, wrapping myself around the carrier to protect her, but the dog is relentless. It is gnashing and snarling. Foam falling from the sides of its mouth.

'Whose dog is this?' I screech. The mothers in the playground do nothing but take their kids further away to protect them from the crazy lady with the cat and the purple dress. 'Help! Help!' I shout as loudly as I can. I'm very scared. This large dog wants to attack my cat, and maybe me too. 'Help! Help!' I continue to shout but no one comes.

I pick up a stick and point it at the dog.

'Get away. GET AWAY!' The dog grabs the other end of the stick, it's now a tug of war. I'm pulling it, but it just won't let go. I only have one hand to use, if I put Pigeon down the dog will have her for lunch.

'GET AWAY!' I shout again. 'AWAAAAAAYYYY!'

'Jesse, Jesse there you are!' says a woman who is running over. The dog immediately softens, starts wagging its tail and skipping with joy over to its mum.

'Were you going to hit my dog?' she says, looking at me with total disgust.

'I thought she was going to attack me, and my cat.'

'What the fuck do you expect dogs to do if you bring a cat to the park? Jesus, put the stick down, you crazy bitch. Come on, Jesse.'

She walks away. Jesse too, as if the whole ordeal never happened. My heart is thumping so fast, Pigeon is wriggling in her carrier. There are quite a few people looking at me. The crazy bitch in the park with the stick and the cat. How is this me?

I leave the park and walk further in these terrible shoes until I find another park. Probably around an hour. I'm in no rush, where am I supposed to go? There is a shop on the corner. I buy water, cat food, a Kind Bar and a Purdy's mineral water because I presume my body needs something. I find a bench that is quite secluded. Nestled in between two large beds full of bushes and trees. There is no playground in this little park, fewer people. A couple of small dogs but all on leads. This feels better. Safer. There is a clip on the strap of Pigeon's carrier so I can detach one end of it. I do that, then unzip just enough that I can attach it to her collar. When it's on, I fully unzip the carrier so she can peek out. She's not an outdoor cat but I have done something similar to this in the garden at home during the summer. She always sat nicely and just enjoyed the breeze on her face. I take her out and pull her onto my lap, she seems nervous but not enough to run away from me. I stroke her fur. She purrs. I wonder when we will ever have our routine back. The bedtime dance, the long intimate sleeps. Our clockwork feeding schedule. Our warm house. The life we were happy with, despite its imperfections.

I get out the letter from Isabella again.

Your cold and brittle demeanour intimidates the staff and makes you impossible to approach.

Is that why I now find myself alone? What I find so hard to understand is that I would describe so many people that way, and yet they thrive. Belinda is such an unlikable person. Insincere, judgemental, selfish. I supported her in ways she didn't even notice yet she's done little but patronise me, make me feel strange, unlovable and unpleasant because of my cat. And still she comes out on top with the husband and the child and even my home. Then there is Isabella; supported by her father's wealth and she knows that no matter how bad things get, she'll always have a home just south of Sloane Square and her celebrity friends to boost her morale. There must be so much freedom when you know you'll always land on your feet. Not like me, in a random park with no job, no home. Just my cat who I have to keep safe and a big purple dress that reminds me of my dead mum and smells of my dead dad.

Am I really so 'cold' that I took on someone else's child and did everything I could to maintain his happiness despite him having no interest in mine? So brittle that I grew a business from nothing and employed staff who deserved opportunities that I offered them wherever possible? Was I really so intimidating that I was 'impossible' to approach when Isabella herself sat spouting inappropriate comments and hardly ever even came to the office, but remained at the helm of a business she had no idea how to run?

I think of the article. Amy Newton's horrible words about us all. How cruel to watch people bare themselves so raw, then take notes and tell the world how sad and lonely they are. How sad and lonely do you have to be to want to do that to other people?

I want to drink. Drinking is what you do when everything goes to hell. I put Pigeon back into her carrier and go back to the shop. I buy a bottle of Oyster Bay Sauvignon Blanc which feels decadent considering I plan to drink it on a park bench alone. I also buy a bottle of Maker's Mark because it's the one spirit I can drink without a mixer and who needs the trouble of cups and measurements when feelings need to be drowned and problems need to be ignored. I have no idea what I'll do after this. But even if I have to sit here drinking on this bench for days, I will, eventually, think of something.

Part Three

Animal

One night I couldn't sleep because the foxes were screeching in the garden again.

I was climbing out of bed to get some milk when the doorbell went. I saw Mum answer it, she was wearing her dressing gown.

'Oh, Mr Hammond,' she said performatively. 'Yes, the broken microwave is in the kitchen, come this way.'

Something broke every Thursday night in our house. Something that Mr Hammond had to fix while Dad was at the snooker hall.

I usually listened from the stairs, but that night I crept down to see what the noises I had become so familiar with really were. The noises of my mother's rebellion. She was lying on the kitchen table and Mr Hammond was on top of her. They were nowhere near the microwave.

I'd seen this sort of thing before on the TV and with animals in the National Geographic magazine. I knew it meant they loved each other. But then Mr Hammond told my mother to turn around. I saw his penis while she moved. It was long and different from what I'd seen before. Quite frightening. It disappeared when she lay on her front, her feet on the floor. Where did it go? He pulled her hair quite hard, and she made noises *that sounded like the foxes that had woken me up. I'd have tried to save her, but she was smiling.*

She kept saying, 'Yes, yes, harder, harder.'

My sister opened our bedroom door and I heard her running down the stairs. I banged on the kitchen door, but I didn't go in. I did it because I wanted my mother to stop. I didn't want Liz to see.

'Girls?' Mum said, opening the kitchen door. She was doing her dressing gown up and Mr Hammond was facing the other way doing up his trousers. Of course, now it all makes perfect sense, but then I didn't understand at all. I just knew that Dad wouldn't like it, and that scared me.

'I saw a ghost, Mummy,' Liz said. My mother picked her up.

'Mia, how long have you been standing there?' she asked me. Both she and Mr Hammond waited for my answer even though they already knew it.

'Not long,' I said, and they seemed relieved that I was at least willing to lie.

'OK, well come on you two, back to bed. Thank you Mr Hammond, I'll let you know if anything else breaks.'

Mum took us upstairs and lay on Liz's bed with her until she fell asleep. She told her Jack and the Beanstalk from memory. I watched them both. It was soothing for me too, to know that she was there.

And even though, deep down, I knew what she'd done that night was wrong, all that mattered to me was how happy Mum seemed when she was with us.

15

I finished the wine and drank about a quarter of the bottle of whiskey. I can't really remember falling asleep, but I wake up on the bench as the sun is going down. A man with lots of keys is trying to wake me. 'Madam, wake up. Wake up madam.' He says I have to leave the park as he is locking it for the night. I ask him very politely if he could just lock me in it. He doesn't seem to want to do that. Pigeon, still with her strap attached to her collar, is lying faithfully in the curve of my body. I pop her back in the carrier and stumble to the park entrance.

'I won't tell if you won't,' I slur to the man.

'Go home, madam,' he says.

'I don't have a home,' I wail.

'Yes, you do,' he says, firmly. As if he knows full well I'm not a homeless woman, like he sees women like me all the

191

time. He seems unfazed by my loneliness, my drunkenness, my cat. I suppose if you are the person who must get people out of a park at night, you've seen a lot worse than me.

'Where to now then, Pigeon?' I say aloud to the sky with the hope the heavens will answer. And, miraculously, I see the word 'HOTEL' in big letters across the road. I walk in and straight up to the reception desk. The woman behind it looks at me, then to her colleague as if to alert his attention.

'Hello,' I say very politely, overcompensating for how drunk I suddenly feel. 'Do you have any rooms available?'

She doesn't answer immediately, trying to find any reason to turn me away.

'I'm sorry, we don't allow cats in our rooms.'

'Do you take dogs?'

'Yes, we do.'

'Great, because this isn't a cat.'

'Sorry?'

'It's a Chihuahua. A small breed of dog. Do you have a room?'

She goes over to her colleague and whispers something in his ear. They both come back over to me. Now the man speaks, because I am obviously a problem.

'Can I help you madam?' he asks.

'No more than she could have, but if she needs you then I suppose she needs you. I'd like a room, for me and my Chihuahua please.'

'OK, I can see the animal and it's a cat. Unfortunately, we don't allow cats into the rooms here.'

It's dark outside now. I have extremely sore feet and literally nowhere to go. I can't get back into the park because I've been locked out of it. I can't go home because my husband might be having sex with his ex-wife in my kitchen. I really need a room in this hotel.

'You're right. It is a cat. I lied. Now can I have a room?'

'I'm afraid not, the situation remains the same. We don't allow cats in the rooms.'

'But I have nowhere to go.'

'Would you like me to search for pet-friendly hotels?'

'But you are a pet-friendly hotel, and you don't like cats.'

'It's not that I don't like cats, we just don't allow cats.'

'Well why not? What's wrong with cats?'

'Nothing, madam, I have one myself. But you can't bring it here because this hotel does not allow them. It's nothing personal.'

'Nothing personal?' I say extremely loudly, gathering the attention of everyone in the hotel lobby. 'I lose my family, my job, my home, I can't get a room in a fucking hotel, but sure, it's nothing personal. This shit just happens to everyone. You're all homeless, just like me.' I point at the woman behind the desk. 'Your husband said your cunt tastes like a dead cat.' I point at another woman. 'Your mum was eaten alive by cancer and died in front of you like a pathetic bear.' And then I swing to the man who is trying to get rid of me. 'And your dad wanked himself to death.' I don't know where that last one came from, but I did always presume that my dad's insistence on being alone had something to do with a sexual fetish. I could be wrong.

The man is now walking me out, his hand on my back, and it's not exactly pushing me but it's absolutely not inviting me back in. 'I'm sorry, and I truly hope that you find a place for you and your cat,' he says. And then I am alone on the street.

There were approximately three murders committed on young women who were alone in London over the past six months. All attacked by men, all women with social lives and families worthy enough to make the news. On top of those cases there were countless 'unworthy' women attacked and raped or killed by men that the news didn't bother mentioning. And yet a man who works in a hotel and is in control of all of those empty rooms literally leads a woman into the dark city to fend for herself, rather than ask her, 'Are you safe, woman with the cat and the bleeding feet? Woman who clearly has nowhere to go, who is scared, and cold, desperate and alone? Can I help you, woman? Save you from the inevitable abuse and violence you will face if you cannot find a place to lay your head?' But no, get her out. We don't let women like that into our rooms.

Rather than society acknowledging women who are struggling and helping them, they put firm hands on our shoulders and push us into the darkness. What kind of woman do you have to be to get the sympathy of strangers? Young? Pretty? Sober? Smartly dressed? Black? White? Upright? On the floor? Who knows? All I know is you're doomed if you show any signs of being affected by a life that's tried to destroy you. People won't help you. They'll let their dogs attack you, they'll skulk away to save their children and pretend you're not there. They'll scream, 'You crazy bitch' at you when you try to defend yourself. They'll make you leave the park. They'll remove you from their premises. They'll fire you for being good at your job. They'll fuck your husband and slam your beloved cat to the ground, so they can have sex in the kitchen that you paid for. They'll write horrible articles about you when you are at your most vulnerable. I think of Martha. Her feelings shared bravely with a small group of people she thought she could trust, yet outed by a nasty journalist who thinks even a woman's tiniest voice must be silenced. What a betrayal. Should we always just presume there is a traitor in every room? And if that is the case, should we never dare to speak our truth?

'IF I GET RAPED IT'S YOUR FAULT,' I shout into the hotel lobby to a sea of horrified faces. They think I am the crazy one, not the man in the old-fashioned servant's uniform who just refused to give me a safe place to stay. I hail a black cab. The driver has lower standards. I get in and give him the address.

16

It's not trespassing if your fob gives you access, is it? I didn't know where else to go. I arrive at the office at 9 p.m. I'll gather my things, sleep under my desk, and be gone by 5 a.m. before the cleaners come. Nothing is more ominous than an office at night. It's almost impossible to believe it's empty. The energy of all of those busy people hovers when they leave, it's not supposed to be idle. A few lights have been left on. That would never have happened on my watch. The inevitable demise of this company without me will begin with extortionate bills. I let Pigeon out of her carrier, and she starts scoping the joint immediately. I close the door behind me so she can't get out.

As I walk in, I see Audrey's pillow is on the floor. I walk around it, not my problem. Her desk is littered with dirty plates, I swipe them to the ground with my arm. From the fridge I take out Isabella's oat milk and pour it down the sink. I take the Post-it note that says 'BELONGS TO ISABELLA DO NOT TOUCH' and write 'FUCK YOU' on it then stick it to her computer monitor. I open a drawer. If I get the angle right, I could piss into it. I close it again. There is a smell. I see that Pigeon's poo is still in the litter tray.

My desk has been cleared; my things are in a black sack in the corner. All just loaded in, no care for any of my belongings. I remember when Dad kicked me out of the house the day after I turned sixteen. He told me everything I owned was his. I left with a backpack full of clothes and my toothbrush and I never went back.

I want to upset people. I take a piece of paper from Isabella's desk, it's a contract she needs to sign. I pick up Pigeon's poo with it and smear it all over the wall. I suddenly know exactly where that kid at my sister's was coming from. This feels really good. There is a noise, the door opening. A cough, a sniff. I fall flat to the ground to hide. I see the silhouette of a man walk into the workshop. I'm stuck to the ground, head up, eyes wide, legs and arms splayed, fingers stretched apart like a giant, terrified gecko. I stay as still as I can, hardly breathing, wondering if I can make it to the safety of underneath my desk without him noticing.

He's moving over to the kitchen. He's left the door open, Pigeon could get out. He's put the kettle on. That's a strange thing for a burglar to do, make himself a cup of tea. I pull myself up a little to try and get a better view. At which point Pigeon makes the absurd move of jumping onto the kitchenette counter.

'Fuck, it's a rat!' he yells, throwing a cup at my cat and jumping onto the nearest chair. I can't leave Pigeon out there with a maniac. Pushing myself up to my feet I run as fast as I can towards the chair and shove the man to the ground. He falls with a thud.

'Mia, fuck. Fuck man, what the fuck.' It's Ajay. I step back. He is rubbing his head. He sees Pigeon again and looks scared. 'What is that?'

'It's my cat.'

As his vision comes into focus, he visibly relaxes.

'Shit. I thought it was one of those giant rats I keep seeing everywhere.'

'You keep seeing giant rats everywhere?' I say, checking the corners of the room. 'Where?'

'On TikTok. They're massive, with long tails. Apparently, there are more of them than humans and if we don't . . .'

I'm not listening. I see Pigeon disappearing through the door. 'Pigeon, come back,' I say, running into the very long corridor. I see her tail turn a corner at the end. This building is a huge warehouse space split into multiple units with a gazillion corridors. I'll never find her.

'Pigeon, come back,' I shout, desperate now. Running down the corridor in my slippers. I notice I have a limp, I'm not sure when I acquired that. I know that no matter how much Pigeon loves me, fear from being in a strange building will override any loyalty. The closer I get the further away she runs. I slow down and lower my voice. 'Pigeon, come on. Pssssst, pssssssst. Piggles, come on.' As I approach the corner, she pokes her head around it. 'It's OK darling, come on.' I reach forward with my hand and rub fingers against my thumb. Here she comes, 'Good girl, come on.'

'I'LL GET IT,' shouts Ajay, terrifying me and Pigeon to the point that we both run away. What happens next is a high-speed chase down multiple corridors as I try to catch up with her. She's so quick, terrified out of her wits. I haven't run like this for ten years. Ajay splits off and disappears down another corner. I follow Pigeon and she stops. I am panting, I don't think I can keep going. Her back is arched, and her tail is huge, the poor thing is petrified. 'Come on, Pigeon. It's only me.' Her back lowers and her tail thins. She hears my voice and it calms her. She flops to the ground, purring and rubbing herself on the floor. I approach slowly because one wrong move and she'll run away again.

'It's OK, Piggles, I'm here . . .' Suddenly Ajay appears from the other direction with a wastepaper basket, edging quickly towards Pigeon. His eyes look crazy, like he's going to catch this cat if it's the last thing he does.

'Ajay, it's OK, I'll handle it.'

He's too in the zone to hear me. 'It's OK kitty kitty, cooomeee to Ajay . . .'

Pigeon's fur starts rising again, her back arching, and Ajay speeds up, running at her with the bin. She takes off again, whipping through Ajay's legs. This time even more determined to get away. Ajay and I run alongside each other. Pigeon hits a dead end and stops, she is cornered by us both. I leap, not realising Ajay is making the exact same move.

We land in a painful heap at the end of the corridor. Pigeon steps into my arms, Ajay is on top of my body. We lie there breathing heavily for a few seconds before both of us start laughing so much that tears stream down my eyes. He helps me up to standing, I have to cross my legs a little so as not to pee on the floor.

'I've never seen you laugh before,' Ajay says.

I stop laughing immediately.

We walk back to the workshop where I close the door to the office, so he doesn't see what I did. Acts of rebellion can feel so freeing when in process, but the regret is starting to creep in. And yet I don't have the head space for that right now, I just want to forget it all.

'What are you doing here then, boss?'

'I could ask you the same thing, *babe*.'

'Maybe we just shouldn't ask questions?'

'Deal. Other than . . . want to get drunk on expensive champagne?' I get a bottle of Dom Pérignon out of the fridge; it's one that Isabella keeps for the rare occasion anyone with a profile pops in to get free stuff.

'Sure. Want to try one of my weed chocolates?'

'Yes, yes I do.'

'Yes boss! I always knew you had a wild side.'

'You did?'

'Yeah, no one is that uptight unless they're hiding something. Let's unleash the Mia beast.'

He passes me a small pack of chocolates. I take two.

* * *

I'm not sure exactly how I end up in Ajay's bed, but the mix of champagne and his weed chocolate numbed my faculties enough to bring me here. I was pretty much up for anything. It was an offer for somewhere to stay, after all, and he didn't seem to mind Pigeon coming along. I haven't had sex with anyone other than my husband in seven years and for the vast majority of those times Pigeon was locked out of the room. Now, here I am in a young man's bed, lying face down with my arms tied above my head, my cat sitting prettily on his desk watching our every move. She doesn't seem worried, so I don't see why I should be. I am aware of what is happening to a point, but my limbs feel like dead weights. Ajay has collected an array of objects from around his room and is inserting them, one by one, into my anus and vagina.

'What is that?' I ask, feeling one very thin thing make its way inside me.

'A pencil,' he replies. Which seems inoffensive enough. If I was to guess what the other things have been so far, I'd say a Sharpie, a toothbrush and maybe the handle of a hairbrush. One item was uncomfortable, and he removed it immediately, possibly a large can of deodorant. It's not particularly erotic. More like a toddler playing with a Duplo set. As he roots around his cupboard looking for more insertables, I feel he's left something inside me. My best guess would be a remote control.

'You don't make much noise,' Ajay says.

'Is that good or bad?' I ask, unsure.

'It's hard to know what you like.'

He comes back and slowly pushes a semi-hard rubber something inside me. It feels all right. Words are quite hard to find. So instead, I make the only noise I can think of to make.

'Meow.'

'Fuck yeah, kinky cat lady!'

'Kinky cat lady,' I think to myself. I suppose it's better than crazy cat lady.

After a few more, I feel like I've got as much out of this experience as I can. I ask him to stop. 'Can you untie me please?'

He does so immediately. If this is a form of S&M it's very gentle, and I'm yet to understand the appeal. Will he wash everything tomorrow? I suppose that's not really my problem. I turn over and shake out my arms. He busies himself for a while, putting things back. I spot the Sharpie and the hairbrush and am impressed with myself for guessing right. It's a bit like a sex version of that game Timmy Mallett used to play with kids on TV in the eighties where he'd put common foods in their mouths when they were blindfolded, and they'd have to guess what it was. It was always so funny; they'd think things like chocolate sauce was ketchup, and bananas were yoghurt. I don't know why I'm thinking about Timmy Mallett. I am still quite stoned.

'Can we fuck?' Ajay asks from the cupboard. I am naked, he is not. Will he take all of his clothes off, or just his bottoms? I say yes, because after the past however many hours that we've been in here I don't see any reason why

202

we shouldn't. He takes off his jeans and his underpants. He picks up his jeans again and finds his wallet. There is a condom in it that he rolls onto his quite small, erect penis. He comes onto the bed and I open my legs so he can get on top of me. He aimlessly thrusts at me as if his penis will miraculously find my hole all by itself. After multiple stabs with it around my vagina and in the top of my thigh, I reach down and guide it in. He becomes excited very quickly. Rocking back and forth on me like a nail file. His head off to the side as if we are doing the waltz.

'I'm gonna cum,' he announces, and then he does. It doesn't go on for very long and he's very quiet compared to the wallowing Tristan does when he ejaculates. Rather than collapse onto me he gets off and removes the condom, which he throws into a wastepaper bin. It doesn't make it the whole way and half of it hangs over the side. This doesn't seem to bother him. He sits on the edge of the bed.

'I've never done anything like that before,' he tells me.

'Like what?' I ask, pulling a cover over my body. Suddenly feeling very exposed.

'All that kinky stuff. Putting all those things up you. Did you like it?'

'You've never done that before?' I ask, surprised. He seemed so self-assured. Like that was something he does. I just went along with it, pleased not be sleeping outside.

'No. I always presumed you were into weird shit. S&M and all that. I don't really know much about it, but I hope that was all OK?'

'Why did you think I was into S&M?' I ask, confused.

'The way you dress, all powerful. And the way you're all, like . . . strict.'

I see on his digital alarm clock that it is getting close to 7 a.m. 'We didn't sleep,' I say. At which he seems unfazed.

'I pull all-nighters all the time. I probably shouldn't tell you that.'

'I don't care,' I tell him. 'I don't work there any more.'

'So I didn't just fuck my boss. That's good, I suppose.'

'I suppose it is.'

I get out of bed. When I stand up my head feels like it weighs fifty pounds. 'I need to go, where am I?'

'Stockwell station is a four-minute walk away,' he tells me. 'Take a left, then a right, you'll see it.'

I stumble as I get dressed. Pigeon is at my feet, she wants to leave too. I realise I didn't even make her a litter tray last night in my drunken state. Hopefully she'll hold it in until we reach our next destination, wherever that may be. I put her in her carrier.

'Ajay, I would appreciate it if what happened remained between us,' I say, in my grown-up voice.

'You got it, boss,' he says. He looks terrible. Exhausted, wasted. I've seen him look this way at work before, was it because he'd been up all night having weird sex with someone else? Maybe. He puts on some large headphones, sits at his computer and starts playing a strange game. He is quite off his box. I have started to sober up and my presence here feels entirely wrong.

I open the bedroom door slowly and creep out. I am aware Ajay lives with his mother and I am not looking to meet her. I sneak along the landing towards the stairs and step carefully onto the first step, it makes a loud creaking sound. The front door at the bottom looks like an eternity away. I manage to get close to it, then spot the door of what I hope is a downstairs toilet. I really must use it before I go, otherwise I will likely get a UTI. I leave Pigeon in the hall and slip into the bathroom. After I pee, I wash my hands and open the door. Ajay's giant Staffordshire bull terrier is sitting in the hall, lifting its gums to reveal its teeth and snarling at Pigeon's carrier.

'No, back off,' I whisper loudly, picking Pigeon up and running to the door, but it's bolted in numerous different places and I can't get out. I hold Pigeon's carrier as high as I can, she is meowing with fear, and I am certain the dog will eat us both alive. I have no choice but to scream.

'AJAY, HELP!' I yelp like a damsel in distress from a 1920s movie. I press myself into the door, Pigeon's carrier held high above my head. The dog is jumping up, trying to get to her. It wants to kill us, why does this keep happening?

'Petal, Petal, get down,' a woman's voice shouts. 'Petal, leave her alone you silly dog.'

The dog retreats and makes different noises. Quieter, gentler.

'She wouldn't actually hurt you, she's all talk,' she says. She's wearing a large t-shirt that comes to the top of her thighs. I can see her nipples through it.

'I think it can smell my cat,' I say, grateful I didn't need to use another stick this time.

'Yeah, I saw you come in with that cat last night.'

'You saw us last night?'

'Yes. I was hoping it wasn't the same girl from last week, she vomited on my carpet.' Does she mean the girl in the green dress from the event? Was she here? What kind of sex did they have? Proper sex, probably. Not whatever the hell I just did with this woman's son. I need to get out.

'I always have to lock up after Ajay, he never remembers. Us girls need to stay safe, don't we? See dog for details.' She thinks that's quite funny.

'I'm hardly a girl,' I say, struggling to look her in the eye.

'Hey look, if I could get a night with a younger man I'd jump at the chance. He's a good kid.'

The word 'kid' makes me want to run for my life. Is this woman – Ajay's mother – not fazed by me being here at all?

'So are you divorced or something?'

'Why would you presume that?'

'Well, a woman of your age out on the pull. I did the same when my husband left me. I didn't have much luck though, good for you! I've given up now. Get everything I need from crap TV and salty carbohydrates.'

I feel like an absolute trollop and feel the need to explain myself.

'My husband has been having an affair. I found out the day before yesterday. With his ex-wife. I'm quite upset because I have a stepson who I love very much and a home that I don't want to leave.'

'Oh God, that's shit. I'm sorry. No wonder you needed a night out.'

'Well yes, exactly. OK, well if you could just let me out . . .'

She gets some keys from a little bowl.

'How old are you, out of interest?' she asks. I really don't want to talk. But I am in her house and just had sex with her son so appreciate the need to be polite.

'Forty-five. If you give me the keys, I can do it,' I say, as she doesn't seem to feel any urgency to open the door.

'I have an older sister who is forty-three.'

'Lovely. Would you mind unlocking the door?'

'I'm forty-one. I started young. I always liked the idea of my son being with a woman who could be my friend. You'd be like an older sister to me. Mine actually died. Can't replace her, pointless even trying. Ajay won't move out, doesn't want me to be alone.'

'I'm so sorry. Please, I really need to go.'

'Oh, yes, of course.'

She finally unlocks the door. She's so close to me. I think I smell. Of her son. A cocktail of stale man sweat.

'Your dress is nice. My mum had one like that,' she says, looking like she means it. 'Next time you come over maybe we can have a takeaway and watch *Gogglebox*? I think Ajay and I would be so good on that but you can't apply, apparently you need to be "discovered".'

'I'm sure you'll be on it one day if that's what you want.'

She smiles hopefully, as if dreaming of that special day. 'It's hard not to get lonely, isn't it? Ajay's dad left a few years ago. He was sleeping with my cousin, can you believe it?'

A moment of solidarity. I stop trying to escape for a millisecond. 'I'm sorry, that must have really hurt.'

'It did. I thought my life was over. But I kept my house, which he tried to take from me, but I wouldn't let him do it.'

'Oh? How?'

'I just refused to leave. The problem with women is we give away all our power. I don't know why we do it. We give all of our power to men all the time. I had to take mine back to show Ajay that he can't treat women that way. Best thing I ever did. He's good to women, ya know?'

I choose not to tell her about the way he just treated me like a stationery cupboard.

'Yeah, he's a good kid,' she says, obviously very proud. There it is again, the word 'kid'. I really need to go.

'Take care,' I say, stepping back out into the world.

'Come back anytime,' she calls after me.

I'm never coming back.

17

It's my house and I have every right to live in it.

I arrive just after 8 a.m. Oliver will have left for school but either Tristan or Belinda could be home, I really have no idea. And I don't really care. I put my key in the door and open it. I immediately let Pigeon out and can feel her joy that she is home. She runs straight into the kitchen. I follow. I get food from a cupboard that is bursting with tins for her, fill her bowl and put it on the floor where she has eaten her meals for the past seven years. We both breathe a sigh of relief. I remember that I am solvent and capable. A woman like me does not need to roam the streets. It feels right for us to be here. I realise I have some negotiations to do before we can stay but that is what I intend. To stay. It's hard to remember, when you are cheated on, that you have actually done nothing wrong and that you don't deserve to be punished. Events of the past forty-eight hours notwith-standing – no one needs to know about that.

I am tired now. Painfully so. The drugs and alcohol have worn off. The inside of my mouth feels furry, my breath stale. I wash my hands, and realise they were filthy. I find apple juice in the fridge and drink most of it straight from the carton. I take a handful of blueberries, then some nuts and eat them by putting my mouth to my hand, as opposed to the other way around. Quite a few fall to the floor, I don't bother picking them up. I run the tap and put my head under it, allowing the water to run through my hair, across my face. I rub my hands over my cheeks, working hard on my solid eyelashes. I hang there for a minute, over the kitchen sink, drenching my head, washing away whatever debris I have collected. I exhale loudly. A mix of exhaustion and relief.

'Jesus, Mia, I thought you were a burglar!' I hear Tristan say as water pours in and out of my ears. I turn my head to the side and there he is, standing a few feet away from me holding a baseball bat. I turn the tap off and stand up, my wet hair now soaking my dress, my legs, the floor. Tristan puts down the bat and instead grabs a hand towel. 'Here. Use this. Where have you been?'

'Here and there.'

'Here and there? What does that mean? And what have you got on?'

'A kaftan.'

'Why are you wearing it?'

'Because it was my mother's. You've never asked me about her by the way, she's dead.'

'I know that. You didn't return my messages.'

'She died of cancer. I watched it happen. I sat with her because my dad refused to come in the room.'

'Have you come to collect your things?'

'When she died I had to call for the ambulance to take her away. Me, a nine-year-old girl. Making the call: "Hello, my mother has died. Please can you take her away."'

'Mia, you don't seem well at all.'

'I'm not well, Tristan. I have had a really difficult life, why have you never asked me about it?'

'You didn't bring it up. Have you come home to collect your things?'

'No Tristan, I have come to go to bed. If you all choose to stay, then so be it. I will be in my room, with my cat. I am not leaving. I am no stranger to feeling uncomfortable in my own home. I'm quite good at it, actually. My dad emotionally abused my sister and me. You've never asked me about that either.'

'Again, you never brought it up.'

'I told you once that I was kicked out when I was sixteen and you said, "What did you do wrong?"'

'What's wrong with that?' he says, still thinking I am the crazy one.

'My father kicked me out when I was sixteen and you blamed me.'

'OK, Mia, we could be here all day with you blaming me for everything. Belinda is moving in in a few days. You can't just . . .'

'I'm not leaving.'

I walk past my husband and go to the bathroom. Pigeon follows me. There are women's products around the sink that aren't mine. That didn't take long. I turn the shower on, Pigeon gets in it as she always does and flies out when the water is hot. I take off my mother's dress but don't put it into the laundry basket with everyone else's. I don't want to wash it. I stand naked in front of the mirror. I look unwell. My toothbrush has gone. I use Tristan's.

The shampoo bar that I use isn't in the shower. Instead, there are multiple plastic bottles of synthetic-based products. I use everything that's there and as much of it as I want. I slather my sore body up with coconut-flavoured foam. I let the suds run between my legs and wipe clean until I squeak. I raise one arm at a time and rid myself of the smell that's been following me for a few days now. I use a pink razor that is not mine to shave my armpits and my legs. I take Belinda's scrub and remove the top layer of skin from my face with it. I use her conditioner for straight hair, even though mine is curly. I sit down on the shower floor and gently clean my feet. They are black with bruises and have large blisters and cuts all over them. Red water runs down the drain. I rest my back against the side of the shower and let water hit me from above. Life can take a bad turn very quickly. It's hard to remember who I was this time last week. I rest my head back and let warm water run down my face.

* * *

'Mia. Mia open up.' I hear banging. Tristan is hammering on the door. 'Mia, are you OK? Come on Mia, answer me or I will have to kick in the door.'

'I'm OK. I'll be out soon,' I say, waking up. The shower still pouring down on me. My body slumped at the base. I stand slowly and turn the shower off. I dry myself. I open the door.

'This won't work,' Tristan says as I walk past him in a towel, holding my dirty clothes.

'Well, I'm afraid it will have to.'

I walk straight to my room and shut the door. I put on a pair of pyjamas. I gather all of the bedding from my bed and walk straight out of my room and up the stairs with it. I drop it onto the floor of Oliver's room and remove all the bedding from his bed. I throw it down the stairs, followed by his mattress. I then go back to my bedroom and drag the mattress off my bed and heave it up the stairs. I repeat this with multiple items. Swapping Oliver's things for mine until I have everything I need. For now. Tristan is dumbstruck and just stands there telling me to stop but doing nothing significant to make that happen. I go head first into the cupboard under the stairs and drag out a black sackful of leopard-print throws that I once wanted to decorate the living room with, but which Belinda referred to as 'whoreish'. I throw the bag up the stairs. I then go to the kitchen and get two tote bags from under the sink. I fill one with food from the cupboards, including some food for Pigeon. I fill the other with bottles of carbonated water. I take a roll of kitchen paper, a plate, a knife and fork. I take it all up to the master bedroom. The last thing I take up is Pigeon's litter tray. I now have everything I need to survive for a few days and don't plan to come out until then.

'Mia, you're crazy.'

I walk right up to my husband's face. 'We're all crazy.'

I go up the stairs. Pigeon follows me. I shut the door and pull a desk across it so it can't be opened. I spread the cat-print throws over the bed, floor and chair. I strip. I crawl onto the bed and fall asleep immediately, holding my mother's dress.

18

It's early evening, I feel like I've been in my cave for days – and maybe I have – and now my phone is flashing with a reminder for the pet bereavement group. It must be Tuesday.

I don't want Tristan and Belinda to know I am going out, so I climb down from the balcony, onto the garage roof, and jump down onto the soft grass of our front lawn. Pigeon watches me through the bathroom window like a human might watch an Olympic athlete. She seems enthralled by my skill. I suppose in the cat world that level of agility is highly commendable. Any human would be less impressed by the way I flopped from post to post. Not to mention how as my feet hit the ground, followed by hands, I realised that I'd forgotten to wash my face, to tie up my hair, or put on a bra. Getting back up requires more skill than I am capable of, so here I am. Looking like shit. Off to group therapy regardless.

I needed the group in some vague, hard-to-decipher way before, but now I need them like my life depends on it. I belong in that group, with Martha, Tiana, Greg, Ada and Lee. My husband could put his penis into ten thousand marshmallows, and I'd still show up on Tuesdays.

I also need to know that they are doing OK after the article. Did they even see it? Surely not everyone reads the *Metro*. I've read it so many times now I could quote it verbatim. I've found myself wondering how Nicole could sit there and lie. And how did she observe me so accurately? How did she see the cat lady beneath, like my skin is made of clingfilm and my skull is made of glass? Did the rest of them see it too?

A woman on the Tube asks me if I'm all right. She just sees a woman in a heap and presumes the worst. Fair enough. I tell her my husband cheated on me. She rolls her eyes knowingly, says 'Fucking arseholes' and gets off the train at the next stop. How many of us are there?

I deliberately arrive three minutes late to avoid attention. It occurs to me that maybe members of my staff arrive late at the office for the same reasons. If I could go back, I'd try to do better at dealing with that. Rather than just feeling anger towards people for bad behaviour, I'd question why they are acting that way in the first place. If someone had told me a few weeks ago that I'd be unemployed and under bedroom arrest I'd never have believed it. Turns out we can all be a bit shit when things get rough. Not judging people is so incredibly hard. Maybe that's why people like Tiana need to go through training. Anti-judgement training. Not many people would pass.

'Sorry I'm late,' I say, walking in. They all glance up to say hello then look notably horrified when they see me.

'No problem, Mia,' Tiana says, exercising her professionalism to the best of her abilities. In another world she would have screamed, 'WHAT THE FUCK DO YOU LOOK LIKE?' But in here, it's just a polite nod. Skills.

The atmosphere in the room is morose. Everyone is here minus Nicole, of course. No one new. Is that because of the terrible press the pet bereavement groups got this week? Who would want to associate themselves with us?

Martha has her hat on again – hiding behind the clothes she wears. Ada is wearing a red velvet tracksuit. Still vibrant, but less than usual. Greg looks no different, maybe more relaxed, happier. Which is odd. Lee is wearing the same clothes. His stubble now a beard, he doesn't have red watery eyes today, but he looks even more gentle than usual. Something is off, I can feel it.

'Welcome again,' Tiana says, holding her cup of tea with both hands. 'No new faces. That's OK.' She has a nervousness about her. Not as unshakable as usual. 'Mia, would you like to begin?'

'I have so much to say, I don't know where to start . . . I've had a terrible week,' I say.

'We see that,' Ada nods, probably referring to my appearance. I know her better now than to be offended. 'What happened, love?'

'My husband has been having an affair with his ex-wife.' Ada stands up and kicks the air. 'What is it with men?' 'It's OK, Ada,' says Tiana. 'Let's let Mia tell us more.'

Ada sits back down, but now she's riled, huffing loudly and clearly agitated. I don't mind, it's nice that someone cares.

'I am the managing director of a jewellery brand. I'd been to a pitch at Selfridges with my boss, a woman called Isabella who, if I am honest, I don't like very much and don't think is very good at running a business.' I lose track of where I'm going, take a deep breath.

'Take your time,' Tiana says.

'I pitched something in the meeting that I wasn't supposed to, and because of that Selfridges said they'd take a collection. But after the meeting Isabella was so angry with me because I'd gone behind her back. Which I had, I suppose, but I thought it was the right thing to do. Anyway, while she's telling me how awful I am my husband calls. But it was a bum dial, he didn't know I was there, and so I heard him and his ex having sex in my kitchen. They even . . .' I am about to tell them how Belinda shoved Pigeon to the ground but stop myself just in time, remembering that these people think my cat is dead. 'I reacted badly, as you can probably tell. I slept with a millennial from work then threw everything from my stepson's bedroom down the stairs and stole his room, where I have been hiding for a few days now. I scaled the drainpipes to get out today. They have no idea I'm not up there.'

'Who is "they"?' Tiana asks.

'My husband and his ex-wife who live downstairs because they are trying to take my house.'

'No. No fucking way,' says Ada, standing up again. 'Nope, not having it. You stay, they can go.'

'Thank you, Ada,' Tiana says, 'sit down.'

'Why would he do that to you?' Lee says. 'Sorry, I don't mean that literally, it's just so awful.'

'I think I have to accept some part in it. I was hardly the world's most affectionate and loving wife. I liked separate rooms, he didn't. That sort of thing. I conformed to marriage; it was what I thought I should do rather than what I wanted to do. Tristan isn't stupid, he always knew that. What's weird is I'm more upset about losing my house and my job than my marriage.'

'I hear that,' Ada says, clicking her fingers like she's on *Jerry Springer*.

'You're unemployed too?' Greg asks. 'Ha. Look at us. Good job these sessions are free.' He seems almost pleased he's not the only one without a job. Greg has changed in the last few weeks. The support is having a good effect on him. Jobless or not, he's getting better.

'I'm unemployed too, I suppose,' says Martha. 'A writer who doesn't write isn't getting paid. It's been weeks since I submitted an article. I just can't think of a damn thing to say.'

'Losing your job might turn out for the best,' says Lee. 'I used to work in an office of all women. When word got out I lived with my mum it's like they all presumed I was some kind of pervert. I got into trouble once for telling one girl she looked nice. She complained about me. It was just a warning, but I couldn't stay, I was terrified all the time, felt I couldn't even look up without someone thinking I wanted to follow them home. I quit soon after, took a job I could do remotely. I was so embarrassed at the time, but truth is I wasn't happy with those women, they didn't want the best for me. They were waiting for me to say something terrible. Trust me, I've tried to be a pervert, I'm just really bad at it.'

I immediately know he's joking and laugh. It takes everyone else a minute, but they do all catch on. Even Tiana, who is trained not to respond to comments like that. Thanks to Lee, the room feels lighter than when I arrived. I feel lighter too, suddenly more aware of how terrible I look. Wishing I had at least put on a bra.

'Did anyone see the article?' I ask, gently.

'Yeah,' says Lee.

'Unfortunately, I did,' says Tiana.

'Poor excuse for journalism,' Martha says.

'What article?' asks Ada.

'Yeah, what article?' adds Greg.

'Oh, it was a silly piece of trash that we don't need to worry ourselves about,' Tiana says, aware of the damage this conversation could cause. 'Mia, what can you . . .'

'No, hang on. What article?' Ada pushes. 'What article did you all read?'

I wish I'd never mentioned it. I mean, I want to talk about it. I want to ask them what they see when they look at me. I want to tell them that I don't think they are any of the things Nicole, or Amy, or whatever her name is, said they were. I think they're some of the nicest people I've ever met. I think they're all brave to come here and expose their souls to strangers, in the hope for genuine connection. But I also wish I'd never mentioned it because what she wrote about Greg was horrible, and I don't think he'll be able to handle it.

'I brought a copy,' Martha says. 'As a journalist I was pretty horrified. You'd never see me selling out like this. Bringing other people down for your own gain, what's the point in it?' She takes the newspaper out of her bag and hands it to Ada. With Greg reading over her shoulder, Ada leafs through the pages until she gets to it. The rest of us look away while they read.

'I knew there was something up with her. Mum's dog my arse,' Ada barks, throwing the paper on the floor.

'It was a very cruel piece. You are all here because you are having feelings that other people might not understand. To come into this circle and abuse the trust in that way is cruel and unkind. I'm very sorry it happened, I'm thinking of ways to better vet who comes here from now on,' Tiana says, as if she's responsible.

'It's not your fault,' says Lee. 'It certainly won't stop me coming again. Although I do realise I wasn't mentioned in the article. But if I had been, I'd still come.'

'Same,' says Martha.

'Damn right,' says Ada.

Greg hasn't said a thing. He is vibrating like he used to. His face getting redder and redder until he can't keep the pressure in any more. 'I told you I was a piece of shit. She sees that. She's right, I am a violent pig. I don't deserve you as my friends and I don't deserve sympathy. I don't even deserve a snake.'

He stands up, makes to pick up his chair as if to chuck it but thinks better of it. 'Might as well just not fucking exist. No one would give a fuck if I live or die.' He leaves, slamming the door violently on his way out.

'I'm sorry, I shouldn't have mentioned it,' I say, so upset. I came here to make myself feel better and in doing so I have made other people feel worse.

'It's no one's fault,' says Tiana.

'I'll go after him, see if I can calm him down,' says Lee, jogging out of the room. Martha, Ada, Tiana and I sit quietly for a few moments.

'I'm going to go too,' I say, standing up and heading towards the door. 'I'm sorry.'

I walk out. I'll not go back. They deserve better than a liar like me.

Part Four

Wife

Mum and Dad were in the kitchen shouting.

'What do you mean, it's back,' said my dad. I wondered if he was talking about the mouse that we had in the kitchen for a very long time. He used to get very angry about it not being in the trap each morning.

'I mean it's back and this time it's not going away,' Mum said, looking at the ground.

'Well, what does that mean? Say it.'

'It means I am dying, for God's sake, you know what it means.'

My dad paced up and down the kitchen, scratching his beard like it was infested with mites.

'What am I supposed to do?' he said. 'What am I supposed to do, huh? Who's supposed to look after things here, do all the cooking and cleaning and shit? And what about the kids?'

'I don't know, how about be a dad and husband for once?' By the look on her face, my mum knew she shouldn't have said that. My dad stopped right in front of her.

'You wanted them, not me. And now you're going to leave me with them?'

'They're your daughters, David.'

'And you're my wife. You were my wife . . .'

My dad cried for the first time in his life, I presume. I remember thinking how strange it was to see him sad. A normal human emotion that seemed so out of place on him. He didn't suit it. And as if he knew that himself, he reverted back to anger as quickly as he could.

He stormed out of the kitchen and passed me in the hall. He pushed his face right up to mine as if he wanted to say the most awful thing he could possibly think of. I closed my eyes, bracing myself for it. His breath launched drops of water onto my face. But he said nothing and left the house. Slamming the door so hard a picture fell off the wall. My mother rushed to pick it up.

'It's OK, Mummy, I'll get it,' I said. I kneeled down next to her. She fell to the ground, her head landing in my lap, and cried.

19

I can hear them talking at the bottom of the stairs.

'I can't move in until that wife of yours is gone,' Belinda is saying, over and over again. Tristan asks her what he is supposed to do. But there is nothing he can do to make me leave. This is my house, I pay half of the mortgage. We are still legally married. There is no legal reason why I should have to leave. There is also no legal reason why he should have to leave. So I guess it's just a case of who buckles first. It wasn't pleasant to hear Oliver crying about his room. I wanted to come out, say sorry and help him move his things back up here. But that wouldn't work, I need to be up here, away from them all. I overheard Tristan telling Oliver there will be a surprise for him after school to make up for it. If I were to guess, I'd say it's a PlayStation or some other hideous form of entertainment that will distract him from me hiding away upstairs.

I like this room. I have running water in the bathroom, a balcony for fresh air, my fleece blanket to keep me warm and the cat-print throws that no one else has to like. There's a TV, a radio and the Internet. I realise it was the marital boudoir of my husband and his ex who he is now back together with but, even so, it's a good room. This isn't their bed, it's mine. I wouldn't sleep on his mattress ever again. Not now I know it's covered in her juice.

I hear Belinda leave for work. Oliver has gone to school. I think Tristan has also gone to work but can't be entirely sure. I've run out of food for Pigeon and she's restless. I need to go downstairs. I put on a long fleece jumper that has a cat playing with a ball of string on it. It falls to around the middle of my thighs. I bought it for myself from a little stall up on the high street. Tristan said it was the unsexiest thing he's ever seen.

I slide the desk from in front of the door and open it slowly. The stairs seem longer and steeper than they ever have before. Pigeon runs past me, excited to venture out. I walk down cautiously. When I get to the bottom, the coast seems clear. I follow Pigeon into the kitchen, I fill the kettle and turn it on, I need coffee. I take some bread from the bread bin and smother it with thick, salty butter. I haven't eaten real butter in longer than I can remember. Why did I do that to myself, it's the most delicious thing in the world. I load up another slice. Crumbs fall from my mouth onto the floor. I'd usually clean them up immediately, but I don't bother. Someone else can do it now. I'm no longer playing the part of the dutiful wife.

There is fresh fruit in the bowl, so I have a banana too. I put the skin back in the bowl, simply to annoy someone. I love this kitchen. I had it done about a year after we moved in. It took much longer than anticipated so we had to cook off a tiny camping stove in the living room for months. It wasn't as bad as it sounds, and was often quite fun. We ate out a lot too, on the nights we didn't have Oliver. We were a happy couple, once. Very. I wonder if where I am buttering my bread is where Tristan and Belinda had sex, and I am snapped back to remembering why nothing is the same.

I scoop a massive tablespoon of instant coffee into a mug and fill it with water. I like it when some granules don't dissolve and sit on the top like coffee croutons.

'You're alive,' says Tristan appearing from nowhere and terrifying me so much that I jump and spill boiling coffee over my arm and thighs.

'Fuck. Fuck fuck fuck,' I yelp, turning on the cold tap and running my arm under it. It's the exact same spot as the oven burn. The skin on my legs is hurting too.

'Here, use this,' Tristan says, handing me a bag of frozen peas that he's taken from the freezer. 'Sit here.' He pulls a kitchen stool over to me and I climb on it. This way I can run my hand under the tap and rest the peas on my thighs at the same time. It's sore, very sore.

'You gave me such a fright,' I tell him. 'I thought you'd gone to work.'

'I haven't been to work in three days, waiting for you to

come out. I thought if I was quiet enough you might. What have you been doing in there?'

'Just lying there, mostly.'

'You didn't go to work.'

'No, I did not. I don't have a job now.'

'What happened?'

'I don't want to talk about it.'

Tristan looks concerned. And then confused. And then concerned again.

'Mia, what are we going to do? Oliver doesn't understand why you took his room and won't come out. He's very upset. And for you and me, this isn't healthy.'

'I'm not leaving.'

I shove another slice of bread and butter into my mouth with the hand that isn't burnt. I lift the peas off my thigh. There is just a little red mark where the coffee burnt me.

Tristan comes closer to look. 'Are you OK?' he asks.

'No, I'm not OK. Are you?'

He fixes his glare at my thighs. He always liked my legs. 'I do love you, Mia. I'd choose you, if I thought you'd want me too.'

'You'd choose me?'

'Yes. If I had to choose, it would be you.'

'Well isn't that what you did? Choose? And you didn't choose me.'

'I just fear you'd never change. I'd always be trying to reach you but you'd never let me in.'

'It's odd that you had sex with your ex-wife rather than talk to me about the problem.'

'I've tried to talk to you about the problem for most of our marriage. You don't want to talk about the problem. You don't really want to talk to me at all.'

'That's not true, we've always had nice chats about all sorts of things.'

'As long as I kept it trivial. Any dive into real emotions and your walls go up and shut me out. You'd come to my room for sex then go. You'd prepare me a meal but want to eat it in front of the TV rather than talk to me. It's hard.'

'You make me sound awful.'

He doesn't comfort me. There are tears in his eyes. He places his hands on my thighs, his head close to mine. The atmosphere is changing.

I open my legs. I am his wife after all.

He kneels down, pushes his face between them. I'm not sure if this is me giving in or taking control but it feels good and so I let it happen. I lean back on the stool to give him a better angle. His tongue takes long slow laps of me. It's the best he's ever done. It's tender and loving rather than frantic and hurried. Men are so strange. I have one of the deepest orgasms I've ever had in my life. He keeps his face there for a while. Breathing me in. He rests his forehead on me, like he is telling my vagina goodbye.

'I'm going for a walk,' I say, getting up and disregarding him. He stumbles and faceplants to the floor.

'And then?' he asks, as if giving my vagina a good lick was going to send me merrily on my way to a new house.

'And then I am coming home.'

The power of his sigh pushes me out the front door.

20

JENNY FRASER
BELOVED WIFE AND MOTHER
1946–1985
RIP

I was too young to have any input about the inscription for my mother's tombstone. I visited the grave once, shortly after she died, but never came back because the words hurt me too much. They made me mad. The kind of mad I couldn't control. I wanted to dig her body up with my bare hands and move it without my dad knowing. I'd carve a new stone, with my claws, and put her somewhere he'd never find her. It would say:

CAT LADY

JENNY FRASER
SHE DESERVED MORE

How did 'Beloved Wife' get there? Those impersonal, cookie-cutter words chosen by a funeral director because my father couldn't come up with any himself. My mother was no such thing as a beloved wife. My father trapped her in his terrible world. She was so talented but he insisted she quit her job at a fashion house when she fell pregnant with me, telling her she didn't have to work. That financially he would take care of everything. By the time Liz was born, she was unqualified and disconnected, with no idea how to break back into an industry that she loved. By this time, alcoholism had got him fired and he worked in a job he hated, bringing his depression, anger and disappointment in himself home every night. Making her life hell as she drowned in a magnified bowl of her own regrets.

He didn't hit her. If he had, I think she'd have left. He kept her there by clever manipulation, but it was hard to understand why he wanted her to stay, he spoke to her with such hate some days. I once heard her shout, 'I serve one purpose and that is to give you power.' I raced straight to my room and wrote it down, so I never forgot it. I was too young to really understand what she meant but the point I gathered was that people try to control other people to serve themselves. I didn't like it.

I presume the reasons she couldn't just go were financial. And when she found out she was sick she didn't have much choice. What was she supposed to do? Move out with Liz and me, then die and leave us alone? Or stay with him so when she died at least we had a home? What a horrible predicament for a mother. Cancer ate her alive in under a year. Maybe there was just no time for big decisions.

What I do know is that marriage can be a trap. Leaving one takes guts. Holding onto your home takes balls. I won't let history repeat itself.

'Hi,' I say when Liz answers the phone. 'I'm at Mum's grave.'

'You are? Why?'

'I'm not really sure. Can you come?'

There's a muffled noise as she covers the phone and then I hear her shout, 'SIMON, I'M GOING OUT. FEED THE KIDS.'

I hear him reply, 'YOU FUCKING WHAT?'

'See you in ten minutes,' Liz says, hanging up.

By the time she arrives I have pulled out the weeds that were drowning the grave and picked enough buttercups to add a patch of yellow. I promise myself I'll visit again with fresh flowers, like so many of the other graves have.

'I'm sorry I never came back,' I tell my mother. 'You deserved better than that.'

'Mia, what have you got on?' Liz says, approaching me. 'You're half naked.'

I look down, I had totally forgotten. The fleece jumper with a cat on it. My legs bare. 'I just walked out of the house, like I was being pulled by a piece of string.'

'Or chasing a ball of string? Anyway, you're here. I'm pleased.'

We stand staring at the stone. Liz takes my hand in hers and I realise it's shaking.

'You must be in some state to come here, you always said you never would. I never really understood why,' she says, gently.

'I've got a lot of anger inside of me, Liz. A lot of hate. Not for Mum, but for Dad and how we were treated. We didn't do anything wrong. All he had to do was love us and he just couldn't do it.'

'He wasn't able to. I feel sorry for him. He must have been so lonely.'

I look at my sister with horror. 'Really?'

'Every other option is just too exhausting. I've been angry, I've hated myself. I've punished myself. I blamed him for everything I ever did. For being pissed off, unemployed, fat, it was all because of Dad. Then one day I had this kid staying. The dad was a right piece of work. Drink, violence, the works. But he got his shit together. He got off booze, found some self-esteem, got his kid back and now he's coach for the school football team and remarried with another baby. All Dad was, was a someone who never got his shit together. Doesn't mean he didn't want to be a better person.'

'Chaos killed him,' I say.

'It did. I believe Mum married a good guy who lost his way and never got it back. She was too cool to marry a monster.'

'She was cool, wasn't she? Those dresses, they were so good,' I say, smiling as I remember her. 'She lived in technicolour while everyone else seemed to be grey. She was her true self until he crushed her.'

'That's true. But also, she allowed herself to be crushed,' Liz says without judgement, because we both know in many ways we've done the same thing. We look back at the grave. Overgrown, unkempt.

'It's hard to see the point sometimes, isn't it? It's all so hard then you end up here,' I say.

'Don't say things like that, Mia. If we don't live for ourselves then we live for the people we leave behind. We all have a legacy of some kind.'

'What's your legacy?' I ask my sister.

'Wiping shit off walls. I'm really good at it.'

We laugh. She looks at me, as if asking mine.

'Walking around a graveyard in a big fleece jumper with a kitten on it? Can that be my legacy?'

We notice a man staring at my legs from a few graves down. 'He seems to think so!' Liz says, laughing. 'Shall we go?'

I pick up the weeds so I can put them in a bin nearby. Liz goes back to her strange family, and I go back to whatever is left of mine.

I hear laughing in the kitchen. I am immediately disheartened by the sound of a happy family that doesn't include me. A little spark inside of me had dared to wonder if what happened between Tristan and me earlier was more real than the other horrors of this week. But as I walk into the kitchen and see the three of them laughing on the floor, I realise my marriage is as dead as the people in that graveyard.

'A puppy,' I exclaim with dismay.

'*My* puppy,' says my stepson. His face so happy it's shining like the sun. 'His name is Buster.'

What a horribly unoriginal name. Nearly as bad as Rover.

'It's so nice to see you, Oliver,' I say, because I am experiencing two things at once. Anger, but also a longing. I miss him. He is too busy to look up at me. That pleases Belinda.

'Where is my cat?' I ask.

'It ran straight upstairs as soon as we got home. Like it always does. It's terrified of people. Not like this little thing, look how friendly he is,' Belinda says, smugly.

The dog is running between them, rolling over and yapping.

'Tristan, haven't I said so many times that we couldn't have a dog because Pigeon would hate it?'

'*We* didn't get a dog. "We" did,' Belinda says, referring to my husband and stepchild. Tristan is yet to look up at me.

'Dad said I could have it because you stole my bedroom,' Oliver says, making it clear that I am the villain here. 'Would you like to cuddle him?' he asks, reminding me he loves me no matter what they say.

'No thanks my love, but he is very cute.' I walk towards Tristan with a large fake smile and growl into his ear. 'This is my home and I'm staying. You can bring five hundred dogs in; I am *not* leaving.' I smile at Oliver as if all is well, and take another tote bag from underneath the sink and fill it with more food for me and Pigeon. I get a clean plate and glass, and another knife and fork. I won't come out for days if I don't have to.

In my room I find Pigeon hiding next to the toilet. She looks extremely cross. I pick her up and put her on the bed with me. With some rigorous stroking she eventually starts to purr.

I don't wake up naturally the next morning. I wake up because I am itchy between the legs. Throughout the night I had been irritated and kept having to scratch, but this morning is another level. I scratch and scratch but no matter how much I do it I just get itchier and itchier. I notice Pigeon scratching too. I pull her over to me and look into her fur, immediately spotting a flea on her back. I've been sleeping naked with her; her fleas must be biting me too. I call my doctor to make an appointment.

'I'm sorry but unless it's an emergency I won't be able to get you in until Thursday,' the lady on the phone says.

'It's absolutely an emergency,' I tell her.

'OK, what is the problem?'

'It's something I'd prefer to discuss with a doctor.'

She huffs far louder than I think is appropriate and tells me to come in between 10 and 12. I say thank you and hang up. I then lie on the bed combing my pubic hair with my tangle teaser to try and stop the itching.

Later in the doctor's waiting room I imagine why the

other people might be there. Do they have fleas in their pubic hair like me?

One man is around fifty and has an enormous nose with warts all over it. Is he here because of his warty nose or is that just how his nose is and he's here for something else? There is also a young woman who doesn't look ill. The presumption will always be that a young woman who doesn't look ill is here for 'women's problems'. A smear test, a sore breast, an STD. She doesn't look pregnant but maybe she is in the early days of it. She is reading a copy of *Cosmo*, which makes me assume she has an STD. Poor her; it must come with terrible shame.

Maybe I should go over and tell her about my fleas. Make her feel less alone. Show solidarity in the sistership. Is catching something from an animal worse? I scratch my vagina despite being around people. If you can't scratch your itchy bush in a doctor's waiting room, then where can you scratch it? That would be funny on a t-shirt.

I do feel quite self-conscious.

The man with the warty nose notices me and turns away as if I am unbearable. I think of the vet's waiting room, a much friendlier place than a human waiting room. Why is that, I wonder. Are we disgusted by each other? Are we too afraid to connect? Are we ashamed of our bad health? Whatever reason it is, I am certain that if a man like Lee were to break down in here, most people would choose to look away.

'Mia Truman?' the doctor calls, coming out of his office. I hadn't thought to request a woman but now I wish that I had. I follow him in and sit down. He's far too handsome for this conversation.

'How can I help you today?' he asks me. I consider lying. Telling him I have a sore ankle, or a reoccurring gas issue. But even as I sit here I can feel fleas running about in my knickers and I really want to get them off.

'I caught fleas from my cat,' I tell him.

'Right, well humans don't really get fleas in the same way, but we absolutely can get bitten by our pets' fleas. Does your cat sleep in bed with you?'

'Yes, nearly every night. She has done for sixteen years.' I choose not to tell him about me sleeping naked because of how much I love to feel her fur against my skin.

'And do you wear bedclothes?' he asks, catching me unaware.

'No.' Damn it.

'Where are the bites?' he asks, as of course I knew he would.

'It's itchy all around my vaginal area,' I tell him as matter-of-factly as I can, questioning if 'vaginal' is actually a word. It didn't sound right when I said it. I see his face change from understanding to concern. It makes me feel uncomfortable. 'I don't have sex with my cat,' I say, abruptly. To which he just shakes his head and tries to remain as professional as he can.

'I think I should take a look. Let me just call in a nurse to chaperone.'

'I don't require that,' I tell him, finding the idea of another person being present horrendous.

'I think it's best,' he says. 'If you could remove your clothes from the waist down and lie on the bed I'll be back in a few moments.' He leaves and I do as he says. I lay a few sheets of blue paper towel across me for decency.

The few moments of being alone in any clinical environment, before a procedure or a check-up, are always nerve-wracking. I think it's humans at their most vulnerable. Unless you are a doctor yourself, you are helpless. You must hand over your body, hand over your mind. Abandon shame and any issue you might have and open yourself for investigation. You just have to lie there, like a slab of meat, while they look at you and poke you and try to work out how you are broken.

I feel broken in a thousand places. Will the doctor notice?

'Are you ready?' he says, knocking and opening the door. I say yes and he comes in with a woman who sits on a chair in the corner of the room. 'This is Esme.' Esme and I smile at each other.

'I have fleas,' I tell her. She smiles again, which is a strange reaction if you ask me. I'd have expected more of a sympathetic nod.

'OK, are you ready, I'd like to take a look?'

I tell him that I am. He says I can keep my legs together and I realise I have assumed the frog position. I know the frog position from yoga. Knees apart, soles of feet together. There is no point in me feeling embarrassed now, he's seen it all.

He snaps on some rubber gloves and moves in with a small metal implement that he uses to separate my pubic

241

hair. He also has what I think is a small magnifying glass. Very quickly he sighs as if he is relieved and says, 'OK, Mia, you don't have fleas. You have pubic lice.'

'I got pubic lice from my cat?' I ask, confused.

'No, you would have got them from another human. Via sexual intercourse.'

I must look visibly horrified.

'It's nothing to be afraid of,' he tells me, all ho hum. 'Crabs, as they are more widely known, are a lot more common than you think.'

I suddenly feel quite ill. 'I have crabs? That's so nineties. Who still gets crabs?'

'You, by the looks of things. OK, you can get dressed,' he says, taking off his gloves and sitting down at his computer.

He tells Esme that she can leave now but she doesn't because I don't make any move to put my clothes back on.

'Are you OK? Do you have any questions?' he asks, realising I have frozen in time.

'All I have is questions. Who did I get them from?'

'Well, who have you had sex with in the last couple of weeks?'

'I had sex with Ajay from work,' I tell him.

'Well then it looks like you caught them from Ajay.'

'But I made sure I peed afterwards?'

'That won't help with lice, I'm afraid.'

I am still lying down. He says he will run a full STD check on me to make sure I don't have anything else. He comes back over and takes a swab. Then he's back at his desk again.

'The treatment is just a lotion. Leave it on overnight and you'll be all cleared up.'

'I have to put lotion on my vagina? I'll feel like Gwyneth Paltrow.'

Esme finds that funny but covers it with a cough.

'If you could get dressed now, we can get this all written up for you,' he says pulling the curtain closed, clearly wanting me out of the room. I hear Esme leave.

When dressed, minus my knickers which I forgot to put on so have in my bag, I sit on a chair and watch the doctor type out my prescription. 'I lost my job and my family and I slept with someone from work. I've been acting very strangely lately.'

The doctor takes a leaflet from a drawer and hands it to me. 'If you need mental health support, call this number, there are people who you can talk to. It's free. And if you don't feel better after that come back to me and I can see about giving you something to help.'

'To help with what?'

'Your mental health.'

'Can I have it now?'

'I'd rather you spoke to someone first. Here, I'll also give you a referral for a therapist. You've been through a lot. Talking might help.'

I think of the pet group: Tiana, Ada, Greg, Martha, Lee. And how I've lied to them all. 'Can I talk to you?'

He doesn't answer me. He hands me two pieces of paper and smiles. 'Use the lotion, set up an appointment with a therapist. There is nothing that can't be fixed with the right people helping you.'

I thank him and stand up.

'And I'm sorry if this is uncomfortable but you really should tell the person that you had sex with. He could give it to someone else without realising.'

That truly is the most horrendous thought. I notice a wastepaper bin in the corner of the room and drop my knickers into it. The thought of little crabs running around in my tote bag is just too much to bear. I go to leave but stop to have a big scratch before I do. 'I'm sorry, it's just so itchy.'

The doctor nods and politely looks away until I've gone.

21

I walk up to the pharmacy and feel irritated that another human on this earth needs to know that I have crabs.

'Hello, I have a prescription,' I say, handing it to the Indian man at the till who has a nice smile. I wonder if he has ever had crabs. If they're as common as the doctor said, then maybe.

'Thank you, you can take a seat,' he says, looking at the piece of paper and not reacting. Which I think is the most incredible skill. The things he must see. I guess you become unfazed quite quickly when you work in a place like this. Does he not look at the prescription for vaginal lice lotion and think, 'How did this silly woman get those?' Maybe he's got more important things to think about.

There is a woman sitting next to me with a horrible cough. 'Not Covid,' she says, turning to me.

I sit down and have a surreptitious scratch. 'Not thrush,' I say. She gets out her phone and reads old text messages.

The pharmacist goes into the room with all the drugs and speaks quietly to his colleague, an Indian woman, who I presume is his wife as it says outside on the sign that this is a family-run pharmacy. Are they discussing how long it's been since anyone needed vagina lotion for crabs? How extremely rare it is for someone of my age to come in with such an ailment? Or maybe he is asking her what they should have for dinner, and not discussing me at all. One night of debauchery. My only night of debauchery in a very, very long time and I got an STD. A mother would say, 'Well what did you expect?' I don't have a mother so I don't need to worry about what she would say. I didn't expect anything that's happened to me over the last week or so.

After a long thirteen-minute wait, the pharmacist comes out and says, 'It's ready for you.' I am pleased to be able to move because I can incorporate a scratch into it. Things are getting extremely uncomfortable down there, and I am keen to get home to begin the treatment.

'Thank you,' I say, taking the white paper bag.

'You're very welcome.'

I turn to walk away but then an irritating impulse consumes me, and I turn back to him. 'I got crabs from a millennial who used to work for me. He's very nice, but very young.'

The man just stares and sees no need to comment further so I go to leave his shop. But just as I am about to, I see someone I recognise standing next to a promotional display unit housing multi-vitamins. It's Lee. I dive behind the antibacterial gels.

'Hello Devaj,' he says to the pharmacist. 'I've come for my mother's medicine.'

Devaj seems to recognise him immediately. 'Hello Lee, how is your mother, any better?'

'Not really. The cat's death has really set her back.'

'Yes well, we love our animals so much. When we lose them it's a very unique kind of grief.'

'It is. Maybe in a way it's harder to cope with than losing people,' Lee says. Devaj pretends to look busy, obviously not agreeing with that. Lee hovers for a little too long.

'And are you all right, Lee? Is there another way I can help you?'

'No thanks Devaj. I'm ticking along OK. I'll see you next month. Hopefully.'

'I'm sure I will. See you then.'

Lee leaves, I follow him down the street until he gets to a crossing. As he presses the button, I tap him on the shoulder.

'Hello,' I say, when he turns around.

'Oh Mia. Look at us, out in the wild. How are you?'

Is he always so kind, so gentle and so nice? It seems so. The little man turns green, so we cross the road together and stop on the other side.

'I was just picking up my mother's medication,' he tells me, holding up the bag.

'Oh, that's very kind of you. I was picking up something

for myself,' I say, holding up my paper bag. 'I'd rather not tell you what it's for if that's OK.'

'I wasn't going to ask.'

I blush. I mean, why would he ask me what my medication was for, that would be so rude.

'What's your mum's medication for?' I ask, going against everything I've just assessed from the situation.

'Her heart.'

'Is it broken?'

He looks really uncomfortable.

'I'm sorry, I think I was trying to be funny. I don't know why.'

'It's OK, I do that all the time. Crack jokes that bomb. It's better than not cracking jokes though, isn't it?'

'I guess it is.' I think of Tristan. My husband of seven years who I can't remember ever telling me a single joke or even trying to make me laugh. Not even once.

'Would you like to get a cup of tea somewhere? My mum is actually sleeping so I don't need to get this back quite yet.'

'Goodness,' I say in a very posh English accent, which isn't how I talk at all. I really should get home to put this ointment on, but I can handle the itching for an hour or so to spend some time with Lee. We find a little coffee shop and order tea.

'Milk?' asks the lady behind the till.

'Do you have oat milk?' he asks, stunning me.

'Oh my,' I say in that terrible posh voice again. 'Are you vegan?'

'God no, but I had to give up dairy years ago. It does terrible things to me,' he says, making a face that suggests those things are not nice to discuss.

'Like what?' I push, not really sure why.

'Oh, you know, gassy. Just not very pleasant.'

'I'm vegan. Dairy is the hardest bit to avoid, it's in so many things.'

'Oh I know, the thing I miss the most is fresh cream in pastries. Mum and I used to have one every Friday after fish and chips. Giving those up was one of the hardest things I've ever had to do in my life.'

I wonder what kind of life you'd have to have lived to be able to say that. 'I miss blue cheese the most,' I say, as we sit down at a table by the window. 'I never really cared about meat but when I was just vegetarian I used to stuff portobello mushrooms with blue cheese and walnuts and they were delicious.'

'Oooh, I loved blue cheese on burgers. There are some OK vegan cheeses now but they're still not as good. I do love oat milk though. Actually, maybe I even prefer it.' He stirs his tea and then takes a bite of his cookie. 'A little bit of whatever is in a cookie is no harm though, is it?'

I smile and sip my tea. I try to imagine having a conversation with Tristan about vegan cheese before he'd start making puking noises and saying how everything I eat is disgusting.

'I bet you're glad you weren't written about in that article?' I ask.

'I won't lie, yes. A journalist's interpretation of a man in his forties who lives with his mother would probably not be very flattering.'

'Why do you live with your mother?' I ask him.

'When Dad died she was alone, I was alone. It seemed ridiculous that I was visiting her all the time and we both just talked about how lonely we were. So I moved back in. Simple. I don't see why anyone should have a problem with that, but people don't like it.'

'I think it sounds lovely. I'd love to live with my mum. I can't though, she's dead.'

'I'm sorry.'

'Thanks. Can I have a little of that?' I ask, referring to his cookie. He's right, a little of what is in it won't hurt. He breaks me off a generous chunk. It's delicious.

'Do you think Greg will be OK?' I ask.

'No, I think it will cause him to really struggle. I hope he doesn't do anything stupid.'

'It's weird, but I care about him. Even though I've only seen him behave pretty badly.'

'Yes, but he came to a group for help and he's trying. That counts for something,' Lee says, being so nice about yet another person who may or may not deserve it.

'It does. The group is quite strange, isn't it?' I ask him.

'I suppose so, but seeing as you and I make up around thirty per cent of it, I guess that makes us pretty odd too.'

That makes me laugh. 'Do you ever feel . . . strange, different?' I ask him.

'No. I feel very ordinary. Which is all I've ever wanted to be. But seeing as everyone seems to want to be a "somebody" these days, wanting to be ordinary can feel extraordinary in itself. Do you feel strange?'

'Honestly, it depends who I'm with.'

'Well, do you feel strange now?' he asks.

'No, I don't.'

My knees start grinding over each other. 'Are you all right?' Lee asks, looking under the table to make sure nothing is bothering me.

I'm so itchy, I can't hide it any longer. 'I'm going to go home; I need to get this lotion on . . .'

'Oh, oh dear.'

'Yes, I have . . . it's, um . . .'

'A rash?' he says, helping me out. 'A terrible rash?'

'Yes, I have a terrible rash. I have to go.'

'See you Tuesday?' he asks as I stand up.

'Yes.'

I walk away slowly, because if this were a romcom, I'd smack into a door right about now.

22

I come straight into the house and run upstairs and into the bathroom, I lock the door. I read the instructions and rub the lotion into my pubic hair and all around my vagina. Just the rubbing alone feels so good. I put extra on because I feel like I have thousands of them. How was Ajay not scratching all night? I wouldn't have had sex with someone who was scratching themselves. Do I really have to tell him? He was the one who gave them to me, can't he work it out for himself? I am so looking forward to not having crabs any more. I'm sure Pigeon feels the same. I find the flea treatment from the vets in the cupboard, open the door and call her. She doesn't come.

'Pigeon?' I call again. 'Piggles.' But nothing. Oh no, please say she didn't get locked in Tristan's room again. I can't take more cat-pee-related shame. I go down the stairs as quickly as I can and knock gently on his door before opening it. 'Pigeon? Pigeon, come on.' But she isn't there. I look in Oliver's room, she isn't there either. Where could she be? A cupboard? The basement? Oh God, the washing machine? And then I hear the sound of laughter outside in the back garden. It's Belinda and Oliver playing with the puppy. My heart sinks immediately, surely they wouldn't be so stupid?

I run now, into the kitchen, calling 'Pigeon' as I go, and then head into the garden. 'You let her out?' I scream at Belinda. 'You let my cat out? Why would you do that?'

'We were just playing with Buster in the garden. I didn't realise the door was open.'

'Pigeon. Pigeon!' I scream frantically into the garden. To my surprise, Oliver stands up and starts doing the same.

'Will you find her?' he asks me.

'I hope so. Pigeon, Piiiiggeeeeeoooon!'

Oliver shouts too. He puts his hands around his mouth to make his voice louder. 'PIGEON.'

I get a stack of Post-it notes. I write 'LOST CAT' and my phone number on as many as I can. 'Walk up and down the street and put one through every post box. OK?'

'OK,' Oliver says, accepting the challenge.

'Wait, we have tae kwon do in half an hour,' says Belinda.

I walk right up close to her face. 'Help me find my fucking cat, or I'll do tae kwon do on you, you understand?'

'Give me some of the Post-it notes, Oliver?' she says, obediently.

I run out the front door.

I tear up and down our street three times calling her name. 'Pigeon, Pigeon, PIGEON!' Then I cover the street adjacent to ours. I knock on every house. 'Have you seen a cat? She's grey?'

'No.' 'Who are you?' 'No, but I'll keep an eye out.' 'I saw a cat, but it was white. Could that be your cat?'

A green door slams in my face.

I'm crying and shouting and shaking. Someone comes out of their house because I am now looking into their garden. 'What the hell are you doing?' they ask me, assuming I am up to no good.

'My cat is missing. Could I just . . .'

'Get the fuck off my wall.'

I get down, run back onto the street. 'PIGEEEONNNNN.'

I head towards the busy London high street. Fruit stalls, clothes rails, buckets, mops, packs of laundry bags, suitcases for sale. Tables and chairs, people's feet. I check among them all. I spot a fishmonger's and go inside. 'Have you seen a cat?'

They look at me strangely. 'We don't allow cats in here.'

I reach the park, there are dogs everywhere. How could she have made it this far and what would happen to her if she did? I look under every bush, call up every tree, run up to every person. 'Have you seen a cat? Have you seen my cat?'

'No.'

'No.'

'No.'

I find myself on my knees. Where do I go now? What do I do? 'PIGGGGGEONN.' My face is in the grass now, my fingernails digging in. My stomach starts to turn. I feel sick again.

Suddenly my phone rings. It's hard to retrieve it from my pocket because my fingers are shaking so much. It's a number I don't know.

'Did you find my cat?' I ask as I answer. 'Please, did you find her?' The person doesn't say anything, but I know they're there. 'Please, did you find her?'

'I had a note come through my door,' says an old lady's voice.

'Yes, for my cat, did you find her?'

Another pause.

'I did find a cat today.'

'Where? Where was it?'

'I found a cat on the road, just outside my house.'

'On the road?'

'I'm so sorry, but if this is your cat, I'm afraid she passed away.'

'What colour was the cat?'

'Grey.'

It will be another cat. It won't be Pigeon.

'It might not be your cat, I just thought I'd call the number to let you know.'

'Where is it?'

'I have it wrapped in a blanket on my step.'

'I'll come.'

I still call Pigeon's name all the way there because she is fine and the dead cat isn't mine. Pigeon can't be found dead in a road, that isn't how it is supposed to be. I've visualised the day, the day I've dreaded more than any other. She'll be in my arms, warm at home. I'll cradle her for her final breaths, and it will be tragic but beautiful all at once.

She is not the dead cat in the road.

I find the house, it's two streets over from ours. I see a blanket on the step, it obviously has something inside it. Part of me wants to run over and rip the blanket off, the other part never wants to see what's inside. I walk towards it slowly and the front door opens. An old lady steps out.

'Whatever happened, I'd say it was very quick. If you want to look, she isn't in a bad way.'

'It's dead.'

'Yes, but intact. If you don't want to look and you have a picture of your cat, I can check for you.' The old lady is frail and is holding a stick to keep herself upright. It can't have been easy for her to get the cat to the step.

'It won't be her,' I say, standing closer now, unable to bring myself to pull apart the fabric to see if it's Pigeon inside.

'Would you like me to unwrap it for you?' she offers.

'No.' I reach down and lift a corner of fabric. It's fleece. Red, with tartan stripes. I owe it to Pigeon to look at this cat.

'I'm sorry,' I say to the woman as I drop the corner.

'Take your time,' she says. 'I understand.'

I inhale as deeply as I can. My heart is thumping in my chest, my stomach hurts. I have to look. I have no choice. I pull back the blanket but keep my eyes shut. Three huge breaths and I open them. When I see her, I can't find the breath inside my body to exhale. My blood stops pumping, my lungs collapse, my eyes close. It seems like hours that I look at her like that, until every faculty I have needs air and movement. And with volume I throw my head back, making a sound so deathly as I drag air into myself, just so I can survive this attack on every cell in my body. I fall forward again, my head on her. My tears drenching her. My hands squeezing her, searching for life. But there is none. I have a hand on her head, another on her body. She is still warm. Every breath in is impossible, every breath out is agony. And then I toss my head back and scream and beg for it not to be true.

'You don't understand,' I say to the woman whose hand is on my back. 'You don't understand what she means to me. She's . . . she's my life.'

'I'm so sorry,' she keeps saying. 'I'm so sorry. She was a beautiful cat.'

Was.

'I don't know what to do,' I say, through tears that will never stop. 'What am I supposed to do? I don't know what to do now.'

The woman kneels down to me, it isn't easy for her. 'Go to the vet, they will take care of it for you.'

'Take care of it?' I don't know what that means.

'Yes, you can get the ashes back. Or you can bury her, in the garden.'

'I have twenty-four hours,' I tell her. 'I know this because I heard a vet say it. I can keep her for twenty-four hours.'

I pick Pigeon up. She feels lighter, somehow. What's changed? No air in her lungs? Her soul has left?

'Thank you,' I say to the woman whose kindness I am so grateful for.

'You will be OK, it will get easier,' she says, like she knows. 'I lost my Charlie quite recently and I never thought I'd get over it.'

'Are you over it now?' I ask her.

'No. But it does get easier.'

I walk away with Pigeon in my arms.

I hold her as close to me as I can while I walk the streets. My tears are so loud and wet and heavy and I can't control anything other than putting one foot in front of the other and holding on so tight. People look at me but do nothing, say nothing. Most people aren't kind like that old woman. Most people just walk the other way or look at me like I'm crazy. *The crazy lady with the cat.* I can hear their thoughts. No one comes to me asking if I'm OK, they just walk around me.

'I AM NOT CRAZY,' I snap at a man who crosses the street to avoid me. A group of teenagers laugh.

When I arrive home Oliver runs to the door. 'You found

her?' he says, excitedly. Belinda is behind him and realises what the look on my face means. I wish it was her that was scraped off the road. I can't think of the words to say, so I don't say any, I go straight upstairs. I lay Pigeon on the bed and pull the desk across the door. I take all of my clothes off and lie down, pulling her against me. I cry loudly and with more pain than I think I have ever felt in my whole entire life.

I've been through so much. I've been dragged out of water. Nothing will drag me out of this. I cry, and I cry, and I cry. I don't want to ever open that door. I never want to leave this room. I never want to admit that this is true. What monster hit her and left her in the road? I don't see a wound, does that mean it was quick? She was stunned and died from shock? I cry and cry and cry. I shout and I beg. I hear a knock on the door, but I scream too loudly to hear what they're saying. I roll around in pain, both in my heart and my body that is aching from the shock. How do I live without Pigeon? Who even am I without her? Whenever people hurt me, she soothed me, I could take on everyone's dismissal because I'd come home to her love. Her heartbeat thumping against me every night. Her loyalty never fading. Devotion. Love. But now she's gone. And all because of Belinda leaving the door open. The one rule of the house that even a child managed to follow.

Another knock on the door. It's Tristan, his words sound muffled like I'm under water. I don't care what they are.

'LEAVE ME,' I screech, I hear him going downstairs. I need this time with Pigeon. This precious time. She looks so peaceful. Her eyes won't close, but they are shining bright. Her fur so soft.

I pull her as close to me as I can. I tell her what she needs to know. 'I wanted this moment to be better for you. I was going to control it, make you comfortable. I'm so sorry, Pigeon. I'm sorry I wasn't there.'

I am quieter now, whispering to her. Tears trying to stop me, but I must say these things while I have her. 'You saved my life.'

Part Five

Cat Lady

'I'll be gone a few weeks this time,' Mum said. And something about her tone told me it would be longer. 'You ask Marie if you need anything, OK? And you can visit me when the doctor says it's all right to. I'll ask Marie to bring you, OK?'

I nodded, but nothing felt OK. Nothing at all. Marie lived a few doors down. She lived alone. She came to play with us when Mum wasn't well enough. I remember she was very kind – but she wasn't Mum.

'I'll bring you food and leave it all in the fridge for you,' Marie said. 'You'll have everything you need. And if you need anything like sanitary towels or new bras, you just ask me, OK? We can go shopping.' Mum smiled at her and they hugged. Liz clung onto Mum and cried.

'I got you girls a little something to keep you company while I am gone, are you ready?' Mum said, her long, thin arm reaching out to open the garage door. Marie was standing next to her, ready to catch her if she fell. When the door opened, I saw a tiny kitten sitting in the middle of the room. It was the cutest thing I'd ever seen.

'Is she ours?' Liz gasped, picking her up.

'Yup, all yours,' Mum said, smiling. So happy to see joy on our faces, even happier to be the one who put it there.

263

'She's got hair like yours Mia, you're the perfect match,' Marie said.

'What will you call her?' Mum asked. Liz and I looked at the perfect, ginger kitten that seemed to love us already, and both of us, without discussing it, shouted, 'Wotsit!'

Mum went to hospital and Liz and I took turns to have Wotsit sleep with us. We fed her and brushed her and cuddled her. We rushed home from school to see her, we played with her for entire weekends.

And then one day Dad was shouting. He said he could 'smell piss on fucking everything'. He burst into our room and picked Wotsit up. He drove off with her in his car and we never saw her again. Liz cried so much she was sent home from school the next day.

'I have a cat, girls,' Marie said a week later when she delivered us some meals. 'And you can come visit her whenever you like.'

So, after school, we started to stop by Marie's house. Her big, fluffy cat called George distracted us from reality for however long we could stay. No one ever talked about what happened to Wotsit.

Mum never came home.

23

I stay with Pigeon as the sun beams through the window and eventually disappears. I lie there, not moving, not letting her go until the sky turns dark. I resist sleep but eventually it takes me.

I wake in the morning, for a second fooled by her soft fur but then reminded by her hard body and my heavy heart. She lies lifeless on the bed and once again this week I remember my mother. I didn't understand death then like I understand death now, but I was taken to hospital to see her. The only dead bodies I've ever seen: my mother's and my cat's. I wasn't with my dad when he died, I didn't want to be. He was the reason I longed for love but pushed it away if it came too close. It got worse and worse and worse, the feeling of inadequacy. The inability to love, to find peace in anything, no matter how much I latched on. And then that night when I couldn't live with the feelings I had been infested with for so long, I jumped. I jumped to what I saw as freedom. I was serious, I wanted it all to end. But it didn't and that made me so angry. I'd decided what I wanted and again humans stopped me living the life I deserved. I was going to jump again. A circle of attempts. I'd be dragged to safety, then I'd do it again and again until no one got in my way. I wanted to float down a river and into the sea. I wanted to be as lost in death as I felt when I was alive. But I only jumped that one time, because I found Pigeon. From the second I picked her up I knew. I knew that I had to do whatever I could to keep her alive. I knew that if I did that, I could also live. *No such thing as just a cat.* The love I longed for had finally arrived. She opened my heart enough to find work, a family. Nothing would ever be a romantic fairytale for me, but at least I was living, at least I was trying. Love opens gateways inside of people, enabling them to take on bigger things. That's what Pigeon was to me: the beginning of the rest of my life.

But now she is dead and that is over. There is nothing I can do. And tomorrow, she will still be dead and there will still be nothing for me to do. I'll just have to exist.

My phone buzzes. A text. I reach for my tote bag, not breaking contact with Pigeon. I have multiple messages from Tristan.

Come down, I can take the cat away for you.

You can't keep her up there.

Come down, Belinda feels awful. She's really beating herself up about it.

Oliver is worried. He wants to know if his notes helped find her.

What are your plans? You can't keep her up there.

Not one single, 'Are you OK?'

I get off the bed and put on an outfit made entirely of fleece. I smooth cream on my cheeks because they hurt from all the tears. In the reflection of the bathroom mirror I see Pigeon on the bed. Lifeless. Grief hits me like a bullet and knocks me to the floor again. Some breathing and I get up. I remove the desk from in front of the door. I pick up my darling Pigeon and I go downstairs. In the kitchen, Belinda looks like she's been crying more than me.

'I'm sorry,' she bawls while Tristan comforts her. 'I shouldn't have left the door open.'

'She's devastated,' Tristan tells me as he strokes her. 'Come on, Mia. Tell her it's OK.'

'It's not OK. My cat is dead and it's her fault.'

'Mia, please,' he begs, but I see no reason why I must bring comfort to a person who has brought me so much pain. I push past them both and go out into the garden. I can feel them watching me through the glass kitchen doors. I lay Pigeon on the grass. Oliver is behind me, the dog sniffs Pigeon.

'I won't let him hurt her,' Oliver says.

'Thank you, Oliver,' I say. I believe him.

I find the shovel from inside the shed. Belinda looks terrified, like I'm going to kill her with it. The thought might have crossed my mind. I head over to a little spot under a myrtle tree. On hot summer days I'd often sit under the tree with Pigeon on a lead. She'd lie in the sun like she was on the most luxurious holiday of her life. I was often crit-icised about not letting her out, but look what happened the one time she did it without me. A mother knows best.

'What are you doing?' Oliver asks me, as I roll up my sleeves.

'When people die you sometimes bury them in the ground. So that is what I will do with Pigeon, I just need to dig a very deep hole.'

I push the shovel into the ground and push it down with my foot, it's much harder than I thought it would be. As I lift it, a few scraps of earth come away. I push it down again, press it back, and lift a little more dirt. I do it again and again and again until I can't do it any more. The hole can't be more than three inches deep.

'You have to help her, we need this to end,' I hear Belinda say. And then Tristan is next to me, he puts his hand out for the shovel and I give it to him. He stabs it into the ground, pushes it with his foot, presses it back and lifts a little more earth than I could manage. He does it again and again and again. Sweat pours from him, he shakes out his hands because they must be hurting. He stops.

'I can't do it,' he says, 'it's too hard.'

'We have to do it,' I tell him.

Belinda steps in, she takes the shovel. She stabs it into the ground, pushes it with her foot, presses it back. She gets less than both me and Tristan. She does it again and again until she sobs with defeat. 'It's impossible. The earth is too dry.'

I get on all fours and kneel over the pathetic hole. I use my hands to dig and dig. Oliver joins me, so does the puppy. We are scratching at the ground, trying to get as deep as we can. My fingers start to get sore; I think I see blood. Tristan is telling me to stop, just give up. But I can't. I've had Pigeon for twenty-four hours now, it's just a matter of time before she starts to turn, and I can't have that happen. I don't want to take her to the vet and never see her again. I want her here, in my garden, so I can visit her every day.

An alarm goes off on my phone. With a muddy hand I take it from my pocket.

Bereavement Group starts in 30 minutes.

I didn't realise it was Tuesday.

'Where are you going?' Tristan calls after me.

I don't answer as I leave with Pigeon in my arms.

24

It's 7.10 when I arrive at the Methodist Church. The door is closed, the session has begun. I look down at Pigeon's body slumped over my forearms. My fingernails thick with dirt. My hands filthy. My shoes, knees, elbows, all soiled.

Rather than risk dropping Pigeon by using the doorknob, I just kick the door open. When I see them all sitting in the circle, everyone but Greg, I fall to the ground and scream through tears. Immediately they surround me. Muffled voices fill my ears.

'You're OK, Mia.' 'We've got you now.' 'Someone make her a coffee, she likes the instant stuff.'

I'm led over to my chair; I am sat down. I can't work out what people are saying. I want to explain myself. I didn't plan this.

'I'm so sorry. My cat wasn't dead. I came because I needed

people. I never thought I'd find you. I listened to you all talk about your losses and I couldn't imagine how it would feel and now I feel it and it's the worst pain I've known. But you were right, Martha. It's not because she was just a cat: my mum, my dad, my past, my future, it's all wrapped up in the love I gave to Pigeon and now she's gone and I'm left with it all but none of the good stuff. Which is what she was. She was the only good stuff, now it's all awful.'

Ada is at my side with her hand on my back, Lee is at the other with his arm around me. I turn my face into his armpit and keep it there, in his warmth. He doesn't seem to mind.

'We tried to dig a hole but the ground was too hard. I don't want Tristan digging a hole for Pigeon. I don't want him near us.'

'It's OK. It's OK,' Lee says. 'I'll dig the hole. Just let me know when and where. I can do that for you no problem, and we will lay Pigeon to rest. OK?'

'OK.'

My breathing slows. I'm feeling calmer just being here with them.

'I think I need you all,' I say, sounding stupid. 'I just needed to be with you tonight. When I realised it was Tuesday I was so relieved. I don't have many people in my life that I can talk to.'

'That's why we are here,' Tiana says. They have all pulled their chairs closer. The circle is getting tighter and tighter. I am so glad I came. Where is Greg?

My phone rings. Lee asks me if he can get it for me from

my tote bag but I say, 'No, it will be my husband.' It rings again, and then again. We all sit in silence while it rings out.

'Are you sure you don't want to answer it?' Tiana says. 'If it is your husband, we are all here to support you through the conversation.'

It keeps ringing. If I don't answer now, he will keep calling. I nod. Lee finds the phone in my bag. It's stopped ringing, but there is a message on the screen saying, 'Five missed calls from SIMON'.

And a text that says: *Come to the hospital. It's Liz . . .*

I walk straight up to the welcome desk.

'You have a Liz Voyce here?' I ask shakily. 'She is my sister.'

The receptionist looks immediately at my hands, which are thick with dirt, and the object that I am carrying. I realise Pigeon's tail has come free and is hanging out. 'I'm sorry, you can't bring live animals in here,' she says.

'It's not alive,' I say.

The woman looks horrified. 'You can't bring ANY animals in here.'

'Please, my sister is here. She's really hurt.'

'Leave the cat outside, and you can come in and I will locate your sister for you.'

I walk back out of the hospital, it's a chaotic scene. Ambulances, people walking, people in wheelchairs. It's grim. Illness and fear. I see a bush in the middle of a little grassy area. I take Pigeon over and hide her underneath it. I cover her with leaves and take the blanket with me, so no one mistakes her for rubbish. 'I'll be back for you soon,' I tell her.

Back in the hospital I am given directions to find Liz. I get to the room she is in and as I go to open the door a nurse tells me I must wash my hands. She looks at me as if I need special care, and rather than make me feel bad for that she guides me to a sink. She takes my hands, one by one, and lathers them up with soap. She massages them with warm water until the dirt comes off and the brown water runs clear. She says nothing to me, but the gentle touch of her caring hands makes me cry.

'My cat died, and my sister fell down the stairs and is unconscious,' I tell her.

'Life can be really unfair,' she says, drying my hands with a blue paper towel. 'But with the right people around you, you can get through anything. Stay close to the people you love. OK, you're ready to go in.'

The kindness of strangers can get you to the next place you are supposed to be.

When I walk into the room, I see Liz lying on the bed, eyes closed, tubes up her nose and in her arms. Her skin is pale, there is blood in her hair. Simon is next to her holding her hand. When he sees me, he gets up and gives me a hug. He's never hugged me before, it's a strange feeling to have known someone so long and to have never felt their body. I stand motionless with my arms dangling by my sides. He squeezes me extremely tightly and sobs into the nape of my neck. I feel his tears on my skin.

'It's OK, it's OK,' I tell him, having no idea if it is.

'He set a trap at the top of the stairs. He said it was to stop people going into his room.'

'Who?'

'The foster kid. You met him.'

'Liz said he was trouble. What has the doctor said?' I ask.

'They're worried she has a vertebral fracture, they'll be taking her for a scan soon. Right now, I just want her to wake up.'

I walk over to the bedside holding my breath. 'I'm here, Liz. It's Mia.' I sit down and press my head to her hand. 'Pigeon died so you can't die too. I need you.'

The machine she is plugged into is beeping. I know from TV that's a good sign but it's not good that she is plugged into a machine.

'She'll be OK, Simon. She will.'

'How do you know?'

'Because she has us.'

I sit with Liz for an hour. She is such a unique woman, but here in a hospital everyone is just the same. Human beings in white gowns in the hands of doctors who don't care who we are or who we love, they just want to make us better.

I must get back to Pigeon. Simon says he will call me after the scan to let me know how it goes. I tell him I can come back with clothes for him or sit with her while he goes home for a shower. I don't think he'd leave her, but it might be good for him to take a walk. It's strange to feel like family with him, but we are. It took this for us to realise that.

It's dark now, there are fewer people around. I scoop Pigeon up, wrap her in the blanket and carry her home. She's feeling different now, not like Pigeon at all. It's been over twenty-four hours at least since she died. I don't have any more time.

When I get home the house feels quiet. The clock says it's 2 a.m. Oliver and Tristan are in bed. I had no idea it was so late. I walked for a long time. Just me and Pigeon walking the streets. Me trying to get as much time with her as I could, postponing whatever has to happen now. I go straight to the kitchen.

'I can't keep you like this any more, Pigeon. And I need a little longer to work out what to do.' I hug her and kiss her on her head. It's wet, from more of my tears. I don't know how my body keeps making them, I can't have a drop of water left. I open the freezer drawer and take out multiple half-empty boxes of fish fingers, chicken nuggets, pizzas and vegetables. I create enough room and I place Pigeon inside. I shape her so she's curled up nicely, just as she would be asleep.

'I'm sorry. I'll get you out as soon as I have worked out what to do. I'll be right here.'

I close the drawer and go up to my room to get a pillow and our blanket. I bring them to the kitchen and put them down next to the freezer. I lie down, wrapping myself up in the fleece, my head on the pillow. I fall asleep on the kitchen floor.

I'm woken by the threat of daylight through the window. Buster is licking my face. There is a terrible smell.

'Off, get off,' I say as I brush him away. The smell is putrid. Did I leave the freezer open? Is it Pigeon? I get to my feet and check but it's closed. I open it slowly, Pigeon is there. She looks so beautiful. Perfectly preserved, I could keep her there forever, who says I can't? I lean down, no smell. I look around and see the boxes of food that I took out. A mix of defrosted fish fingers and chicken nuggets is blending in the air with the smell of a huge splattering of puppy poo all over the kitchen floor, luckily nowhere near me. It makes me laugh. To think how many times Belinda shamed me for Pigeon having the occasional mishap and now look at this, their own beloved puppy's shit all over the floor.

'Thank you, Buster,' I say, leaning down to him.

I see my phone light up on the counter. It's 6 a.m. A text from Simon.

Some good news, she won't need surgery, she's awake and asking for you. When can you come?

I leave immediately.

* * *

When I walk into the hospital room Liz is sitting up. 'Wow,' I say, taken aback. 'This is an improvement.'

'She's very lucky,' Simon says. 'Should make a full recovery.'

Liz looks weak but she's smiling. 'I'm OK,' she says gently. 'Just sore.'

'Simon, why don't you pop home, have a shower and get changed. I can stay with her until you get back,' I say, wanting Liz all to myself.

'I will. And I'll check in on Mum and the kids, I'm sure she's doing fine but I need to hug them all. You know?'

'It's like he fell down the stairs and came back up with a new personality,' I say, when he's gone. Liz tries not to laugh because it obviously hurts.

'He loves me.'

'He does. You scared me.'

'I'm sorry.'

I hug her the best I can without hurting her.

'That kid. What a shit,' I say. 'What the hell did he think would happen? There's no way he didn't mean to do some damage.'

'We're all just a product of what's happened to us. I was going to give him everything I had.'

'Well, you almost gave him your life.'

'I've still got my family, we're all OK.' She smiles. As long as there are people who need her, she'll get through anything.

'How are you?' she asks, breathily.

I wonder if telling her my horrific news is the right thing to do, she's got enough of her own to deal with. But I know

277

my sister, and there is no such thing as an emotional burden for her.

'Pigeon died.'

'No, Mia.'

'Belinda left the door open. She got out and was hit by a car. I'm angry that I can't just be sad, I have so much rage to process too. It shouldn't be like this.'

'Anger doesn't matter in the end.'

'In the end?'

'When I woke up, I didn't know where I was. Simon was in the bathroom and I just saw that I was here and honestly, I thought I was going to die. Do you know all I could think about?'

'Who would make Simon endless cups of tea?'

'Don't!' She's sore, laughing hurts. 'I thought about everyone I loved. I didn't think about Dad, or the people who have hurt me, or the foster kids who have been abusive, or even the one who made me fall down the stairs. I thought about Simon and the kids, and I thought about you. It was all that mattered. That I had you guys. We can't act like we don't need each other any more Mia.'

'I suppose I convinced myself that I don't need anyone. It's easier that way.'

'No, it's not. It's lonely that way. You surround yourself with people who call you crazy and you've learned to believe it yourself. You're no crazier than any of them.' She frowns, as if talking is getting too hard. 'Forgiveness, compassion, kindness and love. It's easier than you think.'

'You sound like a greeting card.'

I take a glass of water from the table and hold it to her mouth so she can take little sips. 'I'm so pleased you're OK,' I say, resting my head very gently on her shoulder.

'You need more love in your life, Mia,' she says with a smile. 'Get some fucking friends.'

When Simon comes back, washed, changed and looking fresher, I leave Liz. She's been sleeping for the last two hours, and I've stared at her that whole time. My incredible sister. The world might disregard someone like her. No career goals. A housewife who takes on more and more domestic chores. Taking in troublesome kids with a husband who is relentlessly distracted by his own ambition. They might not think she has much to offer. And yet that's all she does. Offer and love and provide. Even after this, her heart still adamantly in the right place. I remind myself we are cut from the same cloth. We feel the same pain, we cry the same tears. I could be more like her if I allowed myself to be – and I want to be. I want my heart to be that full. But when it comes to allowing people in, I don't know where to start.

As I enter the Tube station, the headline of today's newspaper that's written on a board stops me dead in my tracks:

THEO MAY. SIX CASES OF SEXUAL ASSAULT

Six former employees of Theo May have accused the mogul of sexual assault. His daughter Isabella May simply says, 'F*ck him!'

279

The front cover shows images of both Theo and Isabella, a rip mark dividing them. I dig around in my bag for some money and buy a copy. I wait until I am sitting down on the train to read it.

Over the past few decades, while cavorting as a philanthropist, Theo May has silenced multiple women over their claims that he sexually assaulted them. But some women cannot be silenced. Six have now made claims that the mogul offered them highly paid jobs on the proviso that they perform sordid acts of sexual pleasure on him. Claims are as varied as one woman being asked to come to work with no underwear on ('he would email me and ask me to take pictures of up my skirt for an immediate pay rise') to being forced underneath his desk to perform oral sex on him while he took 'very important calls' – often to the many female-led charities that he supports.

Multiple accusers have spoken of a toxic work environment. 'Theo May created an environment where to be touched by him was like being touched by the hands of God. He somehow made the women he didn't prey on feel rejected. That is a new level of predator,' said one source.

I stop reading to catch my breath. This is horrific. I feel icky at the thought of being in his presence. To think I liked him. And I judged Isabella for being ungrateful for his money. I spot her name a few paragraphs down so read on.

When asked in an exclusive interview, May's daughter, Isabella, said, 'My father has silenced many women with money over the years, myself included. It's not easy to go out into the world and stand against my own father, but I stand with the women who were brave enough to come forward, and for the many who are too afraid to do so. I see you, and I have your back.'

When asked if she will be supporting her father through his trial, she simply said, 'No, f**k him!'

Holy shit. In an instant, everything I ever thought about Isabella changes.

25

As I come out of the Tube station and walk past the Marie Curie charity shop, I notice a leopard-print dress on a rail inside. It pulls me in in the same way a muffin might lure a child. It's been years since I've come into a shop like this – any style influenced by dead people wasn't part of the remit. But the truth is, my mother's kaftan is currently my favourite dress, and that came from a dead person and was on its way to a charity shop before I intercepted it, so who am I to judge what they have on their rails? Also, I'm not sure what I've been masquerading in for the past however many years constitutes as 'style'. I don't work in an office any more, I can wear whatever the hell I want.

The dress is labelled 'One Size'. It's a huge, floaty leopard-print kaftan and it costs £12. To the right of it is a purple cat-print blouse, and on another rail there's a long, tiger-striped cardigan. There are cat-print shoes, a scarf, even a pair of leggings with tabby cat faces on them. I scrunch them all into a ball and put them on the counter.

'Is someone going to a fancy-dress party?' the old lady volunteering asks me.

'No,' I say, unoffended. 'I'm just very keen on cats.'

'I have a whole box of cat-print things in the back. Would you like to see them?'

'Yes,' I say, enthusiastically. 'Yes, I absolutely would.'

There's so much uncertainty in my life at the moment but I do know that I want to live in my house until I die. I open the front door and walk in with a new determination. Belinda and Tristan are sitting in the kitchen looking stressed. It's not unusual. They always seem stressed and unhappy in some way. Why am I only seeing that now?

'Are you Googling ways to have me evicted?' I say, joking. Tristan shuts his computer suspiciously. I turn the oven on.

'What the hell are you wearing?' Belinda asks, forgoing any attempt to be polite.

'It's a leopard-print kaftan,' I tell her. 'I just got it from the local Marie Curie.'

'You look like a homeless person,' Tristan adds.

'Well, I am not a homeless person,' I say, smugly. 'This is my home, any further comments?'

'Mia, do you really not want to leave? You could get

yourself somewhere nice. It would be a lot less expensive for you to move than us.'

He's talking to me like I'm stupid and I don't like it. 'Your finances aren't my concern. I will buy your half of this house. If moving isn't something you can be bothered to do then that isn't my problem.'

'It's just that . . .' Belinda begins, before I interrupt by mimicking her in a high-pitched, offensive voice, taking us all by surprise. She continues in a lower octave. 'It's just that Tristan and I bought this house together when we got married. We dreamed of living here and raising a family here until we grew old. And now we have that chance again and we are asking you to please not get in the way of that dream.'

'Then why did you have sex with someone and leave him? And when that didn't work out, you and your big spongy fanny got all sad and wanted Tristan back, but by then he was married to me so you couldn't have him. But you hung around like a bad smell until he felt so guilty he got back together with you anyway, even though you're fucking mental and worse to be married to than a dying goat.'

'A dying goat?' Tristan asks. Which is fair, it was a very strange thing to say, but I hold my head up high and act like it's exactly what I meant because I can't think of anything better.

Belinda pinches the top of her nose with her index finger and thumb and breathes in deeply. 'I do not have a spongy fanny.'

'Sorry, marshmallow,' I say, correcting myself. 'You have a marshmallow vagina. Which, when you think about it, sounds quite soft and loose.'

'OK, OK, stop. I can't stand you two fighting over me any more,' Tristan shouts, putting his hands over his ears like Belinda and I are two jumbo jets taking off.

There's a rare moment of solidarity between us as we look at each other quizzically. We've never got on, but I'm not sure either of us would ever describe it as 'fighting' over Tristan. He's hardly Keanu Reeves.

'Keep the damn house, Mia,' Tristan says. 'Fill the freezer with cats, you lunatic.'

Belinda looks horrified. 'What? Tristan, what are you saying?'

'She won't leave, I know her. She does what she wants.'

'But you won't be happy. You said, this house is where you are happy?'

'He doesn't want to be happy, Belinda. He just wants to win,' I say, casually taking a ready-made vegan mac 'n' cheese out of the freezer, stroking Pigeon gently as I close it. I've become quite used to her being in there now, I wonder if I might keep her there forever.

'For God's sake,' Tristan shouts suddenly, becoming physically irritated by something. It distracts him from his rage. He starts frantically scratching his beard. 'This house has fleas, I'm sure of it. We will be better off leaving.'

I catch Belinda subtly scratching herself between the legs. She doesn't think I notice. I recall my husband's head between mine on the very seat she is sitting on. I imagine the crabs transferring from my pubic hair to his facial hair. A small but noticeable smile forms across my face.

'Oh, you think it's funny we have fleas from your cat?' Tristan says, angrily scratching his chin.

'Actually,' I say, knowledgably, 'cat fleas don't live on humans, so it won't be that. You probably have crabs.'

'What?' Belinda says, standing up, crossing her knees a little as she tries to relieve an itch with the top of her thighs. 'No one gets crabs, it's not the nineties. You're completely mad.'

'They do. It's quite common. I had them, recently. Tristan, you probably got them from me when you performed oral sex on me in here. Remember, a few days after I found out you two were sleeping with each other?'

Tristan has gone very pale. Speechless, and almost translucent.

'You did that?' Belinda says, staring at him as hard as she can.

'Oh, there's nothing to be mad about Belinda,' I add. 'I've been sleeping with my husband throughout your entire affair, so really, nothing has changed.' I take the cardboard off my mac 'n' cheese and violently stab eight holes into the foil so it can breathe.

'You have crabs? How?' Tristan eventually squeezes out, Belinda still trying to kill him with her gaze.

'I don't have them any more,' I say, dipping my finger into my cold dinner and sucking the creamy sauce off. 'I did though.'

'How did you get crabs?' he asks, not moving. Not believing.

'I slept with someone, Tristan. A millennial. I had sex with him a few nights before and he gave me crabs and then I gave them to you when you performed oral sex on me. It's not complicated. And there is nothing to be ashamed of, it's easy to treat. I have some lotion left if you want it?' I walk over to the oven, and pop in my dinner.

'You had sex with someone?'

'Yes. I know it's hard for you to understand that. But when I discovered your affair, I went out and I had sex with someone else. It turns out, I am still desirable to men. Very much so. He enjoyed my body very much.' I feel my buttocks clench at the thought of the implements.

'You had SEX with someone?' he repeats.

'Yes, is that a problem?'

'You're my wife!'

'Yes, and you are my husband. Your point?' I am facing him front-on now, I feel very strong. He is absolutely beside himself. Belinda has given in and is now scratching her fanny like the fleabag that she is.

'This is intolerable,' Tristan says.

'Yes, it is,' I agree. 'I suggest you leave Oliver sleeping and the two of you go to Belinda's for the night. You can come back tomorrow when Oliver is at school and we can work out how we proceed with the divorce, me buying you out of the house and the logistics of you moving out. Contrary to what you might think, I have no intention of making this harder for any of us than it already is, I just want it done.'

'I'm not leaving Oliver with you, you crazy bitch,' Belinda spits.

'You have every right to wake him up and take him with you, but we all know he is better off where he is.'

'Well, we are taking Buster,' she says, trying to upset me further.

'That would be ideal.'

'You slept with someone?' Tristan says, still baffled.

'I did.'

They make their way slowly to the front door. Embarrassed and defeated. I got the house and they got crabs, so I guess if we must choose a winner it's going to be me.

'Oliver has swimming tomorrow,' Belinda tells me, asserting herself.

'I know he does.'

Tristan storms to the car and turns on the engine, but Belinda lingers at the gate. I wonder if she's going to come back to me with some sisterly apology. A woman-to-woman moment where she acknowledges our plight at the hand of men. But no, she scuttles back to the door where I am resisting a cheery wave and says, 'Get me that lotion then.' I go upstairs to my bathroom and get it. She snatches it from me with a hiss. When she's gone and the door is closed, I exhale and fall against it. My house is mine. I took my power back.

I eat the mac 'n' cheese alone in the kitchen with the freezer drawer open so I can see Pigeon. 'I'll get you out soon, promise,' I tell her. When I'm done with my food, I wash my plate, wipe the surfaces and turn off the lights. Then I go into Oliver's room, breathe in the smell of him and whisper, 'I love you' to his sleeping face.

26

When you're married for the wrong reasons, the only things missing when that person's gone are the things you didn't realise were slowly destroying you. I spent most of my day with someone who was mildly annoyed with me for seven years. Someone who knew who I was when he married me, but whose disappointment that I was someone else played out in different ways every single day. An argument, a judgement, sometimes just a sigh loaded with resentment. Neither of us married for the right reasons but, in many ways, they were the same reasons. We did it to create a façade. We did it because we presumed it would make us feel better. We did it because we are all led to believe that the traditional family is the route to all happiness, and that any other version of it is problematic or an act of rebellion. For me, the reality of marriage was that it made me play a part. By trying to slot into the role of wife, I could only ever be a disappointment. My need for independence was his problem, not mine. My veganism was his problem, not mine. It's amazing to me that I allowed someone to be so upset about my eating habits when he never even knew how repulsed I was by his. I spared him from so much of himself.

So much of a bad marriage is enabling a partner to behave in a way that you know isn't right. But the truth is, I'm not sure I ever cared enough to try to fix it. The more distant we became, the closer I got to what I wanted. Which was, ultimately, not him. I found the deceit hard to handle at first. Being lied to shakes your nervous system, I reacted strongly to that. But was I sad because I had lost love? No, I was sad because I lost myself trying to find it.

Tristan took the majority of the furniture, and I am left with little but my house, which at this point feels like a lot. I could have fought for more, but every exchange has been so exhausting that I ran out of fight. I presume I will wake one day with the energy to rebuild my life but for now it's quite the achievement to just get downstairs when I wake up. But, today, I am almost out of coffee and oat milk. I have consumed nearly every tin of beans, fruit and vegetables from the cupboards and there is nothing in my freezer other than my deceased cat.

I don't know how long I plan to leave Pigeon in the freezer, but I feel it is my right to decide on when it happens. I find it extremely comforting having her there. I could not control the way she died but I can control what happens now. She is preserved perfectly. Her coat still soft even though her body is hard and cold. I've found myself wondering why human death is handled with so much isolation and mystery. The bodies are taken away from the family. They are treated and dressed and it's illegal to bury them at home or in places that they loved. I'm sure there would be good business for temporary freezing units to preserve dead loved ones while family members take the time they need to plan funerals, while being able to be physically close to the corpse every day. They could set a limit, maybe six weeks until they must remove the body from the premises and make funeral arrangements. If I was to be honest though, I can't think of a single human who I would want lingering around in a freezer after they die. Maybe the current system is right after all. But there is no doubt that grief has been easier while I've been able to open a drawer and feel Pigeon's fur each day. It's helping bridge the gap between her being here and her not being here. Every morning when I eventually make it downstairs, I go straight to the freezer, open the drawer and tell her that I love her.

When I shut it, I see the only thing remaining as evidence that this was once a family home: the picture of our family that Oliver drew for Mother's Day. Five stick figures. One of Belinda, one of Tristan, one of me and one of Oliver, and one of a cat. My hair so fiery and red. A nice detail. Just for me. When Tristan and Belinda came to ransack the place and took everything of any emotional value, this was the one thing they left. It used to sit on the fridge surrounded by more of Oliver's artistic endeavours. They didn't want it so now it stands alone. I take the picture off the fridge and with some kitchen scissors I cut around the picture of me then stick it back to the fridge. Just me on my own. No family, no cat. I'm not sure when and how this happened, but here I am.

I am living the sort of life where no one drops in. There are many things that define a week, and when you remove them, days can carry very little difference from one to the next. There is no Monday morning to prepare for, no weekend to stock up for. No lunches to shop for. There are no meal plans, food deliveries, Oyster card top-ups, make-up applications. There is no outfit composition to think about, no schedule of self-care. Each and every day is the same. On the rare occasion the doorbell goes it's the postman or an Amazon delivery person bringing me the continuous stream of goods that I have been ordering to make up for how much has been taken from this house since Tristan and Oliver moved out. I ordered a desk to put in Oliver's old room but I'm yet to build it. At some point I will need to work but for now there is no urgency to do anything other than make it through the day. I ordered lots of candles to fill the whole house with the smells that I like the most, now they are not confined to my bedroom. I am living in a confused state. In one way the peace, privacy and space are good. The whole house is mine, I consider only myself. But I am realising that I am maybe more like my sister than I thought. I enjoyed taking care of Pigeon and Oliver. There were even some parts of looking after Tristan that were good for me. Needing to keep someone else's life in order can help when trying to do the same for your own. I now have nothing to care for. Yesterday I wondered if I might kick a hole in a wall, just so I had something to fix.

When my doorbell rings unexpectedly I jump and become immediately aware of my surroundings and my unkempt-ness. I am unwashed, the curtains are drawn, and I am quite thin. I am wearing the leopard-print kaftan again. In fact, I've been wearing it for days.

Who could it be? I am not due any deliveries. The ringing is persistent. I stand in the kitchen staring at the door. If I was in a horror movie, I would grab a knife.

'Who is it?' I call as I make my way down the hall.

'If I tell you, you won't open it.'

It's Isabella.

'What are you doing here?' I ask with a defensive tone. Does she have the police with her to do me for vandalism? Is she here to tell me how awful I am? I don't need to hear that.

'Open the door. I'm not here to argue,' she says through the letterbox. 'I can see you.'

I consider making her wait while I run upstairs to wash my face, get dressed, muster an image less troubling than the one I am presenting right now. But what for? She doesn't need any other version of me than the real one. I open the door.

'Woah, Mia,' are her first words, which make me wonder if I should have popped upstairs after all. 'Are you ill?'

'No.'

'Are you sure?'

'Yes, I'm just going through some things.'

'I like the outfit though; it weirdly suits you.'

Her saying that has a surprisingly elevating effect on me.

'Can I come in?' she asks.

'I'd rather you didn't.'

'Oh, come on, Mia. We worked opposite each other for years, it ended badly but it wasn't always awful, was it?'

'What do you mean by "it"?'

'Us, our friendship.'

I've never thought about us having a friendship before. But I suppose it's inevitable when you sit in the same room as someone for eight hours a day, every day for ten years. We stand staring at each other. She looks different too. Much thinner. Exhausted.

'I read it,' I say. 'The article about Theo. I don't really know what to say.'

'It was more than an article. Every paper, website, TV channel in the country, maybe even the world, ran the story.'

'It must have been horrible. I'm sorry.'

'Oh, don't be. It's been a long time coming. I'm just glad people know about it now. Mum and I have strongly suspected it for years but what were we supposed to do, out him? He kept us under his thumb with money, but when those women came forward I just went with it.'

'Your mum knew? Why didn't she leave?'

'Because he did what all rich people do when they have power, he threatened her with her getting nothing. I stayed for the same reasons. I'm not proud of that, but I didn't want to lose the business.'

I always thought Isabella's mum seemed quite cool. Not showing up to all of the events, being happy behind the scenes. I guess you never really know what someone is going through.

'But at least I'm not going to have another little sibling. Apparently, there are around seven of them kicking about.'

'What? Your mum is pregnant, isn't she in her seventies?'

'No, not my mum. God, how did you not work this out? Audrey. That baby was my dad's. They've been fucking for years. Why else do you think I'd employ someone so useless? He made me do it after I walked in on them in my parents' bedroom. She was his PA's daughter. Gross. He said if I gave her a job, he wouldn't leave Mum. I stupidly agreed because for ages I thought my mum would be worse off without him. I underestimated her. I underestimated myself too. Bullies are only bullies because people allow them to be.'

I haven't inhaled since she said the word 'Audrey'. 'I had no idea, I can't believe it.'

'Yeah, I know. I feel bad for her, she was stupid enough to think he actually loved her. She's finding out about all this now too.'

'Have you spoken to her?'

'I was the first person she came crying to. I told her it's OK, he was a manipulative fucker and she was just another victim of it. I told her I wouldn't sack her, but I'm moving her to Marketing which she'll be better at. That girl couldn't design a necklace if her life depended on it.'

'That's really good of you,' I say, meaning it.

'Yeah, well, us girls have to stick together, don't we?' she says, smiling. 'Now the tension has gone I'll be in the office more. I just never wanted to be there because I couldn't stand to be in the same room as her.'

'I thought you were just skiving.'

'I know you did.'

'What about the company? What will you do?'

'I've been offered investment money from three extreme-ly prominent female entrepreneurs. They want to grow the business. They'll do more for me than Dad did. Guidance and money, and I won't feel relentlessly indebted to someone whose eyes I can't look into.'

'That sounds like a sensible plan. Well done.'

She laughs. 'Wow.'

'What?'

'You said, "Well done" to me. You've never said it before. No matter how much I tried to make you say it, you never did.'

'Why did you need me to say it?' I ask, genuinely baffled. I never thought I mattered in Isabella's world of celebrities and multimillionaires.

'Because I admired you. But you challenged me on almost everything I did. You spoke to me like I was stupid, like I didn't know what I was doing. Like I was selfish, ungrateful. I tried to explain to you how hard things were for me. Being a single mum, the pressure of being in the public eye, running the business. Some days I'd list the things I was up against just hoping that maybe you'd say, "Well done, you're doing great." But you never did.'

A thousand scenes of us in the office flash in front of my eyes, and in every single one of them she is telling me how hard her life is and I am judging her for being ungrateful.

'I think maybe I was jealous,' I say, gently.

'Jealous, what of?'

'Because I thought you had life handed to you on a plate. I had a really bad relationship with my dad. Really bad. He was emotionally abusive, he abandoned my sister and me, and I've spent my life just wishing he'd been better. And I thought Theo was better. I thought if I had a dad like that I would be better too. So, when I'd see you challenging him, or not appreciating what he was doing for you, then it sparked something in me and I just . . . I suppose that made me unkind to you.'

'That's the most you've ever told me about yourself,' she says. 'All those years working in the same space and I never even knew about your dad.'

'Well, to be fair, by the sound of things I didn't know about yours either.'

'That's true.'

We smile at each other. The relief of this conversation is palpable.

'It was me in that article. The one you read about the pet bereavement group.'

'I knew it, there's only one Mia! Why didn't you just admit it?'

'Would you?'

'I suppose not. But if we're having a competition about who's had the worst article published in the last month, I think I win? Wait, your cat died.'

'Yes.'

'You never said. I always thought I'd have to give you a month off when that happened, I knew it would really upset you. Why didn't you mention it?'

'Well, she hadn't died at the point the article came out. I was going to the bereavement group anyway, because . . . I don't really know. I just felt I'd found a place I could be myself. But Pigeon is dead now. She got hit by a car. She's in the freezer.'

'What? Why is she in the freezer?'

'Because I don't know what to do. My husband cheated on me with his ex-wife. That means I've lost my marriage, my stepson and my cat. I also, obviously, lost my job.'

'Oh, Mia.' She steps closer and puts her arms around me. 'Look, I'm just going to come out and say it: I want you to come back to Isabella May. I don't want to do it without you. I also need your help. Fliss quit, and I need you to go and ask her to come back too. She respects you, I know I need to earn that from her and I will.'

'Fuck,' is all I manage. This is not how I expected this conversation to go. I'm so stunned that I don't say anything else for a good minute.

'Well? Don't leave me standing here all night.'

I'm surprised by my reluctance to turn her down, but honestly, I miss it.

'If I even consider this, that's *if* . . . I have a few non-negotiables. You need to be more aware of the way you speak to staff members about race and sexuality. Sometimes you say things that are straight-up offensive. It's not OK. I want us all to make an open effort for more diverse hiring and have proper safeguarding in place so that staff feel supported. If we're moving forward then sustainability, diversity and progress have to be a part of what we do. We need unconscious bias training for all of our staff, especially us. We let Fliss down and I never want that to happen again. Will you agree to that?'

'I will. I've done a lot of work on myself in the past few months. I've read a lot, I've listened. I would have spent a lifetime defending any bias I have inside of me, but I see it now. I'm not proud of it Mia, I want to do the work.'

'OK, well then I'll think about it. And whatever happens, you need to apologise to Fliss for the way you've behaved. Will you do that?'

'I'll do it all, whatever it takes to make her feel appreciated and safe. She trusts you Mia, she'll listen to you. And then it's down to me, I know that.'

She looks at me with gentle eyes and I understand that a lot of her behaviour stems from all the turmoil and damage with Theo. But it doesn't excuse her racism. Nothing does. If she truly is willing to examine herself then I will support that. I know I have to do better, too. I never want to stay silent when someone is being treated unfairly again, that makes me just as bad.

'OK, and one last thing if I'm going to consider this.'

A little of the old her shines through with a huff.

'I want to get rid of the Nespresso machine and bring back the French press. It's quieter and better for the environment. If you agree to that, then I'll come back. Yes?'

'Yes, Mia. A big fat yes. I'm a Starbucks oat milk latte kinda girl anyway.'

27

As I approach Fliss' flat in East London I see there are window baskets full of flowers and painted pots going up the stairs to the front door. Dreamcatchers hang in the bay windows and the front door is painted a bright pink. As I am about to knock on the door, I hear arguing.

'If they stay, then I go. It's that simple,' a woman's voice shouts.

'Oh come on, what am I supposed to do?'

'I don't know Fliss, but I can't live like this. I'm not trying to be difficult but look at me. I'm a mess.'

I hear the sound of footsteps, louder and louder, and then the front door opens. A very stylish woman with bloodshot eyes storms out. She sneezes three times as she walks down the stairs.

'Babe, come back. Take another Claritin and see how it goes?'

'I can't live on Claritin, Fliss. I'm going to Mum's, just sort it out or I'm not coming back. Don't make me choose between you and being allergy-free, please.' She walks off down the street, sneezing as she goes.

'Mia?'

For a second, I forget that it must be quite strange for Fliss to see me here. It takes me longer than what would be normal to answer.

'Oh, sorry. Hi Fliss, it's Mia.'

'I know it's you Mia, what are you doing here?'

'I came to see you. Who was that? She seemed very upset.'

'My fiancée. And yes, she is. Why did you come to see me?' She frowns and then looks me up and down. 'Are you OK?'

I'm still wearing the kaftan. I suggested I should change but Isabella insisted I wear it, saying the 'new me' looks more fun than the old me.

'Not really. I've had a really terrible few weeks, but things are looking up. Can we talk? I won't take much of your time.'

'Come in. I've had a terrible few weeks too.'

Inside, Fliss' flat is stylish and beautiful, just like her. There is a cat curled up on the sofa. 'Oh look,' I say, rushing to it and stroking its beautiful soft black fur. The cat looks up at me and purrs before rubbing herself along my wrist. 'She's so affectionate,' I say, adoring being in her company.

'She is, her name is Midnight. Come, look.'

I follow Fliss to a small kitchen where there are four little kittens sleeping in a pile on a bed on the floor. 'Meet

Marmalade, Biscuit, Cookie and Crumble. Midnight is the mum.'

'Oh, your gran's cats, you told me about them?'

'Yes. Sadly Gran's moved into a hospice. Midnight gave birth a few weeks before, she was so happy to be there when it happened.'

'I'm so sorry.'

'Thanks. I knew it was coming but, even so, you can never really prepare yourself. She raised me, so it's hard. She asked me to take care of the cats, but Abby is so allergic. She can hardly be in the house at all. I feel awful about it, but I don't know what to do.' She looks longingly at the kittens, this must be so hard for her. 'Anyway, how can I help you?'

'Oh yes, I almost forgot why I came,' I say, wanting to kneel down on the floor and push my face into the kittens, inhaling their fur, kissing their heads and hearing their gentle purrs. 'Isabella told me you quit,' I say.

'Yeah, it felt like an uphill battle. She knew the only reason she got into Selfridges was because of me but she resented me for it. I figured if they wanted it under Isabella May they would want it anyway.'

'Did you get another job?'

'Not yet. I heard from Rosita directly who said she was super impressed with my stuff, so I thought I'd pitch to Selfridges under my own name, but I haven't heard anything about a meeting yet.'

'Well, I think getting our brand values together is more important than commercial glory right now. The investment has given us some breathing room, so whatever about Selfridges.'

'It all left me feeling pretty shitty to be honest. The last few weeks with my gran too, it's been a lot.'

'I'm sure. Isabella has been through a lot too.'

'No shit,' she says. 'That stuff with her dad was horrible. I suppose that's the end of the company anyway, glad I got out when I did.'

'Actually, no. I'm going back.'

'What? Why? Then why did you quit?'

'Quit? I didn't quit, Isabella fired me for pitching your stuff to Selfridges.'

'Fuck, what a bitch.'

'Yeah, but we talked. She's been having a horrible time with her dad, she's been under his control for so long I think it made her want to grab onto any sense of pride she could. Not that it excuses everything she's done, and certainly not the way she has treated and spoken to you. But it's going to be different; I can feel it. She's got investment to keep the company going, all from women. Theo is out, and Isabella wants to do exactly what you said. She wants us all to tell our stories, and for you to be Head of Design. You'll get a significant pay rise and be credited for everything you've done.'

'That all sounds a bit too good to be true.'

'I know, but it's real. The truth is, Isabella May Jewellery doesn't exist without you, and it doesn't exist without me, and it certainly doesn't exist without her. I think it's worth another shot to see if we can make that work. What do you say?'

Fliss exhales loudly and strokes Midnight as if that is how she copes with stress. It makes me love her even more. 'I'm not taking her shit anymore.'

'No, and I will support you in every way I can, but I truly believe she finally realises the damage she has caused . She's doing proper inclusivity training and she's read *White Fragility* three times. She's quoting it constantly. It's not enough but it's a start. Obviously her actions will be what matters, not her words. I'd like to give her the chance though. And I'm sorry too, Fliss. I should have done more to protect you.'

'I have to admit, starting my own company was feeling really scary.'

'I have absolutely no doubt that one day you will have your own brand, but you can build a name for yourself on someone else's dollar first. She'll give you a cut of your collections too. Everything in writing. Part of the remit from the female investors is that women, especially women of colour, must be elevated in the brand. To be honest with you, I think you could probably ask for whatever you want. You're worth it.'

She thinks for a few seconds.

'Fuck it, OK.'

'That's where I am too, fuck it. Let's just give it everything we've got. I've got a good feeling.'

'We'll see. One wrong comment from her and I'm out.'

'I'll be right behind you.'

'Now what about my shitshow private life?'

'Do you want to talk about it?' I ask, liberated by my

new ability to engage with people on an intimate level. I think of my friends in the bereavement group; they'd be proud of me right now.

'Abby literally can't be in the same room as Midnight, let alone the kittens. I just don't know what to do.'

'You want to rehome them all?'

'I suppose so, but how will I know they go to nice people? You hear such awful things.' Fliss drops to the sofa, so upset.

'Don't worry,' I say, seeing it all very clearly. 'I have an idea.'

28

'Are you sure about this?' Fliss asks as we approach the Methodist Church. 'Should you not have checked in with them about it first?'

'No, trust me. These people are grieving. They don't think they're ready for another cat, but I'm convinced once they see these babies, they won't be able to stop themselves.'

I've deliberately made us arrive a few minutes late in the hope that everyone will be there. Of course, it's never a given. Any one of them could stop coming at any time. And new people might have come, making this a little more awkward than I intend it to be. Although Tiana did say she hasn't received a single request for new members since the article was published. I wonder if Amy Newton knows the damage she did – I hope whatever she got paid was worth it, although I doubt very much that it was.

'It's just in here,' I tell Fliss. 'Ready?'

'Yup,' she says to the background chorus of the kittens and their sweet meows. I slowly open the door and poke my head in.

'Mia!' says Ada, so happy to see me that I can't help but smile. I see Martha next to her, and Lee and Tiana, but no Greg. His chair still there and empty. No one knowing where he is, and if he is OK.

'I hope you don't mind,' I say, opening the door wide. 'But I brought a few friends.' I notice Martha twitch uncomfortably, and Ada and Lee look nervous, as if the idea of more people is too much to bear. But when they see Fliss with the pet carriers in her hands, they all breathe a sigh of relief.

'This is Fliss,' I say as we approach the circle. 'And this is Midnight, the mum. And these are her babies: Marmalade, Biscuit, Cookie and Crumble.'

'Biscuit?' Ada laughs. 'I love biscuits.'

'Is it OK if I get them out?' Fliss asks.

'Of course,' Tiana says. 'I'm always up for a little cuddle therapy.'

The kittens are small enough that they don't want to venture off. Instead, they put on quite the show of climbing on top of each other and rolling over. We all marvel at their cuteness and laugh at how silly they are.

'They're gorgeous,' says Martha, picking Cookie up. 'Oh look, she's licking me.'

Martha's entire disposition changes in an instant. Her face lights up and rather than the deep laugh I have occasionally heard her emit, she begins to giggle. Cookie curls up on her lap and falls asleep almost right away.

'She likes you,' I say, gently.

'I like her too,' Martha says.

Meanwhile Ada has picked up Biscuit and has her right up to her face, kissing her nose over and over again. And Lee is on his knees on the floor playing with Crumble.

'Aren't you lucky to have all these lovely cats,' Ada says.

'And so nice of you to let us play with them,' adds Lee.

Fliss and I stand up straight. 'Well, actually,' I say, 'we were wondering if you guys might like to take them home?'

No one looks at me, as if I've suggested the unthinkable. Fliss goes on to explain about her gran, and how Abby is allergic, and how much she wants to find the kittens good homes, and how I suggested coming here. Everyone looks to be in deep thought, I honestly couldn't guess who will say yes and who won't.

And then all of a sudden, Ada pipes up. 'Why not?' she says, cheerily. 'What harm can it do to bring some joy into my house? It doesn't mean I didn't love Mrs Jones, does it? I have her ashes and a little photo in the living room. Maybe it's time I moved on. Would you like to come home with me, Biscuit?' she says. Biscuit reaches out a little paw and taps Ada with it, making us all laugh. 'I think she said yes,' Ada says.

'Actually, Biscuit is a boy,' says Fliss, correcting her.

'Oh well, even better. I need a new man around the house.'

'I think my mum would love it if I brought Crumble

home. It would really cheer her up,' Lee says. 'And if you really can't keep the mum then I could take them both? It would be nice to keep them together, wouldn't it?' He picks Crumble up and starts scratching her behind the ear.

'That would be beautiful,' Fliss says, getting teary. 'My gran loves Midnight so much, she's heartbroken she can't live with her any more.'

'Well then, I think Midnight would like to send photos of herself to your gran, wouldn't you Midnight? You can tell her that she will always be her cat, and that my mum and I will just be taking the best care of her that we can. Would that help?' Lee says, always so deeply kind and thoughtful.

'She'd love that, thank you.'

We all turn our attention to Martha. 'What do you think, Martha? Is it time?' Tiana asks.

Martha studies the kitten asleep in her lap. She strokes it gently. A tear runs down her cheek and she looks up to us all. 'Yes,' she says. 'Yes, it's time. I'll take Cookie home.'

I let out a huge sigh of relief. This is the most perfect success.

'But what about Marmalade?' Fliss asks.

They all look at me for an answer. 'I can't. I'm sorry, I'm not ready. I still have Pigeon at home. I'm so proud of you all and I know you're going to be so happy but, for me, it's just not the right time.'

No one pushes me. The respect for where people are at in this room never fades. Fliss looks upset and goes to pick up Marmalade, the only ginger kitten, and puts her back in her carrier. 'I suppose I'll have to find someone else for her,' she says. 'She can't come home with me, I promised Abby.'

'You don't need to take her home,' I say, putting my hand on her knee for comfort. 'There is someone else I'd like to ask.'

I find the house easily, its location is etched into my mind. Knowing this is where Pigeon was hit makes my body shake. I must stay focused on the kindness of a stranger, not the awful thing that happened for me to need it. I walk up the steps to the front door. I have Marmalade in Pigeon's old carrier, where she is sitting quietly making no fuss at all. I knock on the door, trying not to look to my left: the spot where Pigeon's lifeless body lay.

For a while, I assume no one is home. I hadn't accounted for that, I thought there would be only one outcome from this visit. But finally, I hear slow footsteps coming towards the door. I have butterflies in my tummy. I am nervous this is a mistake. The door opens.

'Oh, hello,' says the old lady.

'Hello,' I say. 'I don't know if you recognise me but . . .'

'I do, how could I ever forget you,' she says. Of course, I was sobbing and screaming uncontrollably on her doorstep. It's not the kind of thing you just erase from your memory.

'I wanted to come back to say thank you – for your kindness that day. I was in such a state and it would have been a lot worse if Pigeon had been found by someone else.

It can't have been easy for you to pick her up and take care of her like that so really, thank you from the bottom of my heart.'

She smiles at me. A smile that feels warm and familiar. I suppose I took more of her in that day than I thought.

'I did what any cat lover would do. I know that pain, I've been there myself a few times now. How are you?'

'I'm OK. Not great but doing better. Thank you.' I need to commit to what I came here for, so I hold the carrier up so she can see inside. Her face lights up.

'Oh, you got a new kitten, how lovely,' she says.

'No, I didn't. I have a friend who needs to rehome some kittens, and this is the only one left. She's very sweet, her name is Marmalade. I wondered if you'd like to keep her?'

'Oh my goodness. What a lovely idea, but I'm afraid I can't do that.'

With my plan foiled, I suddenly feel quite ridiculous. What will I say to Fliss? 'Are you sure?' I press. 'I know it might seem disloyal to get another cat but . . .'

'No, that's not it. I think it's exactly the right thing to do. But . . .' She looks down sadly. 'I'm afraid it would outlive me. I'm not very well, you see.'

She's an old woman, how could I not have considered this? 'I'm so sorry,' I say. 'This was really foolish of me. I didn't mean to upset you, I'll go. I'm so sorry you're unwell.'

'You know, ginger cats are nearly always boys. She's very unusual, just like you. It seems to me like you two should stick together. You're the perfect match.'

A bolt of something runs up my body. I've heard those

words before . . . I start to walk away but, as I do, I think about the things that have got me through the tough times in life. It's kindness, and mostly from strangers. I turn back to her. 'How are you feeling about your cat who died?' I ask her.

'Not great, I still find it very hard.'

'Do you have anyone to talk to?'

'Not about that, no. People expect you to get over it, don't they?'

'Not everyone. What if I was to come over to chat to you about it every now and then? It might be nice?'

She looks quite taken aback by my offer, but she's also smiling. 'That would be lovely,' she says, gently.

'Great. What about Tuesdays at seven p.m.?' I ask, knowing that the bereavement group as I know it will no longer exist now they have their new kittens. 'We could do it every week, if you want? I'll bring biscuits.'

'Thank you,' she says, and I start to walk away again with Marmalade in my bag, unsure of what to do next.

'Mia?' she calls after me. Stopping me in my tracks as I am certain I never told her my name. I turn and look at her. The familiarity of her smile slowly dawning on me. Surely it can't be?

'Marie?' I say, choking up.

'Yes. It's me.'

I run back up the steps and hug her as gently as I can. Her frail body needing care. She smells the same, I remember it well. Her smell, her kindness, her love. I feel like a child again.

'I knew it was you the second I saw you,' she said. 'That

fiery red hair, I'd never forget it. I didn't want to add more to your grief that day, after everything with Pigeon, but I hoped so much you'd come back.'

I'm crying so much at this point that I can't form words. For the second time on this step, but now there is joy. The shock of this is overwhelming. Mum's friend, Marie, after all these years. The memory of her kindness and care reminding me how loved I used to be.

'Why don't you come inside?' she says, guiding me in. 'I can at least play with the kitten, can't I?'

29

When I called Liz and told her about Marie, she insisted I come over the following night for dinner. I take Marmalade, wondering if I can persuade my niece and nephews to have her. When I arrive, I'm pleased to see that the front door has been freshly painted and the dick and balls have gone. I let myself in and, for once, I see no toys cluttering the hallway. There aren't various sound systems blasting from different rooms in the house either, just the sound of laughter coming from the kitchen, where the scene is so far removed from what I am used to that I wonder if I've arrived at the right house. All of them together.

'Hello love,' says Simon, standing at the cooker wearing an apron and holding a wooden spoon. 'Staying for dinner? I know you won't eat the chicken, but you can have the chips and beans right, no animals in those?' His smile is so enormous it's totally changed the shape of his face.

'Um, yeah, sure, great,' I say, trying not to be rude by showing my amazement.

Liz is breastfeeding my niece. On another chair sits Nate, and on another is the eldest, Tommy. I haven't seen them all in the same room for about two years.

'Well, this is rather lovely,' I say, kissing Liz on the cheek and handing her a small bunch of flowers that Simon takes from her and puts in a vase without trimming. Liz raises her eyebrows at me, making it clear she can't quite believe it either.

'The house seems quiet, it's nice,' I say, sitting down.

'First time in years we haven't had any fosters in. I'm not gonna lie, it's pretty nice to just be with these guys.'

'Yeah, pretty nice to be able to find a seat,' Tommy says.

'We're taking a little break from that too. Six months,' Liz says, swapping boobs. 'Some much needed family time, right lads?' They all nod.

'I think that sounds like a really good idea. Look who I've got,' I say, revealing Marmalade. I pass her to Tommy, who says, 'Cats are weird,' so I pass her to Nate, who holds her like she's an atomic bomb.

'We're not really animal people,' Liz says, foiling my plan to leave without the cat.

I put food into a little bowl and make a litter tray from the baking tray and a newspaper that I shred. She uses it right away. 'Such a good girl,' I say, proud of her.

'Kids, why don't you take the kitten into the living room and play with her while Aunty Mia and I catch up,' Liz says, peeling Layla off her boob. She breastfed Nate until

315

he was five, something tells me she'll keep going with Layla as long as she can. The three of them do as they're told with varying levels of excitement.

'Dinner in five,' Simon calls after them, burning his hand on a pan.

'OK. Now tell me everything,' Liz says. 'Marie, wow, I never thought we'd see her again. Did she get married, have kids?'

'No. Her exact words were: "Until a few months ago, I was a very happy cat lady." Which I obviously found extremely inspiring. She said she had a few bad relationships with men and gave up after that. She just settled into an independent life, well, with her cats. Do you remember George?'

'Yeah, and I remember Wotsit. What the hell did Dad do with that cat?'

'I think it's probably best we never knew.'

I tell Liz how Marie and I talked for hours until she became too tired to carry on. How she told me lovely stories about Mum, of how much she loved us both. 'She had so many photos, which she'll show you when you come with me next time. And she had some of Mum's dresses, look.' I take four colourful kaftans out of a tote bag; they have been perfectly stored for thirty years.

'They'll suit you,' Liz says. 'Your new style, it's just like Mum's, I love it.'

'Marie said Mum had always maintained she married a good man who let life get on top of him and that a part of her remained hopeful he would turn it around. She said she

316

was a very positive person. I told her that sounds a lot like you.'

Liz's eyes fill up a little. This is the most we have talked about Mum in so many years. Maybe even ever.

'It's like staring our childhood in the face, both terrifying and cathartic. I don't know, I feel lighter. Just to hear what Mum was like, it was like getting a hug from her. I know that sounds stupid.'

'It doesn't sound stupid at all,' Liz says, reaching over to me and hugging me. We stay like that for a while.

'She didn't take the kitten though, which is the whole reason I went back,' I say, hinting.

'Well then, that kitten is even more special; because of her you went back and look at where that got us. I don't know what it is about your cats, but they have a very clever way of making your life better.'

'OK, it's ready,' calls Simon, putting plates of overcooked freezer food onto the table. 'Come on kids.'

They trudge back in, Tommy holding Marmalade. I take her into my hands and look at her. She's such a pretty little thing. And Liz is right, this kitten just came to me by chance and took me back to Marie, changing everything. Just like Pigeon did all those years ago. And for that reason, even though I didn't think I was ready, I decide to keep her.

'I wonder what I should call her, Marmalade doesn't feel quite right,' I say.

At which point Layla shouts, 'Yay, Chips!'

'Chips it is,' I say grinning. It's perfect.

We sit and eat, and I watch them talk to each other like

they have never done before. The problem with seeking love from everyone is that the people who need it from you can feel left behind. Seeing Liz with her own kids, and Simon respecting her, is a truly happy sight indeed. It's not the way my life turned out, but I'm really happy that it went this way for her. When we've finished, Liz and I go upstairs with hot soapy water, scrubbing brushes and cloths.

'Glad we're doing this. It would have made Mum really happy,' she says, pushing the hatch up into the loft.

'Need any help?' Simon calls up the stairs.

'Nope, we got this,' Liz says from the eaves. 'OK, you ready?'

'Yup,' I say, reaching my arms up. She gently lowers the doll's house that Mum gave us all those years ago.

'It's going to look lovely when it's all clean,' she says, looking at it lovingly.

'As good as new.'

30

The next afternoon I am sitting in my kitchen watching Chips playing with a feather. Things certainly seem to be improving. I have the house, a job to go back to, I even have a new cat. But what the doctor said is playing on a loop in my head and my conscience will not let it go.

'I'm sorry if this is uncomfortable but you really should tell the person that you had sex with. He could give it to someone else without realising.'

As an act of solidarity to the sistership, I must minimise the risk of further infection. I begin typing out an email:

Dear Ajay, I hope you are well, and that life is treating you kindly. I'm sorry to say that you have crabs. From Mia.

No, I can't tell him like that, I should build up to it better.

Ajay, it's been a few weeks since I last saw you. Thanks again for letting me stay over, I . . .

No, I can't thank him for letting me stay over. I'm not sixteen.

Ajay, Mia here. I hope you're very well and enjoying the Great British Summer.

NO! God, how can I do this without sounding so middle-aged?

Ajay, I do apologise in advance for the content of this email, but I feel obliged to tell you for the goodness of humanity that . . .

Ah! Now I just sound like Winston Churchill. Writing this in an email is impossible. Also, I only have Ajay's 'Isabella May' email address. It could get intercepted or seen by someone else while he's in the bathroom scratching his balls. That wouldn't bother me, but I start back in the office next week and I am trying to reduce my humiliation levels, not increase them. I think I have to go to his house and tell him in person, it's better to get this over and done with before I attempt a professional relationship with him again. That is the grown-up thing to do. There is nothing to be embarrassed about. Really, we peaked when I was face down on his bed with a Sharpie up my arse.

As I approach the front door to Ajay's home, I wonder if this is really necessary. It was weeks ago, if he hasn't sorted it by now then maybe he deserves to have the crabs. He should be able to work it out for himself and go to a pharmacist like I did. But I do know that many people have no idea they even have them. I have since discovered that the humiliating doctor's visit was unnecessary and that there are multiple over-the-counter remedies that would have worked just fine. The whole experience – from going to the office and smearing cat poo on the walls, to ending up in Ajay's bed, to realising I had crabs, to people *knowing* I had crabs – has all been so shame-inducing that coming here to 'do the right thing' will at least end the whole debacle with a strong moral code.

It's a Wednesday evening, I presume he will be home from work. I knock on the door and immediately hear Petal barking. She sniffs around the edges, wondering if what is on the other side is something she should cuddle or kill. I hear footsteps and start to feel very nervous. This visit might be even less dignified than my last. The door opens and Ajay's mother is standing there. Damn it, I was hoping this would be quick. She smiles as soon as she sees me.

'You came back?' she says, which I find alarming. Was she waiting for me?

'Hello, is Ajay home?' I ask politely but not inviting too much connection.

'Yes, he is. Come in, come in.'

'No, it's OK, really. If you could just let him know I'm here I'll stay outside. Thank you though.'

'Ajay,' she calls, holding Petal by the collar so she doesn't run out. Or attack me. One of the two. 'Ajay, it's Mia.'

I don't know why her knowing my name surprises me. I never told her. Did they discuss me after I left? Mother and son, discussing his sexual conquests. I shouldn't have come back. I consider fleeing, but then I see Ajay coming down the stairs.

'Hey babe, what's up?'

Babe. Oh dear, I really did abolish any authority I had with him that night.

'Ajay, hello. Please can I have a word?'

'Er, yeah. OK.' He comes outside and pulls the door shut a little, but his mum and Petal are still right there and can hear everything. Seeing as they have obviously already discussed the fact that we slept with each other, I see no point in holding back.

'Ajay, you gave me crabs. I'm not here to have a go at you or make out like I am not equally to blame for getting them, but I thought you should know so that you can get yourself checked out.'

He doesn't look as bothered as one might think he would.

'Oh, OK. Thanks.'

'Did you know you had them?'

'No, I didn't know. What does it mean?'

'It means you have crabs growing in your pubic hair and when we . . .' I whisper as his mum can hear me '. . . had sex, they transferred to me. Are you not uncomfortable . . . down there? You know . . . itchy?'

'I just thought it was cos I get quite hot.'

I feel a little unwell at the thought of it.

'You can go to the doctor if you want but you can also just get the treatment at a chemist. It's a lotion, just leave it on overnight. I left mine on for quite a long time due to unforeseen circumstances, but you can wash it off in the morning. OK, thanks. I hope everything at work is all right.'

I turn around and walk away, regretting this whole thing enormously.

'I quit,' he says, stopping me in my tracks.

'You quit? Why?'

'Well, I mean. I got fired.'

'Wait, why would she fire you?'

'I told them it was me who put the shit on the walls.'

'You did what? Why?'

The door opens. 'Because I told him to,' his mother says. 'I felt bad for you, with what your husband did and then getting fired. I've been there, I know how it messes with your head. Didn't think you needed to be in that trouble on top of all that.'

'And what about all of the dishes from Audrey's desk that I smashed on the floor?'

'Yeah, I said I got high and knocked them over,' Ajay says.

'Right, and the Post-it with "FUCK YOU" that I left on the computer monitor?'

'No, everyone knows that was you.'

'Sure, no, that's fair.' I don't know what else to say. 'I can't believe you did that Ajay . . . What will you do for work?'

'I already got loads of work. All my mates are establishing start-ups so I'm doing all their websites for them. Earning more money, and more time to work on my weed business. All good.'

'Right. It was a really strange thing for me to have done so I'm surprised you chose to take the blame.' I had wondered why Isabella hadn't mentioned it. I just thought she was turning a blind eye.

'It's no big deal. That's not really my world, it doesn't matter what they think of me.'

'I'm not sure what to say, Ajay. But thank you.'

'They were quite pleased to get a quick confession, I suppose? It's not a very nice thing to talk about,' his mum says.

'I imagine you're right. Sorry, what's your name?' I say, realising I have never even asked.

'Binita. Are you OK, Mia? We've been worried about you.'

'I'm OK, thank you. My cat died and it was awful. I didn't think I'd survive, but I'm all right. I've got a new one, actually, which has made things easier.'

'Have you got a picture?' she asks.

I find my phone in my tote bag and show them a video of the kitten playing with a toy mouse.

'Ahhhhh,' says Ajay. 'You've got good taste in cats.'

'Thanks.' I'm dumbstruck by these two.

'Do you want to come in and have a cup of tea?' Binita says, letting go of the collar around Petal's neck. I brace myself to be attacked but she just sits down and wags her tail.

Ajay and his mum both stand looking at me, waiting for my answer. They're such strange people. Or maybe they are just extremely kind, and I was just blind to it. And to be honest, looking at how my life has played out over the past month or so, I'd say I'm the strange one. And maybe that's OK too.

'*Gogglebox* is on in a bit, you can stay and watch it with us if you like?' Binita says.

'Sure,' I say, allowing my sister's words about making friends to flood my brain. 'That would be very nice.'

I go inside and take a seat on the sofa. Petal sprawls herself across my feet.

31

With so much progress and so much change, I have to face the one thing I've been dreading the most. Pigeon is still in the freezer, and I know I can't leave her there forever. I take Lee up on his offer to dig the hole. He arrives with a shovel even though I told him I have one.

'I like the handle on this one, it was my dad's,' he says. I don't argue with him. It's so kind of him to come and do it for me in the first place.

'I haven't taken her out of the freezer yet,' I tell him. 'I didn't know how long it would take to dig the hole, so I thought it was best to wait.'

'I think that's right. You can have as much time as you need with her before we lay her to rest. Where would you like her to be?' Lee asks, tenderly. He seems to understand every inch of how delicate this is. He's such a large man compared to Tristan, who was small and angry about it. He vibrated and let out a high-pitched frequency. Maybe only Pigeon and I could hear it, but some days it deafened us both. She hated him. In retrospect, I was ambivalent, but going through the motions of what a wife is supposed to do. How many ambivalent wives are there? How many would be relieved to discover their husbands were sleeping with someone else so they could get out of it without being the one to blame?

We go outside. I shut Chips in the kitchen so she can watch us out of the window. Lee's soul reaches every corner of his frame. He takes off his large green sweatshirt, leaving him in a grey t-shirt and jeans with big boots. He has a big stomach, he's not fit, yet somehow extremely attractive to me. I have a rare impulse to stroke him. To rub myself against him. To lie with him. He has even brought his own bottle of water. He doesn't ask me for a thing. There are people who give care, and people who need taking care of. We are both the former and it makes for the simplest of dynamics.

'Can I get you a drink?' I offer, regardless.

'I'm fine, thank you. Here?' He is standing in the exact spot I would like Pigeon to be buried. I think. I don't really know what I want. What I want is for her not to be dead.

'Here,' Lee says, laying down the shovel and rushing into the kitchen to grab a chair. 'Sit here, can I make you tea?'

I sit on the chair. 'No, I'm OK, but thank you.'

He puts his hand on my shoulder. 'This is very sad and you don't have to pretend it isn't.'

'Thank you.'

'OK, hang tight. I'll get this hole dug and then we will give Pigeon the perfect send-off. You'll be able to come out here whenever you want and be close to her.' He picks up the shovel and takes a deep breath. The handle rises high into the air but before it comes down he stops.

'I'm so glad I met you,' he says.

'I'm so glad I met you too,' I say uncharacteristically, but with my whole heart.

He launches the shovel into the hard ground.

Nearly two hours later, Lee is sitting on the ground, sweat pouring from him, his feet resting in the hole which I would estimate to be only a foot deep. He looks beaten. 'It might take a while longer,' he says, not giving in. 'We could run the hose into the hole and let it fill up, and then when the water drains away the soil will be softer, it might be easier to get down another foot or two.'

I look into the hole. I can't imagine laying Pigeon's body in there, then throwing earth over her. I don't want to do this any more. But Lee has worked so hard. And it's not finished. He lies back to straighten out his back. He is obviously very sore from all the hard work.

'I don't think it's right . . .' I say, nervously. 'I'm sorry, but this doesn't feel right.'

'It's OK, I'll keep digging. This is far too shallow for us to . . .'

'No, I mean burying her. I'm sorry. It doesn't feel right. I don't think I want to sit by her grave. I just keep imagining her rotting away out here and it's not right. I'm so sorry.'

'It's OK, I . . . um . . . I can fill it in again.' He stands up, and immediately starts putting the earth back in as if it's perfectly all right. Like it doesn't matter that he just sweated blood to get me to this point.

'Lee, leave it, we can do that another time. I finally know what I want to do with Pigeon.'

'The vet will be closed now. We can take her tomorrow. Apparently you can choose the urn you'd like, it takes a few weeks. I can drive you there if that would make it easier?'

'No. No that's not right either.'

'What then?'

'OK, please, just hear me out . . .'

On Lee's advice, I take a few days to think about the new plan, to make sure this is what I really want. Because once done, there is no going back. My conclusion? This is absolutely the right way to say goodbye to Pigeon.

We waited until 10 p.m. before we came to the bridge. I thought my best shot of not ending up in a cell again was to wait until dark, and hope no one notices.

'I've always thought it's such a shame that London Bridge is so ugly,' Lee says, as we step onto it. It's a warm night, quiet and still. There is traffic, but it isn't heavy. I'm carrying my frozen cat wrapped up in our fleece blanket. My arms are numb.

'It is, but really, it's all about the view not the bridge itself. You can't beat that,' I say, nodding towards Tower Bridge. Lit up so elegantly. So bold and unapologetic. The most spectacular sight. I remember taking it all in just before I jumped. I thought to myself, if the last thing I saw in life was that splendid, then it hadn't been a total waste of time.

'Are you sure you want to be here? It was hard to find anything conclusive as to whether this is illegal but I'm pretty sure it is,' I say to Lee, giving him an out.

'I'm sure. People who throw dead pets in the Thames together stay together, right?'

'That is what they say. OK, this is the spot.' I stop walking. 'This is where I jumped. It's a different view now. So many new buildings. If I'd succeeded, I'd never have seen them.'

'I'm so pleased you didn't succeed.'

'I am too.' I look behind me, checking in both directions. 'It was a long shot to think they'd come, I suppose. It's late.'

'We can wait a few minutes if you'd like?'

Lee puts his arm around me. Something I have become used to now and enjoy very much. His soft body almost as good as a fleece blanket. His large hands pulling me in tightly. We stand looking at the water, the willingness to jump now so hard to imagine.

'I used to think life was predictable. It's quite comforting to know that it's not,' I say, never imagining for a minute I would be back on this bridge feeling as strong as I feel right now. With a man I met the way that I did. With sadness but also so much joy. 'Why is it not until afterwards that you realise every bad thing that ever happens to you makes every good thing feel even better?'

'Time to let the good times roll. After this, of course. Are you ready?'

'Yes, I'm ready.'

Lee places a hand on my back and I step closer to the barrier. Tears fill my eyes, my lips shake. I put my face to the blanket that has Pigeon inside. The words flow.

'I never knew love like the love I felt for you. You saved my life and then you changed it. I'm sending you off this way because I want to set you free. Not to rot in the ground or to burn in flames, but to drift down a river to the wide open ocean. To dissolve and feed the fish that you always wanted to eat. There was no right way to say goodbye to you, so I'm bringing you to the place where it all began. I love you, Pigeon.'

I raise her high enough to get over the barrier.

'Wait,' Lee says, gently pushing my arms back down. 'Look.'

I turn to the direction he's facing and see the figures of seven people walking towards us. As they come into focus I make out Martha, Ada, Tiana, even Greg. And behind them is Liz, Simon and Marie. Simon is helping her walk. They came.

As they gather behind me, the timing feels perfect. I step forward. I hold onto the blanket and stretch out my arms over the edge. A long, deep breath as I roll her out. The blanket becomes light and blows in the gentle breeze. I hear a very quiet splash.

'I love you,' I say, as a multitude of warm and caring hands find their place on my back. We stay like that for a while, I'm not sure how long.

'I don't mean to ruin the moment, but we should probably go,' Lee says. 'Every time I hear a siren, I think they're coming for us.'

I feel the hands leave my body, but their support stays with me.

'I'd say I'd done it if they come. I've been in the nick before, could do it again,' Greg says. Still down on himself, but still here, and that's the most important thing.

We all walk slowly back towards the Tube station. Me, Marie, my sister, her husband, my new boyfriend, and my very strange group of friends.

Epilogue

It's a warm evening in September. The sky is getting darker now and the moon is ready to take over. I'm wearing one of my mother's kaftans and my long red hair is out and messy. Lee and I are sitting in my garden drinking wine, watching our cats all cuddled up on their bed inside the glass doors. Mama – formerly Midnight – is licking Chips' ears. And Flip-Flop – formerly Crumble – is lying on her back.

'We need to make sure we always bring them to each other's houses so they are happy in both,' I say to Lee.

'The same goes for us. We must always be happy in both houses.'

'Deal.'

I reach over and put my hand on his knee.

'How's divorce going?' he says, with a cheeky smile.

'Better than marriage. Who knew?'

'I couldn't share a room with someone every night, I don't know how people do it. I'd be so hot.'

'Well, exactly. I didn't. I'm not sure that worked out great for me in the end but seriously, why would anyone want to deal with someone else's sleep noises?'

'Or stealing the covers.'

'Or their farts!' I say as my eyes stream with water. 'The average person does five farts a night. How is that good for a relationship?'

'I only ever want to hear you fart by mistake, or I'm leaving you!'

'Fair enough. I think we're on the right track. Maybe separate bedrooms don't work, but separate houses, well, that sounds like the dream.' I take his hand in mine. 'I hope we live in separate houses together forever.'

'Me too.'

We sit peacefully, watching the cats.

'OK, we're done for today,' says a very sweaty Greg, coming outside. 'We got most of the unit done, Alec is gonna paint it tomorrow, right mate?' he says encouragingly to Alec, Ada's son.

I decided I'd like a new built-in wardrobe in Tristan's old room. Something substantial to hold the colourful dresses I can't stop buying. I offered the job to Greg, seeing as he was unemployed, and when he said he'd need some help Ada volunteered her son, Alec. They're doing a great job and make a good team. I heard Greg saying earlier that he's booked another job, and that he'd like Alec to join him on that too.

'We're off for a pint, if you want to come?' Alec asks.

'No, but thank you,' I say, excited for their budding friendship. 'But have fun.'

The two of them leave, Lee and I smiling emphatically like proud parents.

'Sorry I made you dig that huge hole. It was such a waste of your time,' I say, staring at the ground.

'Don't be sorry,' he says, taking my hand in his. 'Nothing is a waste of time if it gets you to where you're supposed to be.'

I rest my head on his shoulder. My life feels like a series of complicated events getting me to this moment. Exactly where I am supposed to be; right here, with him.

The doorbell rings. 'Are you expecting someone?' he asks.

'No.'

Whoever wants to come in is ringing the doorbell repeatedly. It's urgent and frightening. I walk towards the door nervously.

'Do you want me to open it?' Lee offers.

'No, just be close.' I open it slowly, but whoever is behind the door pushes it. Before I have a chance to realise what's going on, Oliver is clinging to my waist.

'Mia!' he says, with total joy.

'Oliver!' I bend down so his arms can reach around my neck and breathe him in as he gives me the biggest cuddle he has ever given me in his life. I realise Belinda is standing behind him. I don't let it distract me.

'He misses you,' she says, with an air of defeat. 'He's been begging to come and see you for weeks.'

'Oliver,' I say, looking him right in the eye. 'You can come and see me whenever you want, OK? I am always here for you, and I've missed you so, so much. Do you want to come in? I've got a new kitten?'

'YES,' he beams.

'You can come too, Belinda. If you want?' She closes the door and looks warily at Lee.

'Oh, this is my boyfriend, Lee. Lee, this is Belinda.'

'Hello Lee,' she says, shaking his hand when he offers it to her.

'Hello Belinda, I've heard a lot about you.'

'Oh God, I can only imagine.'

'Well, she let you in, didn't she?' Lee jokes.

She follows us into the kitchen.

My kitchen.

In my house.

Where I live alone, with my cat.

Acknowledgements

Thanks to my entire team at HarperCollins for getting me to the point of loving this book like it's another pet. Kimberley and Charlotte for the edits. Liz for making sure everyone knew about it. Claire for the cover and everyone in marketing and beyond who have done such a brilliant job.

Thank you to my agent, Adrian Sington. We've now worked together for almost twenty years, isn't that wild? I love our phone calls and long lunches. I love how much you encourage me and how honest you are whilst also making me want to write more and more. I'm so very lucky to have you.

Thanks to ALL my friends. I am not listing you this time because you know who you are, and I always miss someone out and feel awful. But I love you and I know I'm a terrible bore and extremely dramatic when I'm on a deadline so please know I appreciate your encouragement. When I said, 'No, this time it's bad. Like, really bad. I've totally fucked it. I hate it and I hate myself,' thank you for reminding me I always say that and to keep going.

Saying that, I am going to call out one person, my darling Shawnta. You've become integral to my life in so many ways. I simply have no idea how I functioned before we met. I love you endlessly and beyond. Tuesdays forever!

Thanks to Rachel Jackson for helping me set the scene at Isabella May.

Thanks to my Patreon subscribers for supporting me. I love writing for you and am so grateful you've allowed me to create a space where I can work hard, get paid and therefore buy kaftans.

Thanks to Aunty Jane and Uncle Tony for introducing me to having pets when I was a kid. Looking after animals is truly one of the greatest joys of my life and it started at home.

Thank you to the great furry loves of my life. Sniff, Acre, Fluke, Nin, Tiku, Minu, Lilu, Potato, Twiglet, Suska, Myrtle and Boo. My pets over the years.

I had a hard time when I was a kid. My mum died. It was absolutely awful and I struggled in ways I'm still not really honest about. Animals saved me. It's as simple as that. Whether it was Nin, the Siamese cat we had when I was a kid, pawing at my cheeks, or the hours and hours I spent at Fermain Bay with my beloved bearded collie, Acre, the joy I got from animals was unparalleled. And even as a forty-three-year-old happily married mother of two, my moments alone with my cats are still so very, very precious, therapeutic and essential to my wellbeing.

In the last two years we lost our cat Lilu and our dog Potato. It felt like life would always have them in it. Lilu defined my adult life, Potato was really our first baby. He needed so much from us and every morning we'd wake up willing to give him whatever it took to make him feel like the happiest, most loved little guy in the world. I can hardly mention his name without crying and I honestly wonder if it will always feel this way. There is no such thing as 'just' a pet. They are family, our heart and soul. It's not fair that their lives are so short, and even worse when their lives are cut shorter than they should be.

I wrote this book because pet grief is real, and it deserves to be written about. Be there for your friends when this happens, they really need you. Thank you to all of ours who hurt with us, sent things, showed up and held us tight. It meant more than you know.

To my family, Chris, Art and Valentine. The home we have created makes doing this much easier. I feel very lucky to have you all. We will always have each other.

And thank you to myself for not giving up, because I know you wanted to. You often don't take the easiest route, but you always get there in the end. So well done, from me. x

A Note from Dawn

Thanks to my Patreon community for giving me a place where I can happily overshare. I absolutely love writing for you all. Here is a special page mentioning the names of everyone who signed up to the tier to get a shout-out in this book. I appreciate you all so much.

Melodie Rae Storey
Caoimhe Ryan
Meral Kilinc
Theresa Bell
Laura Belbin
Mandie Pontin
Gill
Becci Martin
Jessica Cullum
Emma Reid

Amanda Hobbes
Sarah Cassidy
Vanessa Wilderink
Mandy Morgan
Eva Gaynor
Lucy Gable-Thom
Laura McGregor
Rebecca
Katherine Christian
Rachel Jackson

Annie Perry
Carina Hummel
Hillary
Sharne
Karin Bessent
Lisa Vizia
Melanie Cameron
Nicola Frye
Debbie Martin
Lyndsay Hynd
Laura Johnston
Milica Coles
Claire
Sophie Termeer
Katherine Morgan
Kate P
Penny Calley
Ali Childs
Lisa Dawes
Olivia Atkinson
Emily Macmillan
Laura Quinn
Nicole Fraley
Louise
Sarah Garratty
Tash Hudson
Sara Moss
Bonnie Cookson
Mairead Gleeson
Lisa Simpson
Vicky Osborn-Buchholz
Angie Hung
Iciar Arostegui

Katharine Richardson
Amberley
Joanna Van
Kerry Picolla
Jenny Fraser
Amie Klapsia
Paula Murray
Darcy Cox
Alison Corfield
Sarah Wright
Laura Harris
Roisin Munnelly
Amanda Cartlidge
Tori Miller
Christine M
Eileen Maguire
Tregaye Lacey
Morissa Thorn
Mig
Ann-Marie
Suzanne Hart
Cheryl Douglas
Barbara Costello
Cheryl
Laura McPope
Emma Cantrell
Laura Featherstone
Emma Cowell
Gemma Feeney
Ella Whellams
Kylee Sims
Caroline Quinton Smith
Hayley Walsh

Jo

Roisin

Sue Baron

Alexis Lumbly

Jo Lee

Laura F

Annie Robinson

Belinda B

Donna

Ross Mckechnie

Katie Webb

Katherine Hucker

Sally

Carla

Elena

Pamela McQuarrie

Nia Roberts

Lizi Jeffery

Nicole Grint

Holly Marlow

Negar Ghadiri-Zare

Fionnuala Crowley

Catherine Twidle

Deb Banner

Alison Brooks

Catherine Meechan

Laura Redfield

Hat Peart

Laura Domek

Tania Usner

Holly Abbott

Jody

Oonagh Doyle

Jaqui

Rachael Corn

Jenna Davis

Cassie Lowes

Sarah Coomes

Nicola Roberts

Sarah Donohoe

Vanessa Holford

Aimee Cavalier

Hannah Keens

Jesnie Barrecott

Jac Hardy-Heeley

Jane Stuart

Katrina Cullison

Anne McGuire

Kate

Darcey Lily O'Shea

Kaz

Lauren Bennett

Lulu Johnston

Angharad

Dee

Tracy

Alex

Tara Stewart

Emma Bahl

Laura Sullivan

Ellen Bowden

Sarah Haddon

Sam Tannahill

Emma Hegarty

Jane Hamilton